RICH GIRL

FAÎTE FALLING
BOOK THREE

MARY E. TWOMEY

MARY E. TWOMEY

Rich Girl

Book Three in the Faîte Falling Series

By

Mary E. Twomey

COPYRIGHT

DEDICATION

For Sara-Beth

Whose laughter, kindness and friendship makes me feel like the richest of all girls.

1

———

MOTHER DEAREST

My fingers twitched as they tugged and pulled on each other in my lap. Despite the gentle light from the oil lamps hanging in the four corners of the long, hollow throne room, I felt as if there must be a spotlight on me. In hindsight, barging into my mother's castle after having punched one of her soldiers may not have been the most princess-like move on my part.

I hadn't seen her since I was a year old, but there she was – me, with a few alterations. Our matching brown, wavy hair, heart-shaped face, slender button noses, and hourglass figures were spot on for a genetics test, but I had a few freckles on my right cheek, and her skin was creamy and spotless. Her curvy frame was far more exaggerated than mine – her waist smaller and her hips wider – but the blueprints were there. While my eyes were blue and hers green, they were the same shape. Her hair was pulled back into one long braid that ended at her waist, and her hands were smooth and unused.

I was more built for the soccer field, and had the thick thighs to prove it, but my mother was made for the very throne she sat on as she stared at me. She took in my humble demeanor with a scrutinizing eye that seemed laced with a hint of longing. I knew the look well, as it was most likely mirrored on my own face. I'd been taken away from her so young; it was strange to think that, were she not wearing a gold crown and all the queenly trappings, I might not know I belonged to her.

Well, really I belonged to her youngest sister, Lane, who took me from the castle when my mother started getting power-hungry. Lane raised me as her own.

Morgan's voice was composed and even, lower in tone than mine. I wondered if she'd ever considered becoming a jazz singer. "Duchess Elaine of Province 9 confirmed that you are the child she stole. Have you anything to say to that?"

I worried that when I opened my mouth, a frog might pop out. There were a dozen soldiers lining the walls of the throne room, plus one official-looking dude to the side near the base of the throne, and his page boy, all staring at me with wide eyes. Why wouldn't they be here? Totally normal to be well-guarded when meeting your daughter for the first time in twenty-one years. "Um, yeah. Lane raised me up in Common. I only just found out about you and Avalon and all of it, so here I am. Thought we should meet each other. Maybe you could stop sending people to try and abduct me."

I didn't see much of a point in pulling punches. She hadn't welcomed me with opened arms, and the sting of her first words to me were still fresh. "Get that filthy peasant out of my castle," was hard to bounce back from. But what mother-daughter relationship didn't suffer a little turbulence from time to time?

Morgan watched me with narrowed eyes, her red painted pointy fingernail touching her lips. I felt like she was studying every square inch of me. I wished we could get to know each other a little less formally. I mean, there were a dozen guards lining the walls, for crying out loud. She was in a red gown on a golden throne, and I was in jeans and hadn't bathed or had a proper meal for days. She looked mildly amused by my blatant "let's deal with this" attitude. "I had every right to try and rescue you. Elaine was foolish to think I would forgive and forget after all this time. You are *my* rightful daughter, not hers."

"My dad sent me with her. She didn't steal me." I really hoped Lane hadn't stolen me. I wanted to believe that my life with her had been the right kind of good, and not a twenty-one-year joy ride. I'd been permitted to see Lane for a total of one minute when the exchange was made upon my arrival to the castle – Reyn for me. Lane begged me to come to Province 9 with her, but I refused, giving her a look that told her we were sticking to the plan, and she would accept it. "It's time I got to know my birth mother," I told her, acting as coolly as I could. "You should go to your province and do your thing. I'll keep in touch."

Lane knew how to read my eyes – always did. It's the rite of motherhood or something. When I would lie and say "I'm fine," she knew to start popping popcorn and gear up for a long venting session after I'd had time to process whatever it was that got me down.

When I kept my distance and gave her no more than a cool handshake, we both studied each other's trembling chins and nodded. "I'll look forward to a weekly letter from you. If I don't receive one, I'll pop by for a friendly chat, so you, me and my dear oldest sister can catch up."

"I think that's a great idea." Then I whispered quickly, "Aunt Avril has your gem. Roland is trying to capture it back. Find Bastien. He can help you get your gem back from her."

And that was that. I didn't get to hug her, to fall in her arms and tell her all that I'd been through. I didn't get to blubber away all my problems and lay them on her capable shoulders. I simply waved goodbye, watching as she left with Reyn, and left me with my birth mother.

Morgan's mouth was in a firm line. "If you hadn't been taken from me, you would know that when you're in court in front of the queen, you don't fidget. You stand up straight and conduct yourself as if you've been raised with some sense of decorum."

I tried to obey all her commands, keeping my chin

high to show her I wanted to make this work. Oh, how badly I'd wanted this to work. "I'm sorry, Mom. I can do better. You might have to be patient with me. I was only a year old when I left the castle. You can take my lack of decorum up with my dad."

"Would that I could. Your father fell ill just after you were taken. Province 2 invaded our kingdom on the eve you went missing. Elaine took you to evade capture on his orders, but she should have returned with you the second I rid Avalon of my late sister Tyronoe's greed. Urien's grief was so great over losing his only daughter that he never recovered." Then her voice sharpened, jerking me from false sweetness to the edge of the ever-ready knife of her threatening tone. "And do not call me 'Mom'. You may call me 'her majesty most high', since that's who I am. You are too old to call me 'Mom', and I am too young to be seen as one."

My face pulled at the gut-punch I hadn't realized she could do in the span of a few sentences. "Okay, your majesty most high. Sorry about that." I bit my lip and didn't argue about the very different version I was being spun of my escape from Avalon. Lane had told me Urien was worried Morgan was trying to slowly kill him, so he instructed Lane to take me and run. My gut pulled me in the opposite direction of Morgan's words. As much as I wanted to believe the best in my mother, my gut had never once lied to me. "Oh. Lane was waiting until she was sure all the sisters who were a threat to me were gone. Then she brought me back to you." I cleared my throat through the lie. "I'd like to meet my dad, when he's feeling up to it."

She looked at me like I was a bug with a convenient excuse she couldn't shoot Lane for. "He won't even know you're there, but I see no problem with you spending time with a useless stump."

I reared back, but kept my mouth shut so I didn't voice a contrary opinion so early on in the game. She knew as well as I that we were locked into a long con. She assumed the goal would be to get me to work for her to find the last four gems, but my end game was to steal the gems she'd hoarded from her sisters and return them to the fallen provinces. That way all of Avalon could flourish, and not just Province 1, where Morgan le Fae held far too much power. I'd already found three of the jewels, and they were most likely tucked in Province 8, where my Aunt Avril was returning with her own Jewel of Good Fortune. She'd stolen the jewels from us, so either they were there, or my mistrustful cousin Roland had managed to take his late mother Heloise's gem back to his home in Province 4. Better he hunt her down than keep trying to prove that I was manipulative and prone to jewel thievery.

Well, I mean, I *was going* to have to manipulate Morgan to try and steal her jewels, but it really was for the greater good. Honest.

When the silence between us was too thick for me to attempt busting through it, Morgan stood, a fake smile plastered on her face out of nowhere. I'd known the woman all of half an hour, and I could tell plain as day that the smile was fabricated. There was too much saccharine in the corners, too much planning in her eyes to really seem joyful. She clasped her hands together and took the stairs down from her throne's elevated platform so she could stand five feet in front of me. "My daughter, home again. Avalon shall have a celebration like it never has before. Rigby, see to the details. The fledgling provinces shall be invited to see the Lost Princess, returned to me at last." She clicked her fingers to the official-looking man who was standing at the base of the throne. Dude had perfect posture, and was dressed in beige fitted trousers, a white dress shirt, and a red suit jacket. The crimson with gold threading matched Morgan's long robes and the guards' stiff uniform tunics.

"Right away, your majesty most high." Rigby gave a slight bow to his head and snapped his fingers to a page boy who kept tight to his heels. "Summon the heads of staff to await instruction in the galley," he told the boy, who ran off after bowing to Morgan, and then shockingly, to me.

Morgan was apparently just getting started with her to-do list. "A grand celebration for the entire kingdom in two weeks' time, so Rosalie can meet her suitors. That should be enough time to get word to the provinces and give them the opportunity to travel to us. Then in a month, we shall have a royal ball where Rosalie will pick her husband. But only invite the heads of the provinces and notable guests to the ball. No need to pretend the peasants own gowns well enough for a dance. No, no. They can stay at home for that. Give them something to long after, aspire to. Do you think two weeks is enough time to groom her?" She asked of Rigby, ignoring my dropped jaw. "If you need more, take it, but let's not stretch it out too long. The people will want to see her settled in our province as soon as possible. I can't imagine how many people have seen her like this already. It'll be an uphill battle to groom all of this out of her." She motioned to my entire being, and my heart sank.

"Yes, your majesty. I'm certain two weeks won't be a problem." Rigby had a long nose, dark wavy brown hair that curled at his neck like a forty-year-old Disney prince, and closed off eyes that didn't give anything away. My gut didn't so much know what to do with him. He scrutinized me from head to toe, no doubt assessing what sort of major damage control he'd need to pull to get me to look like a princess.

I held up my finger to pause the nonsense train that was already leaving the station. "Um, let me stop you right there. I'm not exactly ready to pick a husband. I appreciate the party and all. I mean, that sounds awesome. The Avalon-wide celebration will no doubt be a blast. I've never been to a royal ball, obviously, so I'll be glad to go to whatever you like. But I'm not even dating anyone, so getting married inside a month is where I draw the line." I shrugged a simple, silent apology.

Morgan blinked at me, and up close I noticed her

eyelashes were unnaturally long. Not like when Jill wore fake eyelash extensions, but like, a whole knuckle long of mascaraed, curly lashes. They jutted out from her eyes like dark spiders trying to crawl their way out of her eyeballs. I blame the dim lanterns' light for not picking it out before. Her words came out slow and measured, as if responding to someone who was stupid. "A husband is necessary for you. You're of age, and it will look poor on my household if I have a daughter no one wishes to marry."

I raised my eyebrow at her. "Because I don't get married in a month, it means I'm an old hag no one wants? I hardly think it's that dramatic. I'm new to Avalon. Blame it on me settling in. Blame it on be being an old hag at twenty-two, I guess. I don't much care. Point is, I'm not marrying a stranger just because people will think it's weird I'm single. I don't care if people think I'm odd." I offered up another shrug as if to say, *This is who I am. Deal with it.*

She brushed off my protest with a wave of her bejeweled hand. "You won't be married off to a stranger. Suitors from all over will make their offers for marriage when you're announced at the celebration feast for Avalon in two weeks. They'll offer their hand to you in marriage, and you can pick the one who offends you the least. We'll announce your choice at the ball."

I tried to fight back my grimace, but I'm pretty sure I lost that battle. "Look, I'm out of my element here, so I'll defer to you in most things about your culture and what-not, but marriage? That gets to be my call."

Morgan's eyes skewered me with laser-like focus. "I see you've spent far too much time with my sister. Willful and foolish. Though, you're still young. There's hope for you."

I brushed off the slam on Lane, who I loved like a mother. I could tell any protest I made to Morgan would fall on deaf ears. "Is Lane alright? You two worked things out?"

"She's returned to the barren wreckage of Province 9 to resume her post, though none of her people will follow, I assure you. I don't see her in twenty-one years, and all of a sudden she's on my castle steps, demanding I give her the judge's son from Province 2. She was never a fool for a man's love, but I saw the desperation in her eyes." Morgan pfft'd, as if the notion was ridiculous. "I guess some people can change. I expect her to marry him soon, with the way she pled for his life. He will suit her well, since Reyn is of noble quality, young though he is."

The castle, while spacious and vast, started to feel like it was closing in on me. I didn't think I could wait the one-week mark to communicate with Lane. Call me a baby, but in that moment, I needed my mommy. I didn't want to get married to someone I didn't know. I didn't want to get married at all just yet. "Can I borrow a horse and a guide to take me to Province 2? Just to make sure she's alright."

Morgan frowned. "Surely you don't need a guide.

You're the Compass. If you want to find her, there's no doubt you can."

My plan wasn't totally well thought out, but I went with it all the same. "Yeah, I didn't even know about that ability until we came to Avalon." Okay, that part was true, but a lie bubbled on my tongue. "I'm about as useful with finding lost things as the next girl." I didn't want Morgan to know I could be her ticket to finding the additional Jewels of Good Fortune. I wanted her to like me for me, not for what I could do for her. "Maybe it was a gift that went away or something. I don't really know how all your magic works. But yeah, I'm not a gleaming GPS to finding lost keys or wallets or whatever. Got turned around four times on my way here." I shrugged in a *what can you do?* kind of way.

Morgan's nostrils flared, and I began to debate the awesomeness of telling her my gift was a dead-in-the-water duck with no hope of resurrection. "Master Kerdik, that snake. I'll try summoning him, though I'm not sure what good that'll do. He never comes when I call anymore." She cleared the distance between us, and brave as I wanted to be, the reappearance of her fake, coiled smile made me jerk back before I remembered myself.

This was my mother. I was supposed to want to be near her. What the crap was wrong with me?

She gripped my shoulders with fingernails that were far sharper than they looked. "Beauty, don't you worry. Your queen will fix what's broken in you. Master Kerdik will put you back together, and your Compass will be good as new. It was your birth blessing; I highly doubt it simply vanished. Perhaps you just need to be taught how to use it. I can certainly help with that."

I nodded, unsure what else I was supposed to do. "Sure. Some mother-daughter bonding time sounds nice."

Morgan glanced down at my dirty clothes and retracted her hands from me, as if I was covered in feces. She snapped her fingers at Rigby without looking at him. Rigby was ready with a handkerchief he placed in her expectant palm. She all but snarled at me as if I was a disgusting bug she needed to wipe her hands clean of. "Straighten her up, Rigby. See to it the seamstress gets her a properly fitting wardrobe. Something grand for the celebration, and a few gowns in the colors of my crown for the courtly meetings when potential suitors come to call." When I opened my mouth to shut down the noise about suitors, Morgan reached out and snatched my lips, holding them shut. In a command that was quiet but firm, she instructed me with two words that made me recoil. "Be beautiful. That's what's required of you. Do not disappoint me."

Lane had never done something so disrespectful to me. I knocked Morgan's hand out of the way, not even pretending to play nice. "Dude, don't put your hands on me, and don't shut me up like that. It's friggin' rude."

It was as if all the soldiers stopped breathing as one. Rigby was motionless, watching the exchange with widened green eyes that were suddenly expressive with a silent warning for me to behave. I kept my chin up, and tried not to look defiant, but instead to appear calm and rational. I tried to look like Lane – a woman who didn't need to prove herself, or fight to get her point across.

I didn't understand the assault that was coming when she pulled her hand back and let her palm smack across my face. My cheek stung with betrayal, anger and a deeply slicing wound that might never heal. Morgan's words came out cold, sifted through lips that barely moved through her flaring anger. "Rigby, see to it my daughter is educated on our ways."

"Yes, your majesty most high."

"Remove her from my sight before I strike her again and leave a mark on her petulant face. It would utterly ruin the celebration." She raised her finger to me in a threat. "But don't think I won't take a switch to your backside, little *bête*."

I didn't know what that word meant, but I'm guessing it wasn't "daughter" by the disgusted way she said it. I felt the pressure of moisture building behind my eyes, but I refused to let them fall.

"Yes, your majesty most high. Come with me, your grace," Rigby said to me with a slight bow of his head in my direction. He gave Morgan a deeper bow before extending his elbow to me.

I took the gentlemanly offer and moved with Rigby out of the throne room and out into my new home in the cold, stone castle.

2

THE AMAZING GIRL WHO BATHES HERSELF

"Dude, you don't need to wash me. Is that seriously part of your job?" I probably wasn't supposed to talk back this early in the game, but Rigby was a man in his forties offering to help me in the bathtub. *No. Just, no.*

"It's my job to oversee all aspects of your care. I do this for your mother, as well. If you prefer another servant, I can summon one for you." His overly formal demeanor did nothing to put me at ease. He stood perfectly erect at all times, his chin elevated and shoulders back with one hand behind him, resting at the small of his back.

"Um, that's alright. I can bathe myself. I'm sure you people have better things to do than help a grown woman in the tub."

"Are you certain? It's not proper for a princess to do peasant work."

"Peasant work, like... bathing? You think bathing is work? Man, Avalon sure is a trip." I offered him a smile, knowing I was probably being a little rude. I mean, dude was just offering what was normal for his world, and I was making faces like a brat. "I'm sorry. I'm being a jerk. This is all a little strange for me, so you might have to be extra patient."

"I can do that, your grace."

I pinched the bridge of my nose. "Could you just call me Rosie? 'Your grace' is really throwing me."

This, apparently, was a big conundrum for him. I watched his composed expression fall into disrepair. "I shouldn't like to argue with you, your gr—Rosie, but her majesty most high would not approve."

"Oh, would calling me by my first name get you into trouble?"

He nodded, grateful I understood the bare minimum. "Apologies, your grace."

I glanced around the fancy bedroom I was given. It was three times as large as our entire apartment, and decorated like a Victorian dream in gold and dusty pink hues. I felt like I'd stepped into a middle-ages dollhouse. "Well, when it's just us, would it be okay if you called me Rosie? Then when we're in front of everyone else, you can call me whatever Morgan likes."

Rigby's debate was plain on his face, the small devious diversion from Morgan's rule a grand step for him. He checked that the door was shut twice before he said, "As you wish it, Rosie."

My grin spread wide across my face. *Progress.* Perhaps there were humanoids here after all. "Thanks. Um, I hate to ask for stuff right off the bat, but if I could get some clean clothes to change into, I'd be grateful. I also need to send a message to Lane, if that's possible."

"Of course, your gr—Rosie." A flicker of a smile caught his lips before it disappeared. "I've already sent for a dressing gown to be worn in here while new clothes are being made for you. I would have the tailor take your measurements right now, but her majesty most high has requested we limit your audience until you're presentable."

"Ah. Mommy dearest doesn't want me seen looking like crap." I ducked behind the partition and started peeling off my filthy clothes. The bath had already been drawn, and was warm. The water smelled like roses, complete with fresh pink petals resting on the surface of the ivory claw-footed tub.

I dipped into the luxury and sunk beneath the surface, exhaling out the dust of the road and letting the rose-scented water seep into my pores. When I came back up, I realized Rigby had been talking to me from the other side of the partition. "Sorry, what? I was underwater. Didn't catch that."

"I asked if you changed your mind and needed assistance. I can still summon you another servant, if you prefer someone else."

I chuckled and started in on the soap, which was pink with flecks of gold in it. "Oh, Rigs. Man, is this going to be the best job of your life. You're used to bathing grown women and doing every little thing. I'm used to doing everything myself. It's going to be a relaxing vacation for you."

"Are you scorning my help because you assume me incompetent? I assure you, I'm quite capable of tending to anything you need. It's my joy to serve the crown of Province I. I'm her majesty most high's *soumettre*."

I laughed, covering my mouth too late. "That's the biggest load of crap I've ever heard. Of course I don't think you're incompetent. I just know how to take a bath without help. Be real, Rigs. It's your joy to wait on Morgan and me? There's nothing else you'd rather be doing with your time than tying our shoes?" I looked up at the painted ceiling that features women in various stages of idyllic, curvy nudity, staring down at me with cherubic smiles of serenity. "You're funny, Rigs. Sit down and rest a little. You've probably been on your feet all day. Take a load off and chill."

The elongated pause didn't give me much hope that I could be myself in at least one room of the castle. Finally, Rigs replied, "Is that your wish, Princess?"

I smirked at finally gaining some ground. "It's my wish and command, if that's what you need. I demand you have a seat and relax a little."

"Yes, your grace."

I heard the chair shuffling, and continued soaping myself, mildly satisfied that he'd conceded for the time being. I was so filthy, that once I finished washing myself, I started all over again, just to make sure I was clean. I idly examined the large square-shaped aquamarine stone on my right ring finger, counting the matching clusters of three diamonds each in a triangular shape on both sides of the square. It was so pretty, the white gold band twisted like vines around my finger, gleaming against my tanned skin. I'd never owned real jewelry before, and the change on my hand was heady. Kerdik had given it to me during the freak storm in which I'd asked my gut to lead me somewhere safe, and it had taken me straight to him.

Rigs didn't know how to sit in a chair and do nothing. He fidgeted kind of a lot, which was good for me, because then I knew he wasn't going to sneak up on me and try to wash between my toes or something. Bastien was the first and only man to see me naked, and I didn't look forward to adding Rigs to that short list.

I gulped hard at the memory of the least sexy moment of my life. Roland, my jaggoff cousin, thought I was smuggling the three gemstones when they went missing (and mysteriously hopped into Aunt Avril's pocket). Bastien thought the best way to clear my name was to search me, which involved me stripping down to nothing in the most humiliating moment of my existence.

It wasn't that I was ashamed of my body. I spent most of my free time on the soccer field, or playing whatever sport happened to have a slot open for me, so I'd always been fit. A few months ago, I'd gone from having a hump, a lazy eye and acne, to now looking more like Lane, who had always been gorgeous. But my body was mine, and I hadn't been given the right to call the shots on who saw every nuance and curve. I'd had deep and real feelings for Bastien – a first for me – and he hadn't trusted me. What should've been a meaningful and passionate moment when he someday saw me naked was tarnished with betrayal. He was the only man to ever see me so vulnerable, and I couldn't trust him now because of it. It should've been my choice to show him my body. There should've been kisses, flowers, promises, and, if Lane had any say in it, a wedding ring. After the humiliating betrayal, I couldn't stomach being around him anymore.

It was as fine a time as any to turn myself over to Morgan and try my luck at finding the gemstones.

3

THE GIRL WHO CAN'T BRUSH HER OWN HAIR

"Hey, Rigs?" I was nervous in the tub, wanting privacy, but also needing more information about all I'd missed.

"Yes, your grace." He cleared his throat. "Rosie."

"Can I send Lane a letter? Is that possible?"

"Of course. We can send it out in the morning for you."

"How was Reyn when Lane took him home? Was he alright? The guards didn't lock him in a dungeon or anything, did they?"

"Master Reyn was ill with a bone sickness before he came to us. That's from giving his sister half his magic to keep her alive in the limbo in which she was left. That wasn't our doing, and he won't be restored fully from that until his sister passes on someday. He left after being humbled by our guards during a round of fruitless questioning. That much we can claim."

I let that settle in for a few beats. I didn't like the thought of Reyn hurt. He was a sweet guy who'd taken a shine to Lane. I hoped they were holed up somewhere nice, and that she was helping him heal up. He'd been sick on our journey a couple times. I hadn't known it was from giving his sister half of his magic, so Rachelle could stay alive in the coma she'd been locked in after Captain Burke left her for dead. "Do you think he'll be alright?"

"Indeed. He's the judge's son from Province 2, which is one of our allies. We couldn't kill him without just cause, and we didn't have it. He was released after the guards had their fun. He'll heal. He's no doubt either at home, or in the arms of Duchess Elaine in Province 9."

I chewed on that information, filing it away in my brain to keep track of how things worked around here. "So this castle's got a prison in it? Like, an actual dungeon?"

"Indeed. It keeps the people honest, for the most part."

"Where is it in the castle? Like, underground?"

"Once you finish with your bath, I'd be delighted to give you a tour."

I yawned, stretching my legs under the water. I loved Cheval, but riding on him for days left my body a little jarred. The warm water was a soothing balm to my aching muscles. "That would be great. I'm a little exhausted, though. Any chance I could catch a nap?"

I heard the chair shuffling as Rigs stood. "You require sleep?"

I yawned again. "Yeah. Every night, chief. The birth

blessing that stuck is that I can hear the animals who talk to me. Drains my battery right quick." I decided there wasn't a ton of jewel thievery Morgan could make me do with that knowledge. I had to give them a solid reason why I needed to sleep every night.

"Of course, your grace. My oversight. I didn't realize, but of course. Good to hear one of your birth blessings is still intact. What else do you require?"

"Require?" My face pulled. I considered his request as I debated between making another request and appearing high maintenance. "That's more than enough. Just the bed would be great after I send out a note to Lane. I haven't had a solid eight in a while, Rigs."

"I didn't realize you'd used enough magic to exhaust yourself. Forgive me, your grace. It won't happen again."

I waved off his apology, though he couldn't see me through the partition. "It's fine. How would you know something like that? We only just met today."

"I wasn't under the impression you understood how to use your magic yet. You've lived in Common mostly, no?"

"Yeah. And I don't know how to do your spells or anything like that. I can only talk to the animals, as far as magic and blessings and all that goes. I can't help it. I love talking to them, but apparently that's the thing that makes me super way tired. So I try to sleep eight hours a night. I get pretty crabby when I miss out."

"Eight hours a night. Yes, your grace." He opened the

heavy bedroom door, the wood creaking as he poked his head out. "The Lost Princess requires the bed be made for sleep, and parchment to write a letter." He shut the door again and set a gauzy beige folded outfit on the table near the tub atop the towel, averting his eyes from me so he didn't see anything too sexy for his own good. "Your dressing gown, your grace," he said as he stepped to the other side of the partition to grant me the privacy I needed.

"Thanks, man. I haven't worn anything that wasn't covered in road dirt in ages." I squeezed some of the excess water from my hair and let the droplets run down my back. "Are you sure it's okay with Morgan that I'm here? I thought after all this time, my mother would be excited to see me, but I think I'm only pissing her off."

Rigs spoke slowly, each word carefully chosen. "The Queen most high is glad to have her daughter back, safe and sound. Perhaps you're more used to Duchess Elaine's exuberance, and were expecting something more to that caliber?"

I tried not to let my voice sound too despondent. Despite all the warnings about Morgan and how awful she was, I still wanted my mother to like me. I tried not to let my tender wounds show. I was Lane's daughter, after all. I had a mother figure who wanted me, and loved me for the weirdo I was. "Morgan and I will find a rhythm, right? She won't always look at me like I'm something icky stuck to the bottom of her shoe?"

"I'm sure no one looks at you like that. Her majesty most high is... She feels a great many things, not the least of which is lonesome. I'm sure she'll be glad to have another family member under the roof."

I stared into the water, which now had bits of dust floating on the surface. "You're a good bullshitter, Rigs. Thanks for trying to make it smoother than it is. You're a nice guy."

A knock at the door interrupted his reply, and I heard something metal sliding onto a wooden table out there when I stepped from of the tub. I wasn't expecting the gauzy white dressing gown to be a legit gown, but after I toweled off and tugged it over my head, I was shocked to see how pretty it was for such a simple thing. There were no sleeves, but thick tank top straps holding it up. The dress cut below my bust, revealing just enough cleavage for me to feel weird stepping foot outside the bedroom. The gown was loose around my hips, and the hem fell to my bare toes. They wiggled happily, feeling liberated being out of my shoes, free to dance and roam at will.

My stomach rumbled loudly when I stepped out from behind the partition. My hair was tangly and wet, but I was clean, and the feeling was marvelous. I couldn't keep the grin off my face and beamed at Rigs, who broke his professional demeanor to smile at me. "Thank you. That bath was exactly what I needed."

"Of course, your grace." He ducked his head out again

and snapped his fingers, giving short commands to whoever was out in the hallway. Then he shut the door and turned back to me. "Supper will be brought up to you tonight, but usually her majesty prefers to eat alone in the dining hall. Perhaps tomorrow you can join her there. Give the two of you a second chance at the reunion you'd pictured."

"Sure. Thanks. Yeah, I'm kind of starved." I meekly explained my vegetarian dietary restrictions, apologizing for the hassle.

Rigs waved off my apology and let in a dude who looked to be just a few years older than me. He carried a silver tray with a quill, ink, parchment, a comb and a bottle of oil on it, setting it on the wooden table in the center of the room. He kept his eyes averted and bowed to me, his black, feathery hair dipping forward slightly. Rigs held his hand toward the man when he spoke to me. "Your grace, this is Demi. He is to be your *soumettre*. Should you need anything, you can summon me, or ask Demi to see to it."

My mouth drew to the side when two men came into the room and put fresh sheets on the bed. They spread atop them a lush satin comforter that looked to be at least five inches thick. It was then I realized that I had not seen a single woman apart from my mother in the castle thus far.

Demi lifted his head to give me a demure nod, blasting me with a full view of his beautiful face. I suddenly remembered being told that my mother populated her castle with the best-looking men in Avalon, sometimes taking them forcefully from their homes so she could have something pretty to look at. I nearly choked on regular oxygen when I took in all of Demi. He had long black lashes framing startlingly bright green eyes. He had the perfect soccer player's build – muscular, but not too bulky. He was a good five inches taller than me, but the subservient tilt to his head made him seem not too towering. His sharp, high model-like cheekbones played nicely with the peak in his left ear. He looked fairy-ish, and too handsome to be real. Ian Somerhalder, in the flesh. I'd admired the elite like him from afar in my classes, but was always way too shy to speak a word to them (not that the hot guys ever looked my way with anything other than a grimace).

When Demi picked up the comb and advanced toward me, I held my hands up and took a step back. "Hold up a second. Are you... Is he going to brush my hair?"

Demi shot Rigs a look of confusion, silently asking why I was being a dork. Rigs held his hand out to me like a gentleman. He sat me on his chair that had been pulled out from the circular wooden table near the center of the room. "Yes, your grace. Demi will see to your personal needs. He's your *soumettre*. Anything you wish. He'll brush your hair, shine your shoes, help you dress, warm your bed, see to your meals, escort you around the castle, and do whatever you wish."

My eyebrows pulled together. "Um, okay. Sorry if this

sounds rude, but shouldn't a girl help me if I have trouble getting dressed?"

"Are you displeased with me, your highness?" Demi asked, his head bowed and shoulders downcast in defeat. Actual defeat. It was the first thing he'd said to me, and we were already off on the wrong foot. I knew I'd been right in never venturing a try at conversations with the hotties in school. I was screwing it up all over the place.

I scrambled to cover my unintentional faux-pas. "No! Nothing like that at all. It's just that where I'm from, it would be weird for a dude to help a girl he doesn't know get dressed. And no man's ever brushed my hair before. That seems a little bananas in my mind."

Rigs nodded in understanding, clicking his fingers for Demi to get started on my hair. The comb was gentle as Demi worked meticulously to unfurl my tangles that hadn't seen the business end of a brush in weeks. Best of luck to the new guy. It kept him situated behind me, though, which was a good thing, since he was too pretty to look at directly. He made me nervous, and I hoped he would leave just as soon as the arduous task of tending to my hair was finished. I pulled my knees up and hugged them to my chest, resting my bare heels on the edge of the seat. I bit at my nails anxiously, hoping my cheeks weren't noticeably red.

Rigs' voice was kind, like a friendly tour guide through a museum where everything was slightly different than it should be. "The other provinces employ female servants, as well as men, but her majesty most high prefers only men in her castle to do her bidding. Other women get jealous of her majesty most high's beauty. You're the first woman to live here with her."

I blinked up at Rigs and took in the tightness in his green eyes. His words started to settle in, and I poked behind the hidden meaning there. Morgan wanted her pick of the men in the land, since my father was incapacitated. "I see. Um, well it's nice to meet you, Demi. I'm Rosie, and this is going to be the easiest job you'll ever have, I hope."

"Nothing is too difficult for me to handle, your grace. I assure you, I'm at your beck and call. Don't be afraid to put me to the test." It was nice to hear his voice. Demi's cadence was gentle, and his voice pleasant and kind with a hint of richness to it, like a radio DJ on a jazz station.

"Well, you've got your work cut out for you with my hair. Been on the road since I got into Avalon. Sorry about that."

I picked up the fancy quill with what looked like a peacock's feather sticking out the end. Though I desperately didn't want to ask for help, I couldn't write a letter without Judah or someone to read it over to make sure it made sense. I pursed my lips and hoped they couldn't see my inner turmoil start to roil in my gut. I didn't want them to know I couldn't write a letter without help.

"Um, I'm real sorry to ask. You're being so nice already, Demi. Would you mind taking a break from sorting out my hair to write a letter for me? We don't have quills where I'm from, so I don't totally feel comfortable using them." My nerves calmed at the totally logical reason even I bought. Hopefully they wouldn't know that I was a hardcore dyslexic.

"Of course, your majesty." Demi set down the comb and picked up the quill, awaiting my instructions.

I hoped he didn't know I was stupid.

I dictated a quick, coded note to Lane, letting her know that I was safe, that Morgan was disappointed that my Compass ability had faded during my time in Common (total lie to make sure she knew the party line). I tried to keep my whining to a minimum when I wrote that I missed her terribly, that I loved her, and to wait until the big party to see me again.

Being introduced to the woman who gave birth to me had been a hard smack to take. I wished Lane's sweetness and fun were around to take the edge off. She would get how weird all of this was.

I also put in a few lines to Draper, telling him to please come to the grand unveiling or whatever, so that I could see him again. I'd only just got him in my life; I didn't like him gone so easily.

The second note was written with careful wording to Reyn.

Dear Reyn,

I hope you're well, though I've heard from my new mother that you were not treated kindly in Province 1. I'm so very sorry, and I hope to visit you soon to see if you need help.

I swallowed and tried to keep my chin steady and my face composed.

I'm returning your hermit crab to you in the state he came to me. I wish him all the best in the long life he'll have with you, far from me. I guessed "hermit crab" was a decent code name for Bastien.

"I think that should do it. Thanks, man." I handed him a fist bump, but he looked at my hand in confusion, unsure what to do with it. I molded his hand into a fist and mashed it to mine. "Like that. It means we're awesome." I was extra nervous around him, and it didn't help that I couldn't remember the simplest thing – that we were from two different worlds.

"Oh. Yes, your majesty. Thank you. I'll have these sent out tonight, if you wish. The journey to Province 2 is only a day, and we'll send our fastest rider out. The letter to Province 9 is a bit longer. If Reyn isn't in Province 2, his letter will be forwarded to Province 9." Demi sealed the two letters in envelopes and handed them to a page just outside the door before returning to my hair.

"Sorry about the rats' nest I've got growing back there."

"It's my joy to serve, your grace." Demi paused combing my hair to tie the ribbon that stretched under my bust into a tight bow at my back. His movements were controlled and efficient. When I glanced down, my breasts were more prominent, and my waist visible – all with the simple tie of a ribbon.

"Rosie. You can call me Rosie, Demi."

There was a long pause, and I could feel Demi and Rigs going back and forth silently behind me. "Yes, Princess Rosie, your grace."

I sighed and slumped in the chair, resigning myself to this new life, however isolated and strange it may be.

4

MY MASSEUR

After an amazing meal of potatoes, root vegetables, a squash soup served in a hollowed gourd, rolls, freshly churned butter, water and a warm drink called *vin chaud*, I was finally full. I'd been surviving on apples and berries for so very long. To stuff myself with the luxuries (in my very own new bedroom) made me slightly giddy. That, coupled with being overly exhausted, brought my feet stumbling to the bed. "Goodnight, guys. Thanks so much for everything. The food was awesome. Haven't eaten a real meal in forever."

I expected them to leave, but nothing in this castle turned out the way I expected. Rigs turned down my sheets while Demi took my hand and helped me into the tall bed. The intimidatingly high frame was sitting on a raised platform in the corner of the room near the window. The platform had three steps to it, so when my feet were planted on the floor, the mattress was as tall as my nose. It was like the bed itself was its own throne. The king-sized mattress sat atop a dark wood four-poster canopy bed. Despite my insistence that I didn't need help with normal things, I didn't turn down Demi's hand when he offered it to help me up onto the super high mattress.

I rolled to the middle of the bed atop the comforter, smiling up at Rigs when he asked me for the millionth time if I needed anything else. He stood on the platform at the side of my bed, looking down on me with a polite, capable expression of one who had control of his household. "You thought of everything, Rigs. You saved the day. Be sure to spread it around the watercooler that I said you were the most awesome of all the dudes ever." My eyelids drifted shut, and I didn't even bother getting under the covers. The mattress was as soft as a cloud, and I felt cradled in the sheer luxury of it all.

When I opened my eyes, a small smile lightened Rigby's formal demeanor. "I'll do my utmost. Goodnight, Princess Rosie. Should you need anything, Demi will be right here."

Demi waited until Rigs showed himself out before he took out the bottle of oil, stealthily climbed atop the mattress and started rubbing my feet. I jerked to wakefulness, my eyes shooting back open at the contact I hadn't been expecting. "Um, whatcha doing, Demi? I thought you'd be going out of the room with Rigs, there."

Demi looked down at the glass bottle in his hand and

then to me. "I'm rubbing oil into your legs. You rode in on a horse, and you mentioned you've not been eating well. You must be sore."

I watched his movements that seemed like a guy honestly just trying to do his job, strange as his position was to me. "Um, okay. I guess that would be alright. Thanks. I've never had a foot rub with like, oil. You sure you don't mind? I mean, you really don't have to."

Demi managed a small smirk. "I don't mind doing my job, no." He knelt on the bed in between my feet and started on my right arch, digging his thumb right where I needed it.

My protest flew right out the window, and my head fell back on the gold satin-covered down pillow. A gratuitous moan flew out of my lips, making me sound like rent-a-girl, and not so much like the princess I'd been marketed as. "Oh, that feels amazing."

"Good. Let me know where else you're sore."

"My legs for sure, and my shoulders a little. But I'm really fine. I'm just being a baby about it. I've never had a real massage before."

"Truly? Her majesty most high has one every night and each morning. That's where Rigby's headed now."

"Huh. So how'd you land yourself this gig? Drew the short straw, did you?"

Demi's black eyebrows furrowed. "The short straw? No, your grace. I'm the envy of all the servants right now. I was chosen for you because I'm the best there is, aside from Rigby, of course."

"Oh. Congratulations?" I wasn't sure what the appropriate sentiment was when the dude was boasting that he was the one who got to rub my feet. Boy, if Judah could see me now. He hated feet. Whenever Jill showed off her pedicures to him, his blanch was unavoidable.

Demi had a charming grin and dramatic arches to his lips that made each expression he did worth watching. He had the face of the hot guy artist in any school, but the humble deportment of the band dork you couldn't help but love. "Thank you, your grace." He worked my right foot until I was a puddle of indulgence, sprawled out on the bed. Then he moved to my calf, massaging the meat with deft fingers and perfect pressure. His eyes met mine when his fingers trailed over my knee, digging his knuckles into the sore thigh muscle. I couldn't help but groan, feeling totally self-conscious that I'd just met him, and he'd already touched more of my body than guys I'd played soccer with for years. I started to understand that the cure for Hot Guy Introvertedness was a massage. If only all the hot guys of the world knew this.

"That feels like the best kind of amazing. Riding a horse for that long is no joke. Especially when I was just learning how to ride."

His voice lowered conspiratorially. "Is it true you were living as a mere Commoner all this time? There've been rumors floating around the castle."

"Uh-huh. I gotta warn you, when you're doing that to my leg? Me and conversation? Not so much. I'm practically drooling over here."

His chuckle was light and indulgent. "Glad to hear it, your grace."

When his fingertips brushed over my underwear, I stiffened. "That's a little too high for me."

Demi frowned, but recovered quickly. "Yes, your grace." He started in on my left leg, asking questions about Common, and if I had any siblings.

"Nope. You?"

"The oldest of us was named Danniell, who ran away to the Forgotten Forest years ago."

"I'm sorry." I tried to be a normal person in conversation, but man, his touch was like honey on my skin. The oil was rose-scented, and after weeks of no lotion, the pampering felt divine. "Why'd he go to the forest?"

Demi was quiet a moment, and I realized my mistake too late. "It's a long story."

I grimaced and bashed the heel of my hand to my forehead. "Oh! I'm sorry, man. That was probably a rude question to ask. I shouldn't have said anything about it. I don't even know you, and that's personal. Totally thoughtless of me."

Demi's hands stilled on my calf. "You're apologizing? You're apologizing to me?"

"Well, yeah. Whatever reason Danniell had for going to the Forgotten Forest couldn't have been a good one.

Here I am, asking you to spill your guts when we don't even know each other." I waved my hand around to clear the air. "Ignore me. This massage is scrambling my brains." I crossed my eyes to demonstrate my point and lighten the mood. "Totally uncool of me."

Demi didn't even muster up a giggle at my crossed eyes, but stared at me like I'd started talking gibberish. "Never in my twenty-five years have I heard a Daughter of Avalon apologize. And for something so small? You apologized for... stepping on my feelings?" He acted like the notion was preposterous.

I clumsily sat up on my elbows to get a better look at him. "Of course. That's what friends do. If we're going to be spending a ton of time together, I can't imagine you'd be happy if I didn't give a crap about your feelings."

His reply tumbled out wary as he leaned back on his heels. He glanced toward the door, as if he wished Rigby were here to translate for us. "I don't think you're supposed to care about my feelings, or my happiness."

I was too tired to argue the fundamentals of basic human decency, so instead I donned an ominous, self-righteous queen voice and thundered, "You dare tell a royal how I should care?"

Demi looked horrified at what I'd thought was a pretty funny joke. He jumped off the bed, stepped down from the platform, and crouched down on all fours on the ground, his forehead pressed to the floor and his butt up in the air.

"A thousand apologies would never be enough, your grace!"

"Oh, jeez!" I fretted, feeling terrible. I totally sucked at all things Avalon. My relaxed limbs made it difficult to maneuver off the bed, but I managed to fumble my way to his side ungracefully. I knelt on the floor and picked up his head, scared that one of my stupid jokes could go south this fast. "Demi, I'm sorry. I was only kidding. I didn't mean to scare you. I was trying to act all evil and scary to make you laugh. Do you really think I'd be mad about something stupid like that?"

Fear was plain on his handsome features. His high cheekbones and perfectly symmetrical face were twisted with distress. "Your majesty, please forgive my insolence."

"Only if you forgive me for telling a crappy joke." I held his face in my hands, my thumbs rubbing out a crease that formed between his eyes when he worried. "Oh, man. I really scared you." I felt horrible. I pulled him into my arms and hugged him tight, unwilling to let him live in so much fear around me. "I'm so sorry, Demi. I don't understand Avalon. This place isn't for me. You're going to have to be crazy patient with how behind I am with all of this."

Demi was frozen for a second, but then banded his arms around my torso, resting his head on my shoulder. "Princess, a sweeter soul I've never known. You're right to say this place isn't you. We haven't seen a smile like yours in ages."

5

DEMI IN MY BED

I quickly learned after Demi's fourth hinting insistence that I make any request known to him, that he was expecting me to ask him to take his clothes off. I didn't even think it was out of any sort of animalistic desire, since he'd been a decent guy most of the time, talking to my face and not my breasts, and staying engaged in whatever conversational trail we ran off on as we sat together on the floor. I was totally out of my element here, but I was determined to make a friend in this place. "Can I ask you a question?"

"You can ask me anything." He seemed grateful I was taking him up on his hinted offer for sexy times, which I was not.

"So, Rigs said something in a roundabout way that made me wonder if Morgan is taking guys on the side while my dad's out of commission."

"Of course. She can take whomever she wishes, any day or any night. She fills the castle with the men she most desires. It's a high honor to be chosen for work in the castle."

I swallowed my acerbic response. "Is that normal? Like, I got the impression that any little declaration of feelings for someone was a big, permanent thing here. How is it Morgan can just take whoever she likes while being married to someone, but everyone else treats a first date like it's till-death-do-us-part?"

"Her majesty most high can do as she pleases. She works hard to make sure Province 1 is most profitable, so she takes her spoils where she can get them."

"And you, you're my mother's spoils?" My heart sank when it dawned on me that my mother had sent one of her former gigolos to do the wild thang with me. *Ick.* Of all the things I wanted to share with my new mother, penises wasn't one of them.

Demi shrugged. "Of course. I was one of her favorites for a time. I've warmed Duchess Avril's bed, too. Her majesty most high loans me out as a gift when things get tense between the provinces and need smoothing over. There are a few of us who serve that purpose."

My mouth dropped to the floor. "You've had sex with my mother and one of my aunts?"

Demi nodded slowly, as if I was stupid. "Of course. That's my purpose. I'm here to make the crown easier to bear."

I motioned between us, needing to spit out the thing I was dancing around. "Is that why you were sent to me?" I jerked my thumb toward the bed, unable to say "sex". Somehow the word choked my throat and deserted me completely, as if it knew it had no business being anywhere near my body. I mean, hello. I'd only just had my first kiss. Sure, I was a late bloomer, but that didn't mean that just because I got my training wheels off, suddenly I was ready for a motorcycle.

"Of course. But if you prefer one of the others, it's completely within your rights to request someone else." He angled his chin toward the empty bed. We were still on our knees on the floor, his eyes boring into me, begging me not to send him away. "I get the feeling that I may not be pleasing to you."

My eyes widened as I chewed on my bottom lip. "You're supposed to be here to help me chill out, and show me the ropes, right?"

"Whatever you need."

"And it's some big deal to get chosen for this? Like, this is what you want out of your career?"

"It's the greatest honor, second only to Rigby's position serving her majesty most high."

I nodded, trying to take it all in. "Okay. Can I be honest with you?"

"I'm superb at keeping secrets, yes."

I couldn't look at Demi through my totally embarrassing confession. He was too handsome, and I was all kinds of awkward. "I... I... I just had my first kiss last month, and it ended in a crash with no bang. I'm still a little shellshocked from it all. So you and I? We're, um, we're not hitting that bed in the way you're used to." My voice dropped to almost a whisper, chagrinned that I was actually saying these things to the rock star-level hottie. "I sleep at night, though." I rubbed the nape of my neck, nervous at asking for something so forward from a stranger I didn't have any business flirting with so awkwardly. "Any chance you feel like catching up on your reading or whatever in bed with me while I sleep?" My cheeks turned pink at the blatant invitation, asking the stranger to be my Judah Band-aid. "Never mind. Forget I asked. That's too weird. I promise I'm not like this – asking a guy I just met to snuggle me in bed. Ugh!" I held my forehead, wishing I could friggin' be cool for one whole minute. "Just shut me up."

Demi's mouth fell open. "Surely you can't be a Daughter of Avalon and have never known a man's touch." When I didn't take it all back and tell him I was joking, he shook his head, completely flummoxed. He seemed to come to himself when he took in my embarrassment, and softened. "Your majesty, of course I can stay with you while you sleep. I'm your personal servant." He reached out and placed his hand on mine. "Don't be afraid to do with me as you wish."

Would that Demi had a giant wart on the end of his

nose or something that would make him less beautiful. My cheeks heated whenever he looked at me directly. "That's what I wish. I just need someone to be nice to me. Morgan and I didn't exactly hit it off. I don't think she likes me. I could really use a friend who doesn't bullshit me right about now."

Demi met my eyes and something clicked. We finally seemed to be on the same page, despite our worlds of difference. He stood gracefully, lifting me with ease and helping me into the tall bed. He pulled down the covers for me and even went so far as to tuck me in, as if I was five years old. "You really want me to read a book while you sleep? That was a genuine offer?"

"Sure. Why not? I'll just be sleeping. Super way boring for you."

He crossed his arms and stared at me in confusion. "Wow. I wasn't expecting you to be so easy to deal with. Usually I'm going all night long." He caught himself and tried to course-correct. "Of course, should you change your mind, nothing would give me more joy than guiding a beautiful maiden such as yourself. Your loveliness is—"

I waved off his babbling. "Yeah, yeah. I'm the shiz. My vagina holds the keys to the Magical World of Wonderland. You don't have to be so perfect around me. I need a friend, remember? You can relax."

Demi's genuine grin was a thing of beauty. It took over his whole body, lifting his shoulders and painting his model-like face with pure light that seemed to glow from within. "Thank you, your majesty."

"It's just Rosie. We're having a slumber party, so do what you like to relax, and enjoy your night."

"I'll be right back. Can I get you anything, your grace?"

Instead of shrinking from what I wanted to say, I decided to be brave and let it fly. "Just your smile. Best thing I've seen all day."

"You've given me that, and far more. Thank you." He bowed to me, and then disappeared out the door.

Immediately I tore out of bed and ran to the window. I popped it open, letting loose a whistle to summon the nearest birds to me. "Hey, guys. Come on in here." I gusted out a sigh of relief when four birds came racing in through the opening, lighting on my arms in the blue moon's light that filtered in and mingled with the dim oil lamp in the corner. They chirped with gusto all the typical astonished greetings that I was the *Voix*, and all the joy this brought them.

"Tell me about the water supply," I asked, cutting to the chase. If the water in Province 1 had been tainted by a rival region when I first entered Avalon, I needed to make sure it wasn't still happening. The birds assured me that the water was safe, and the animals in Province 1 were well-fed and had plenty of protection from the larger predators. They had plenty of complaints about the Queen's Army, though, tromping through the woods and leaving their homes in ruins. There was an overwhelming consensus that the army didn't respect the nature in the land they'd been entrusted to protect.

"I'll see what I can do, guys. Anything else I should know about if I'm staying here for a while? How can I help?"

The birds didn't waste any time tattling on the soldiers, tell me there was a spot in the woods where the soldiers took their spoils of war to defile them against their will. My voice darkened. "First thing tomorrow, I want you to take me there. Show me this spot."

"No! No! We would never take you there. You're the Voix! *We wouldn't risk you like that."*

"I won't risk the women like that. If I'm there, that nonsense won't go down. I have to shut it down. Thanks, guys." They chirped their happiness to help. I whispered to them, checking over my shoulder to make sure I was alone. "I know Morgan's stolen the jewels from the other provinces. Any chance you might know where she's stashed them?"

The birds looked at each other in confusion, admitting that they didn't pay attention to things like jewels, but they'd do a search of the grounds for me, first thing. They even went so far as to promise they'd rally the other animals to enlist their help.

"You guys are the best. But nothing conspicuous. You have to stay hidden from Morgan and her people. She can't know what I'm looking for."

I loved the energy of birds. They were so chipper and

happy to help. Plus, the aerial view of things was dead useful. "It's too dark out to search for the jewels now. Why don't you come sleep with me?"

"We can sing you to sleep!" They offered, winning my heart and making me swoon with their sweetness.

"You guys sure know how to make a girl feel at home. Thanks, babies."

I laid back down in the bed, making myself comfortable against one of the thirteen pillows. Like, actually thirteen pillows. Bonkers.

The door opened, and the sound of Demi's voice made me smile. "No! Shoo! Get away from the princess. I didn't realize the window was open."

"Oh, I did that. These are my new friends. Do you mind if they stay with us?"

Demi swore in astonishment. "You really are the Lost Princess. I mean, I knew it, but to see it in person? Incredible. They can truly understand you?"

"I told them you were going to read to us," I teased, hoping he would read to me without me having to admit my giant flaw to him. I couldn't handle going from revered princess to Remedial Rosie in a night. Not in front of the hot guy.

Demi grinned. "Well, with an audience like this, how could I say no? And how did you untuck yourself already? I was gone for only a few minutes." Demi locked the door, and then latched the window before he settled into the bed beside me. His arm wrapped under me to bring my body tight to his, propping me up with pillows against the tall headboard, so we were cuddled together in our cave with the comforter pulled to our stomachs. My arm draped over his lap in a snuggly hug and squeezed his hips, our budding friendship starting on a much better note.

He opened his dusty hardcover book and handed me a second one. "I didn't know what you would like, so I brought a second option. I wasn't sure you'd enjoy what I read. I don't know any Commoner tales."

"Not even the classics? What about Romeo and Juliet?"

Demi shrugged with a blank expression. "Why don't you tell it to me?"

I didn't know how condensed to make the whole play without pissing off Shakespeare himself, so I started at the beginning and took an entire five minutes to work my way through the Cliff's Notes version of the plot. By the end, Demi was gasping at all the right parts, enraptured by the story that Ninth Grade Literature professors everywhere never tired of teaching.

"That was incredible! How very sad. So they both die? They never get to truly be together, as they were meant to be?"

I shook my head. "Sometimes Juliet doesn't get her Romeo. Shakespeare didn't sugarcoat it for the viewers. Sometimes love stories end up in tragedy."

Demi reached out and held my hand, running his thumb over my knuckles. "I should hope that your love stories have happier endings than that."

We shared a sweet smile, letting the cozy atmosphere knit us closer together. "I hope that, too."

"My turn. Which book would you like to read tonight? Something from Avalon, this time. I'm afraid your Commoner tale was too sad for me."

I swallowed hard, skating around my limitations with a breezy expression. I leaned forward and tapped one of the books on his lap. "Could you read me a few pages of whatever you're into?"

He settled down into the pillows, pressing a sweet kiss to my forehead. "Of course, my princess. Nothing would make me happier." And darn it, if I didn't actually believe him this time.

He had a page marker halfway through, but thumbed back to the beginning for my benefit. "'Most tales of Ardennes started with 'Once upon a time,' but the tale of Michel Fourniret should never have started in any time, and after this account, shall never be spoken of again.'"

Demi was a cuddler, pausing to sink further down into the covers so he could bring my head to his chest and scoop my body to wrap around his. He had a swimmer's body, lean and agile, but muscular, too. He seemed to know what I wanted, which was for someone to hold me, to make me feel safe, and to keep things G-rated while I figured out how this new life worked. His sweetness endeared me to him. The safety of his arms nearly threatened raw emotion to spring up in my eyes, but I held it back so I wasn't the freak who cried just because someone was nice to her. "Are you quite certain this is what you wish me to read you? It gets quite dark toward the middle. I brought a collection of romantic poetry you might enjoy better."

I hated poetry. It's a dyslexic's nightmare. All the flowery language I have to decipher and decode, on top of the words having multiple meanings, makes for a traffic jam in my mind. A simple sentence, which takes far more work for me than for others to get through, loses all meaning by the end. Judah tried to read poetry to me when he was tutoring me through the Shakespeare section in our Freshman Lit class. He liked to do an old lady warbling voice that tried to be British, but usually ended up sounding like a cackling witch by the end. When he'd wrap up a poem, I still had no friggin' clue what it had been about. "I don't really understand poetry," I admitted quietly, sharing a portion of a secret with Demi, who didn't laugh at me for being stupid. "Dark and scary is fine by me."

"One day, I'll read you some poetry." One of my birds hopped on Demi's shoulder, judging him to be safe, now that I'd vouched for him by cuddling the man. His eyes widened as he marveled at the tiny creature, completely enraptured by the small miracle of my birth blessing. "This is incredible, your grace."

"Rosie," I reminded him.

Demi was fond of kissing my face, indulging us both in the cuteness when his lips grazed my cheek. "Rosie it is, then." I held tight to him, my one beacon of sweetness in the sea of uncertainty.

6

MY NEW FRIEND

When I awoke in the morning, Demi had breakfast waiting for me. He was making it all too easy. With him rubbing oil into my feet while I ate my meal in bed, I could almost forget the urgency of my mission, and the ill feelings I had toward Morgan for making him think being a gigolo was an appropriate grand ambition.

I refused to be turned from Lane's daughter into Morgan's. I so desperately wanted for Morgan to be a great woman I could model myself after, but the more she revealed of her personality, the less I saw that as a thing worth striving after. I finished scarfing down as much as I could of my grand breakfast, which consisted of tea, eggs, rolls, fruit I'd never seen before, freshly-squeezed juice and a piece of candy that tasted like mouthwash and raspber-ries. Avalon didn't so much understand candy, if the raspberry mouthwash treat was any indication. I pushed the rest of the platter to Demi. "Here, dude. You finish the rest. I think I stuck to my half, but I may have eaten more of the berries than my share."

Demi quirked his eyebrow at me, his sculpted lips curling into a half-smile he often wore when I did something he thought was cute or funny. "I've already eaten with the servants in the kitchen, your grace."

"Rosie," I corrected him for the millionth time. "And I know you're still hungry. You've been eyeing the eggs. Have at it." One of my birds brought me a piece of ribbon he'd found outside to lace through my hair. I had six birds total working on a single braid after Demi had brushed my curls that morning. Demi had, for the most part, gotten used to the animals that flocked through the long window, but he was amazed that they could braid my hair.

"I couldn't possibly eat off your plate. It's not appropriate for a servant to share food with a royal."

I rolled my eyes at him and handed him the fork. "Be a rebel. I won't tell. I don't want all this breakfast to go to waste. Especially not when some of the other provinces are low on food. Doesn't seem right." When he still was hesitant, I taunted him with a guilt trip. "If you don't eat it, the starving children in all the provinces will cry. 'Demi! Demi! How could you let all that food go to waste?' they'll say."

"Well, if it's for the starving children." I moved the tray to his lap, and he forked a pile of eggs. Demi looked around guiltily and shoved them into his mouth. He chewed so fast and swallowed them down, I thought he was going to choke them right back up. "Oh, those are amazing. The chef adds purslane to the royals' eggs. It's harder to find, so it's reserved for only you, Morgan and important guests. Keeps you from falling to everyday illnesses and keeps your mind sharp."

"Huh. So that's what the green stuff in the eggs is." I clapped my hands together and held them out like I was getting ready to catch a football. "Give me your foot."

Demi obeyed on instinct, but retracted it when I started rubbing oil into his heel. "Oh, you can't do that, Rosie."

I grinned at him, tilting my head to the side. "Hey, you called me by my name. I almost feel like a person now. Thank you."

"Yes, well, I've already broken enough rules. I'll not have you rubbing my feet."

I quirked my eyebrow. "Um, perks of being a princess. I get to do whatever I want. I want to rub your feet. Makes me feel like we're on a level playing field. You scratch my back, I scratch yours. Or, well, rub your feet, anyways." When he opened his mouth to protest, I shrugged. "It's who I am, Demi. I don't have servants. People who are very lucky have friends. You were cool to me last night when I was all turned around. You held me while I slept. That's a big deal to me. In my world? That's about as intimate as I get. This is my way of saying thank you."

Demi was cautious, but finally rested his foot on the

bed between us, his eyes going from wide to rolled back when I started working on the arch of his right foot. "Oh, you're dangerous. You can't tell anyone about this, Rosie. It'll be my head, for certain. I'm your *soumettre*, remember."

"You sincerely overestimate how many friends I have if you're worried about that." I mulled over my plan while he moaned, losing himself in my touch. "So how long do I get to spend with you today?"

"I'm yours every day and every night, unless Rigby or her majesty most high tells me otherwise. What did you have in mind?"

"A tour of the grounds?" I requested, hoping that would be the least conspicuous way of seeing where my gut pulled me. I needed to find the Jewels of Good Fortune and set Avalon right again. I kept my eyes on Demi's long and manly foot, circling his ankle with my thumb while my knuckles dug into his heel. "And I'd like to meet my dad, if that's okay."

"Of course, Juliet," he teased me with a charming smirk. "I'll have Rigby set something up with his majesty most high's attendants to make sure he's presentable. We can tour the grounds while we're waiting. Though, the castle's quite large. It would take days to see all the rooms."

"Should I like, meet the soldiers or something? I kinda want to see Avalon's spin on female armor."

"Female armor? We don't have anything like that. Only men serve in the army."

I frowned. "That's weird."

"The population's stilted – two men to every one woman. Men are expendable." He said it so frankly with no hint of frustration at the unfairness that anyone should be seen as expendable.

"I don't like that. It's mean."

Demi smiled softly at me. "No, I don't imagine you would. You're new to Avalon. It hasn't hardened you yet. I pray that day may never come." He scratched his forearm, which he managed to do so gracefully, he looked like a work of art with an itch. "What parts of the castle would you like to see first?"

"The spot where the soldiers take women against their will. I feel like that'll be a good place to set up camp for a bit."

Demi frowned at me. "I can't imagine under what circumstances you could convince me to take you there. For what purpose?"

I shrugged. "If I'm there, they can't get away with that sort of thing, right?"

Demi tilted his head at me, as if I was a strange bird. "If you'd like that behavior to stop, I can tell Rigby, and he'll take it up with her majesty most high. That's how the chain of command works. Her majesty wouldn't allow me to take you there, though."

I was bummed that I didn't have as much power as I was hoping. I wanted to change the world in a day, but perhaps that was overshooting things a bit. After a few beats, I moved my smile back into place, pacing myself for the jewel heist job I hadn't realized would be such an ordeal with absolutely no backup. "Finish your breakfast, Romeo, and then let's get to it. I'm sure there's a room around here filled to the brim with legit candy. No point in hiding it. You know I'll find it. I've got a nose for good chocolate."

Demi shoveled in a bite of eggs. "I wouldn't dream of hiding a thing from you. First stop, the room with all the sweets."

7

KICKING THE BALL, AND PUTTING MY FOOT IN MY MOUTH

I was ready to go the second Demi finished off his last bite. My travel clothes had been washed, so I traded the dressing gown I'd slept in for the comfort of jeans and my purple Andre the Giant t-shirt that felt like a second skin. Demi helped me secure the closest thing Avalon had to a soccer ball, which was a leather ball used in the practice sessions for their annual polo events. I tried to explain soccer to Demi, but decided the basics were the best place to start. We went outside of the castle, staying between the large expanse of land that fell between my new home and the moat that encircled our fortress. It was just enough space to dribble the ball back and forth as we started to trot along the perimeter.

I kept a smile on my face while I tried to listen intently to my gut. I wanted to find those jewels and get out of here. I had no plan for after I discovered the gems, but decided not to let that bother me. Something told me like a creeping tap on the shoulder that if the jewels went missing, and I took off, Morgan would only increase her hunt for me. I hoped she believed that I had no Compass ability left to speak of.

"No, no. Try to kick it with your instep, Romeo. You're going to hurt your toe always kicking it head-on like that."

Demi obliged, but I could tell the adjustment felt unnatural to him. "Like this?"

"Yeah. Try it for one lap around the castle. You'll have more control over the ball like this."

He kicked the ball back with slightly better aim this time while we trotted a few meters apart. He wore beige pants and a white t-shirt, looking like a model from a Gap ad. "Is this what Commoners do for fun?"

"Sometimes. It's what I do. I love playing sports. I do soccer most of the time. That's my favorite. But I play basketball, sometimes rugby, and baseball if I need some extra stimulation. Just depends on how much free time I have after school and work, how many sports I can cram into my schedule. What do you do for fun here?"

My gut was still pleasantly settled, and we were already halfway past the front of the castle. I hoped I could find the jewels soon.

"We go hunting for game. The royals play polo. Some of us play *les coup de poing*. We find ways to entertain ourselves."

"Cool. You'll have to teach me."

Demi shook his head, fielding one of my kicks with surprising agility. "No. *Les coup de poing* is no game for a woman. You could get hurt. It's quite rough."

"Clearly you've never played rugby before. Trust me, I can handle it."

"Her majesty most high would never let you play, and the men would be afraid of a swift beheading if they touched you wrong or injured you."

I grimaced, cradling the ball with my instep and dribbling it a few feet before kicking it back as we progressed along the perimeter of the castle. "Oh. Well, I don't want that."

We bantered for a while, and I learned that Demi was the second oldest of seven children, and that he'd grown up in Province 8. "When our province was surrendered to her majesty most high, I was chosen to serve in the mansion."

"Surrendered? What do you mean?"

"Before she died, Duchess Avril couldn't feed us all, so her majesty most high made an offer to provide for the people in the portion of Province 8 where I lived. It helped the duchess because there were less mouths to feed, which benefitted all of Province 8. So the region was absorbed by Province 1. Then when Duchess Avril died, the rest of the province was absorbed by Morgan."

I guessed it was a big secret that Aunt Avril hadn't been killed, but managed to escape into the Forgotten Forest with her Jewel of Good Fortune. I decided it was best for all involved if I kept my mouth shut about that one. "And everyone in the province was cool with that?"

Demi shrugged and kicked the ball back as we passed a stone parapet with a lion statue growling out at us on the ledge. "There wasn't a choice. We went from barely making it day by day to feasting when her majesty most high took us in. Her payment was her pick of the men to serve however she saw fit. Some were chosen for the army, while others of us were groomed for serving her in the mansion."

My mouth hung open. "So you're a spoil of war? You were taken from your family?" I stopped the ball underfoot when it came to me, and closed the gap between us with a crushing hug. Demi's body stiffened on first contact, but I couldn't let him not be hugged through the awful confession. I nestled my cheek to his chest and squeezed him tight until he softened in my arms, melting like pliable chocolate. "Demi, I'm so sorry that happened. What can I do? Can I give you your freedom and send you back to your family? Like, do I have that ability?"

Demi's arms finally wrapped around me, rubbing up and down my spine while he inhaled the scent of my curls. "I'll go home when I've served my sentence. We're to give the queen ten years from the time we're taken, and I'm seven into mine. Life before this was so long ago, I barely remember the feel of a family. I made my peace with it all years ago. My parents are healthy, I'm told, and my brothers and sisters are fed. There are many of us like me here, so we lean on each other when it gets difficult, but over the years, we've grown numb to it all."

"That's like, the worst thing I've ever heard! You're numb to being without your family? I'm a couple weeks without Lane, and I'm falling apart."

Of all things, Demi's chest rumbled with a quiet chuckle. He thumbed my cheek and cupped the underside of my jaw so my face was angled up toward him. "My sweet princess. How fair you are. You needn't worry about me. If I'd not been taken, I wouldn't be able to serve you now."

I blew out a childish raspberry. "That's an awful consolation prize. Can I talk to Morgan for you? Can I ask to get your sentence reduced?"

"No, my sweet Juliet. If I displease you enough that you send me away, I'll be beaten and sent to do hard labor in the fields with the other shamed servants, or I'll be beheaded. There is no other way for me."

I looked up into his bright green eyes, appreciating anew how vastly different our worlds were. "I'm so sorry my mother did this to you."

Demi squinted in mild confusion before his lips parted in wonder. "You're being sincere. You truly wish me free so I can return to my family."

"Of course. I don't want this life for you. I want you to be happy and have a good life that has nothing to do with bowing."

He glanced worriedly around to make sure no one heard us. "You cannot say such things out in the open. Her majesty most high will think I'm filling your head with foolish dreams." Demi's thumb slid across my cheekbone, his gaze thickening with intensity and intention. "And surely you cannot say things like that to me and expect me not to kiss you."

My eyes widened when it occurred to me that I was in the arms of a man I'd known one whole day. My lips were close enough to clear the distance and taste his. Demi had the look of being a great kisser. He'd kissed a few of the top women in Avalon, so he had to be pretty good at seduction.

I didn't mean for the words to tumble out of my mouth like a clumsy punch, but I found I couldn't stop them. "You kissed my mother and my aunt. I can't kiss a guy who's kissed my mom."

Demi flinched as if I'd slapped him, which I guess my words kind of had. It wasn't his choice to be with Morgan or Aunt Avril. He didn't have a choice in his life at all. He was in survival mode, just trying to keep his head attached to his shoulders, and I was being a princess about the whole thing. Demi released me from our tender hug and went to pick up the ball. "Yes, your majesty. Perhaps you'd like to continue the tour of the grounds?"

His professional demeanor was exactly what I deserved. I lowered my chin and nodded, taking with grace the distance he needed to give me. We didn't kick the ball back and forth anymore, but walked with a division the size of a grizzly bear between us. The ball was tucked under Demi's arm. He talked about how old a few of the towers were, and I let him fill the awkwardness that settled between us. When he finally ran out of things to say, I reached out and gripped his hand, looping my pointer finger through his. "I'm sorry, Demi."

He shrugged. "You've nothing to be sorry for. You're right. I am a whore. I'm a whore and you're a princess. For a moment, I forgot."

I couldn't respond with anything other than a meek, "You're not a whore. You're my friend. I'm so sorry I was careless. I was so mean. Please forgive me."

Demi gave me that same odd bug look he did whenever I apologized. "If you need my forgiveness, you have it."

I was about to say something to further debase myself, but my gut chimed in with a tug toward the moat. It was a gentle nudge at first, but as I steered us closer to the water's edge, the nudge became a shove. My gut was screaming at me that this was the place, and that beneath the water was a jewel. I leaned over, and Demi's hands on my waist secured me in place. "Careful, your majesty. It won't do you any good to fall into the moat."

"'Your majesty?'" I turned in his arms, the hurt plain on my face as I cast my eyes up at his. He let his arms fall down and took a step backward, his hands tucked behind his back, like he was waiting for an order. I shook my head at him. "Ouch, Demi. I made one slip. I told you I'd only ever kissed one guy my whole life, and it went up in flames. I'm not good at the whole sweeping romance thing, but you don't have to go all formal on me. It was an accident."

He dipped his head and replied quietly, "I hear someone coming. I only used your title so as not to be punished."

I dropped my fight, chagrinned. "Oh, sorry about that." I pinched the bridge of my nose. "I'm screwing up all over the place."

"Be patient with yourself and with me, your grace." He stood straighter when Rigby rounded the corner at a trot. He gave Rigby a slight bow.

"Her majesty most high has requested the princess not be seen in peasant attire outside the castle. She's to be taken back inside and properly dressed straightaway."

I sighed at the loss of my jeans. I should've known that was coming. Everything here was so formal. "Okay. Hey, Rigby. How's your morning going?"

Rigby ignored me completely, and it was then I realized he only looked at Demi and hadn't spoken to me at all yet. "Take her through the south entrance. She's not to be seen like this. The suitors are already responding with letters of intent. Her majesty most high will want to approve of her appearance before she's seen by them."

I looked down at myself, confused. "But I look fine. And I told her I didn't need any suitors. She's still on that? I told her I'm not ready to get married, much less to a stranger."

Again, Rigby didn't look at me, but only spoke to Demi.

"Take her quickly, and see to it she doesn't speak her mind. Her majesty most high is in a state this morning."

"Yes, sir. Right away."

I felt unbearably sad that for no reason at all, my friends in the castle had been cut by fifty percent. I didn't know what I'd done to make Rigby hate me so much. "Rigby? What's going on? Why won't you look at me? Did I do something wrong? Whatever it is, I'm sorry!"

I watched the vein in Rigby's neck tighten and pulse as he fought to ignore me. "Demi, please explain her majesty most high's temper to your charge. The princess has been permitted to keep you, but should anyone else in the castle look the princess' way, they shall face her majesty's wrath."

My eyes snapped to Demi in alarm. "Come again? Rigby, why are you mad at me? Please don't hate me. I don't know what I did!"

Demi nodded, his body rigid as he wasted no time pulling me tight to his side. "Come, Princess. We'll take the back corridors to your chambers to avoid her majesty's whims."

Before I could respond or get a straight answer, Demi was shoving me into the nearest castle door, his body stiff and on high alert. He wrapped my hand around his elbow, taking quick and quiet steps, pausing before we rounded each corner. He pressed his finger to his lips, but I was already too turned around and upset to speak my mind. It felt like we were hiding from someone, though I wasn't sure who.

8

THE PUNISHMENT FOR JEANS

Demi gusted out a breath of relief when the door to my bedroom closed behind us. The small reprieve was all he allowed himself before running to the tall oak wardrobe in the corner and flinging the double doors open. He yanked out a dress at random and laid it on the bed. "You have to change now, Rosie. Quick as you can. It would really be faster if I helped you."

"Huh? I can get dressed by myself, but thanks." I went behind the partition with the new dress where a pile of white ruffles lay draped over an upholstered chair. "Why is Rigby mad at me? What did I do?" I jerked my shirt over my head and kicked off my shoes, socks and jeans.

"Rigby adores you, which is the only reason he thought to warn us. Her majesty most high hasn't permitted another woman in the castle in ages. You're the first. Her temper tends to flare when men look anywhere other than at her. Rigby is her most trusted servant, so he must be careful if he wants to stay in her majesty most high's good graces."

"But Rigby's gotta be like, twenty years older than me. She's not actually jealous of me. You can't be serious. I'm in old jeans and sneakers."

"Yes, and even in peasant clothing, you're going to turn the eye of every man in the castle. We've been starved for true beauty."

It was the closest Demi had ever come to out and out dissing Morgan, so I chose not to comment on it. "Okay. Then how is making me dress up going to help men not look at me?" The heavy pink material almost fell clean off me when I worked it over my head. I fumbled with the lacing in the back, but it was being stubborn, and had too many loops.

"Her majesty most high is quite proud. It won't do to have suitors come to see you, only to think Morgan cannot run her household and look after one small girl. You're Master Kerdik's blessing to all of Avalon, so it's important you're presented as royalty. Her majesty most high fears only Master Kerdik, and there have been rumors that he's been seen in Avalon. First time in decades. If he thinks she's not presented you properly, he might pass judgment on her." His tone turned grave. "Even the strongest and bravest don't get back up once Master Kerdik's judgment is passed."

I gave up on the laces and came out holding my dress

up with a look of apology on my face. "I don't know how to lace this thing up. I know I said I didn't need any help, and I swear I'm not trying to make things weird, but could you lace me up just this once? Maybe teach me how, so I don't have to bug you about it again?"

Demi's expression vacillated between amusement and panic that I'd wasted so much time doing it all wrong. "You forgot your undergarments, Rosie."

"Huh? I'm wearing underwear. What are you talking about?"

A crooked half-smile played on Demi's lips. "Let me help you. Otherwise her majesty most high will see you like this, and she'll be terribly displeased with us both."

My face was burning crimson when he led me back to the pile of ruffles I'd dismissed as somebody else's. He kept his eyes locked in on mine as his thumbs tucked under the edges of my dress' neckline and slowly peeled down the gown until it was a puddle of material on the floor. My hands moved quick to cover my bra, but Demi only smiled softly at me. He picked up the mountain of beige and white alternating ruffles and slipped it over my head. My arms were expertly threaded through the capped sleeves after Demi popped my bra off. He kept his eyes focused on mine so I didn't freak out and run away, but I was still on the brink. "Demi, I don't think I like this dress," I warned, panicked.

"These are your underskirts. They keep your dress in place." He lifted the corset thing that Scarlet O'Hara had worn in *Gone with the Wind*, and began to fashion it around my waist. His hands gently moved under my breasts to plump them out, but his touch was kind and as respectful as possible. I didn't feel the fear I assumed would rise up like bile in my throat at the way too intimate contact. I tried to remind myself that this was Demi's job, and I needed to chill out about it. He tied the corset just tight enough that I could still move freely and breathe just fine. The pink and red dress was slipped over my head, but this time it didn't droop off of me. The poofy ruffled under-dress thing held it in place. I held my breath while Demi laced up the gold ribbons on the back of the gown.

Demi leaned down to whisper in my ear. "It would do well for you not to mention any temper you have about your suitors today. They're coming, whether you like it or not. On the days her majesty most high is in a temper, it's best not to provoke her."

"Oh, jeez. I told her no, though. Don't I get a say in any of it?"

"No," Demi answered flatly. "And when she gets here, I'll do my best not to look at you, so as not to provoke her. Try not to be offended. It's only to make sure my head stays in place." He turned me to face him so I could see his sincerity. His hands cupped my cheeks, reminding me that he'd just seen me almost naked. My cheeks heated in his capable hands. "But I'll be counting the minutes until I can look on your lovely face again."

I'm sure it was probably a line. I mean, dude had been

taught to tell royals whatever they wanted to hear. But darn it, if I didn't believe the sincerity in his pleading eyes as they drank in my features. He looked at me as if I was beautiful.

I don't know why I did it, but for once I decided not to stop myself from being brave. I took a chance, leaned up on my toes and brushed my lips to his, just once, light as a feather's touch. I wasn't sure if it was romantic, or a very flirty platonic gesture, but it was enough to scare me away from him entirely.

Demi's eyes were wide with shock that I'd initiated the kiss I'd sworn I didn't want. He judged the space between us to be way too much, and took a series of bold steps in my direction, backing me up until my shoulders pressed against the wall, my chest heaving against his. "I shouldn't have..." I began, confused that I was thinking of Bastien now. A pang of disloyalty pinged in my chest, though I didn't fully understand why. Bastien wasn't in my life anymore; I didn't owe him fidelity after what he'd done. Still, there was some undiscernible part of me that felt sad that I'd kissed someone else. Maybe this was what moving on felt like.

Demi sized up my uncertainty and played along the edges of my daring, his lips brushing against mine from left to right, daring me to take a bite of the forbidden fruit. "Rosie," he whispered, filling my lungs with his sweet peppermint breath. "I thought you said you didn't want to be kissed."

"I d-don't. Or I didn't." I turned my chin away from his to stop the slow seduction that oozed naturally from him. "I don't know what I'm doing!"

The knock on the door was well-timed, and broke us away from the point of no return. He shot me a look that told me to be cool, and puffed his chest before opening the door. "Good afternoon, your majesty most high. The Princess is overjoyed to see you now."

Morgan wore a red dress that showed off her exaggerated curves. Her lips were smudged in red, and her eyes seemed to spark with temper that came out of nowhere. "I thought I told you to be expecting suitors, and yet I hear reports of you running around in peasant clothes outside for anyone to see. How is it you're this much of a problem already? I gave you one order: be beautiful. How is it you can't remember one simple thing?"

My mouth fell open, stunned that this was how she was starting out our second conversation. "I didn't know I wasn't allowed to wear jeans."

Her voice was shrill as she yelled for everyone who might be walking down the hall to hear. "Were the dresses my tailors made for you not to your liking? Is it possible you're this stubborn?"

I stiffened, angry that she was treating me like I was a spoiled brat. "No. I told you I didn't want to get married yet. I wasn't expecting to have to perform like a monkey for men I have no interest in. I'm wearing the dress now, so chill out about it."

Lane had never hit me before, so I wasn't expecting Morgan's hand that flew out at me, slapping me across the face. My cheek burned with too many layers of betrayal, stunning me with the reality that this was my life now. Demi and Rigby kept their eyes resolutely on the floor, and I knew I was on my own.

I had hurt on my face and venom welling in my soul, but luckily, I didn't have to compromise myself by fighting back. A flock of birds came zooming in through the open window, attacking Morgan with their beaks, wings and claws. They tore at her hair, ripping pieces out and pecking at her face in my defense.

As much as I appreciated the gesture and the knowledge that I wasn't alone in all of this, I didn't want to give Morgan yet another reason to hate me. I whistled for them to leave her alone. They'd been docile and decidedly not homicidal when I'd first met them, and now they'd turned dark for me. *No, no.* On my whistle, the birds flocked to me, forming several rows like little kamikaze soldiers between myself and Morgan, each of them chirping foul things that were better left unheard by human (or Fae) ears.

"What foul magic is that?" she seethed.

I tsked her. "You want me to 'be beautiful'? Well, my birds don't think your behavior is all that attractive. Birds don't care about looks as much as they do about kindness."

Morgan's voice was shrill. "You have no clue how to stay on top in this world!"

"Being pretty means *nothing!*" I roared, more at life than at her. I wanted to scream it in the face of everyone who'd grimaced at me before I'd lost my magical necklace. I wanted to shout it at myself most of all, as a reminder that if I lost myself in the chaos of life, there would be nothing. *I* would be nothing if I tried to be Morgan's daughter instead of remembering that my greatest adventure was me. Not this castle. Not a beauty contest. Not finding some guy to marry. Just plain me.

Morgan was livid, her face dotted with bloody marks as she fumed. Her fists were clenched like they wanted to lash out at me, but knew they couldn't without incurring more wrath from my feathered homies. Spittle flew out when she spoke to me through clenched teeth. "You will select a suitor, and dress like a daughter of the highest throne. You will behave with the decorum I would have raised you with, were you not taken from me."

I held up my hands. "You know, I always wanted to meet you. You're starting off on the way wrong foot with me. I already want this to work, but I'm twenty-two. I don't need someone to map out my life who's just now meeting me. Maybe you and I should spend some time getting to know each other. That way I won't piss you off so much."

"Not possible. I knew upon first glance that you would be just as foolish, reckless, and unpolished as Elaine." She snapped her fingers to Demi, who came to her side in a blink. "Her figure hasn't been trained. Tighten that corset."

"Yes, your majesty." Demi didn't waste a second coming around behind me, unlacing the ribbons on my dress and tightening the stays on the corset beneath. It was uncomfortable now, but I could still breathe, so you know, bonus.

"Tighter," Morgan demanded, an angry fire in her eyes. I knew that fire; it was the same flame that kindled irrational action inside of me whenever anyone made fun of Judah. I'd been suspended a couple of times for fighting on his behalf – totally worth it.

Demi jerked me when he whipped the cords back. I didn't mean to cry out, but dude, oxygen is kind of a nonnegotiable. "That's too tight!"

"Nonsense. You're just not used to it. You'll adjust in time. Tighter, Demi."

Demi led me around my birds and over to the bed while Rigby looked away. Demi's long fingers positioned my hands on the pole. He wore dead eyes and had no words of reassurance on his lips. He pulled until I was sure either one of my ribs or the corset was going to break. Each cry from my lips made Morgan snider, satisfied that she was winning because I was suffering.

When she finally decided I'd had enough, Demi laced up my dress and stood behind me, awaiting further instruction. I was scared to breathe for too many reasons. All of it was too much. I tried to keep my voice calm. "Whatever point you're trying to make here, I already get it. I'm a disappointment. You're the queen, and I'm a nobody. I get it. I'll stay out of your way, and I'll play along as much as I can." I shook my head at her, drawing in the shallowest of breaths. "But a corset won't make me more yours. Hurting me won't make me love you."

Morgan squared her shoulders to me. "I've no interest in love. Queens don't have that luxury. In time, you'll see the lengths I'm going to are for your own good. Avalon needs a strong, unified monarchy."

"Unified? You've been living alone for too long if you think this is how you and I will get on the same page. I'm not one of your subjects out there. All I wanted was for you to be nice to me. Tell me you like my hair because it looks like yours. Play catch with me. Take me shopping. Tell me about your life. You know, girlfriend type of stuff. This?" I motioned to the dress, and then my line of birds who had their tails up in anticipation of another attack. My breasts felt pushed to their limits, my dress straining around my chest with each barely-there breath I managed. "This isn't the way. I'm your daughter first, and a princess second. I think you forgot that."

It was as if I hadn't even spoken. "Rigby, take Demi down to the post and have him disciplined for letting the princess out in peasant clothing. If he's to be entrusted with her care, he must understand the level to which he must rise. There will be suitors here from all over Avalon. Mistakes like that could be costly."

"Disciplined?" I was panicked that something as

simple as jeans could be cause for punishment. "What does that mean?"

A small smile played on Morgan's lips. "He'll be tied to a post and whipped until he spills enough blood to satisfy me."

The worst was that there was no reaction from Demi, only compliance. He bowed his head to her. "Yes, your majesty most high."

When he moved toward the door, I grabbed his arm, dread and regret crushing any bravado I might've had. "No! No, Morgan. *I* wore jeans. Demi didn't tell me to. We didn't know how crazy your standards were, or I wouldn't have done that. I'm not trying to make you mad, here. You can't attack Demi for a mistake *I* made!"

"I can do as I please, and it pleases me to watch him bleed for his mistakes. Serving the high princess is the loftiest honor any servant in all of Avalon can have, aside from serving me. I'll not have him treat the privilege so callously."

"Then I'll take his place," I offered, scared and half out of my mind. I held tight to Demi, my hand in his as I moved forward to shield him with my body.

"No, Princess," Demi admonished me quietly. "It's alright. I'll go willingly. If it pleases my queen to watch me bleed, there can be no higher honor than to delight her majesty most high."

I could barely move, and air was hard to come by, so

panicking wasn't helping matters. I ignored Demi's canned response I knew he had to produce to avoid a worse beating. "Whip me instead until you're happy. It's me you hate, obviously. It's me you're disappointed in. Don't take it out on him."

I couldn't believe I caught Morgan off her guard, but that seemed to do it. She took a step back, trying to figure me out. "You can't possibly mean to offer yourself in his place. He's merely a slave."

"He's a person!" I roared. "If you think punishing him will help anything, you're dead wrong. It'll only divide you and me more. You want a unified kingdom? Then don't attack my servant." I hated that I used the word "servant," but guessed that if I said "friend," it would only drive her to hurt him more.

She rolled her shoulders back, looking every bit the queen people feared. "Men do not matter in our world, least of all slaves. Look at this as your first education on what's important in this kingdom."

I blanched, recalling the many modern-day countries that treated women with that same calloused hand. "That is the most disgusting thing I've ever heard! If you don't love the people you rule over, then what's the point?"

She threw out her hands to the sides incredulously. "To rule them! That's the whole point. My job is not to coddle them or give them more importance than is necessary. My job is to rule. If you're to sit on the throne one day, then you must stop your pathetic heart from constantly bleeding over nothing."

I slowly turned my chin from side to side, utterly destroyed that this was what my mother thought she had to do to keep her kingdom in check. Maybe there was logic in her way, but I couldn't stomach any of it. "I'll take a heart that bleeds and breaks over having none at all." I tapped my chest, utterly broken that this was the sad life my mother led. "I wanted more for you than this."

"Do not pity me, child." She snatched at my face again, pinching my jaw with her nails to hold me in place. "You have one job: be beautiful. Whatever this is that you're doing? It's weak, not beautiful."

The second she released my cheeks, Demi whirled me around to face him, his expression composed while he chose his words carefully. "It gives me pleasure to serve her majesty most high. I would not allow you to take my place, even if we had that choice. To take pleasure from my queen would be a crime I couldn't abide in myself." He seemed to be saying something more with his eyes, pleading with me to be cool, and that this was all kosher. Then he met Morgan's eyes with a firm nod. "I'll go now."

Morgan composed her face and rolled her shoulders back, exposing her cleavage proudly. "Very well, Demi."

Demi didn't need an escort to take himself to the post. He walked out with grace and dignity befitting someone light-years above me. I knew tears would start to well in my eyes, so I did my best to calm myself down. I wouldn't degrade myself in front of that hateful woman.

"A guard will escort you around the castle until your *soumettre* is returned to you, no doubt wiser this time." Morgan sneered at the birds, kicking one before she made her exit, slamming my door behind her.

9

NEW HUSBAND, NEW VOICE

ears poured down my face, but the second I realized I couldn't wheeze and carry on with the corset so tight, I did my best to calm down so I didn't pass out. I was afraid to go out of the room looking anything less than perfect, lest Demi be punished for me being a loser. I made sure my nose wasn't red, and the birds re-braided my hair, assuring me that I looked like a princess. A heavy weight settled on me that Demi would pay the price if I screwed up even the smallest detail. The corset was too tight, and my fingers started to tingle from the unbearable constriction.

Rigby, not a guard, greeted me when I stepped out into the stone hallway, though he still did not look at my face. "Where shall I escort you, your majesty?"

"I'd like to visit my father, please," I said quietly. The bird on my shoulder cheeped encouragement to me. It was sweet, but I couldn't feel anything but doomed. "Is that okay? Is that beautiful?" I wasn't sure what I was allowed to do anymore.

It was then I realized I just asked a man for permission to move around in my own home. I just asked someone if my actions were beautiful – a thing I would never have cared about, were there not the threat of violence to cage me in like a frightened animal. I was sickened at my obeisance, but couldn't stomach getting anyone else hurt for my freedom.

"Of course, your majesty. Follow me."

There was no charm to him anymore – not that he'd had a ton to begin with. I'd thought I'd caught a glimpse yesterday, but Morgan had stamped out his personality, ironing him into the drone she desired. I wanted desperately to ask Rigby if Demi was alright, but I knew he couldn't be. I kept my bluebird with me, letting him nuzzle me every few steps to keep me going. I was beginning to understand the whole fragile princess trope. The corset was so tight, I could hardly breathe. Walking only exacerbated my dilemma.

Rigby led me past dozens of guards in leather armor, who all turned their backs on me when I approached. While I knew it was because Morgan was having one of her infamous jealousy days, I couldn't help but feel like a leper.

Rigby took a heavy skeleton key from his pocket when we reached wooden doors that stretched from floor to ceiling. He nodded to the two guards who stood post just outside, and unlocked the door, heaving it open with a heavy shove. The creaking told me the room wasn't well cared for, and the thick coat of dust inside confirmed that fact for me.

There was no flourish to the space, just a simple narrow bed in an unlit, windowless room, next to an end table. The man on the bed had a mostly unlined face with crinkles around his eyes. After meeting Morgan, I wondered if those were from stress. His hands rested at his sides, and if I didn't know better, I would guess that he'd been merely sleeping. I resisted the urge to poke him.

I don't know what I'd been expecting, other than Clark Kent. He was a man beginning his fifties, by my guess. My steps felt weighted as I neared my father's bedside, shocked that I was meeting my own personal rock star, and he hadn't been disappointed in me yet. Granted, he was unconscious, but still.

He'd sent me to live with Lane because he knew Morgan was bad news. Though he couldn't express it all to me, there was something inside that latched onto the hope that my father loved me, once upon a very long time ago. I reached out and brushed my fingers through his chestnut hair that had wisps of gray at the temples. There was dust in his hair that wafted out with my simple touch. I don't know why, but the fact that he'd been so abandoned that his body had begun to collect dust angered me. He had a longer nose than mine, but my breath caught in my throat when I saw the three freckles on his left cheek that were identical to my own.

I was too nervous to talk to him yet, especially with an audience, but for a first encounter, we weren't doing too badly.

Rigby locked the heavy doors behind us and sighed, releasing his tight shoulders with visible relief. "Princess, are you well?"

I pried my eyes from my father to look at Rigs incredulously. "Are you serious?"

He motioned me to come to him. "Let me loosen your stays while we're in here. I can't imagine you can breathe like that."

I almost gusted out a sigh of relief, but my ribs couldn't expand all that far. I turned around and nearly cried when the laces fell slack. I held my dress up and let Rigby adjust the whole getup so I could move around more comfortably. "Thank you."

Professional Rigby was put on hold when he spun me around and placed his hands on my shoulders, looking me seriously in the eye. "You must never do that again. Demi and all the slaves in the mansion understand that her majesty most high does what she wishes. Standing up to her only ever makes it worse."

"But Demi is getting hurt because of me! All because I wore jeans? That's ridiculous! You have to help him."

"The only help I can give him is to educate you on how to survive here. You cannot contradict the queen. You will wear your stays tight. You will choose a suitor. You will do as you're told, otherwise Demi will suffer for it. She knows she cannot harm you, not now that the announcement's been made to the provinces that the Lost Princess has been returned to us. And especially not now that she sees the full loyalty your gift garners from the animals." His voice lowered. "There have been rumors that Master Kerdik has returned to Avalon. He was friends with King Urien, and her majesty most high knows he wouldn't tolerate her killing King Urien's offspring. So you will obey, or Demi will suffer for your freedom."

"I have to get married? Like, there's no other choice?"

Rigby nodded solemnly. "Yes. You must get married. If I were you, I'd choose a suitor before one is chosen for you. Duke Henri has the most land that's been bountiful enough to sustain its people. It's close to Province I, and it would behoove her majesty most high to absorb his land without a fight. Duke Henri is who she'll choose for you. It's the most advantageous move for her because it will add to her kingdom. The Duke has already agreed to it. He's put up a fight to remain independent from her for years, but now that Master Kerdik might be back? He'll want you in his household so Master Kerdik's blessings might fall on him. Morgan and Duke Henri stand to gain a lot from this union."

My mouth fell open at the blast of insider information. "She wants me to marry Draper or Damond? But they're my cousins! Isn't that against some sort of law or something?"

He shook his head. "No, no. Draper's been cast out, so he holds no royal claim. He's royal only in name, but not by inheritance. Damond is promised to a judge's daughter from Province 3. You would be married off to Duke Henri himself."

My mouth fell open and my stomach churned. Now that I could start to feel my fingers again, since my stays had been loosened, my hands started to vibrate with fear. "No. You can't be serious. He's old! He's my uncle! He's got to be more than twice my age. He hit Lane right in front of me!"

Rigby exhaled when he saw he was finally getting through to me. "Exactly why you should be proactive and choose a suitor for yourself. Duke Henri has far more terrible traits than striking a woman, I assure you. I couldn't live with myself if I let you get married off to someone like him."

There was nowhere to sit, so I dropped to my knees on the floor while I tried to sort things out. "I have a month before I have to get married, right?"

"Yes, but you must choose a suitor well before then. All of Avalon is coming to the celebration of your return in less than two weeks' time. You have to give the queen your decision by then."

I knew I wouldn't be able to sneak out all the jewels in two weeks. I was under such scrutiny that I could barely go outside without wrath raining down on my head. I closed my eyes and swallowed the bile in my throat. "There's no way out of this."

"I'm afraid not. But there are ways to make your life bearable. Duke Henri isn't your only option."

"That door's locked?"

"It is. We're alone."

I reached for Rigby's pant leg and tugged him down to sit next to me. His movements were stiff and unpracticed at tenderness, but he managed to wrap his arm around my shoulders, allowing my head to fall on his sturdy shoulder. "Do you think my dad would've liked me?"

Rigs' body softened around mine, his chin resting against my temple. He reached for my hand and threaded his fingers through mine. "I have no doubt he would be most pleased to see what a compassionate, willful woman his daughter turned out to be. To offer yourself like that for a mere slave? I've never seen anything like it in all my years serving her majesty most high. No doubt Demi will be the envy of all the servants now."

I snorted my disbelief. "Yeah. I bet they all wish for a beating like that. She's sick to send Demi there."

I could hear Rigs' gentle smile in his tone. "They wish a royal would care for anything other than territory or themselves. They wish to catch the eye of a beautiful princess, as all men do. Demi will be envied because a princess offered herself up for him after bedding him only one night. It speaks highly of his ability to please you if your connection is already this strong."

"Okay, first off, Demi and I aren't having sex. I want my first time to be special, not something that my mother arranged. I mean, seriously. Demi's my friend, and he's been super way nice to me. After the culture shock this place is? I need a friend to keep me sane. I can't believe she's hurting him. Is it bad, the punishment?"

"Oh, it's most severe. It has to be to keep us all in line and under her thumb." At his brazen words, he checked the door again to make sure we were alone, and that no one witnessed him mouthing off. "But rest assured, Demi will be glowing when word spreads of your intended sacrifice. With that single act, you've already won the hearts of the slaves here."

"Well, I didn't do it for that. Demi's my friend. Of course I'd take his place. He didn't even do anything wrong. It's me Morgan's mad at." I let out my worries, since finally someone was around who understood the rules and would explain them to me. "What am I going to do about this marriage thing, Rigs? I can't marry Duke Henri. Just the thought makes me want to ralph."

"Then you must choose your own suitor. Someone you can stomach, preferably."

"But I don't know anyone in Avalon well enough for that. And how does this even work? I just go up to some dude on the street and be like, 'I'm Rosie Avalon. Nice to meet you. You're bipedal and seem like you might not be an axe murderer. Will you marry me?'" My nose scrunched in distaste. "I can't even picture myself doing that."

Rigby chuckled at my ineptitude. "No, no. Nothing like that. The announcement's already been made, so eligible suitors will come to make their offer to you for marriage at the celebration for Avalon. You simply select whom you like."

"But how? I don't know anyone. How will I know who's a good guy?"

Rigby took a few beats to think this out before responding. "Did you think her majesty most high was good when you first met her?"

"No," I admitted. "Though I wanted her to be."

"Trust your instincts. Pick someone you like the sound of. If he has a voice that stirs something in you, investigate that offer."

I reached out and coiled my fingers around a handful of his shirt, needing someone to stay with me when life was too weird to be livable. "Will you be there? Like, when I have to meet these guys, will you be with me?"

"If the queen wills it."

"Can we work out a signal or something? Like, ask me if I want potatoes when a guy you think is good comes around?"

"If I'm there, I can come to your room the next morning and give you my thoughts on which of them would make the best mate for you. The list of people I would approve of isn't long, I'm afraid. It would have to be someone strong enough to stand up to her majesty most high, and those are few and far between." He gave me a slight squeeze before standing to his feet and pulling me along with him. "Come, now. I've indulged you too long. Princesses don't sit on the floor. This room is dusty and hasn't been tended to in a long time. I'll see to it that it's cleaned if you're wishing to make visits here a regular occurrence."

"I do, yes. Could I have a minute with my dad?"

"Of course, your grace."

"Rosie," I reminded him.

Rigby looked deep into my eyes, saying things I didn't expect over so small a thing as asking him to call me by my first name. He held my hands in his, my knuckles to the ceiling, and kissed the backs of both of them. "I saw your face when I had to keep you at a distance this morning. Know that it's always for your own good."

"I know that now."

"It causes me pain to see you suffer. I'm sorry I hurt you."

I nodded once, my chin lowered, and I migrated into his arms for a quick hug to center us both. "Thanks, Rigs. See you in a few."

I waited until the doors shut behind him before I made my way back to the bedside of the man who hadn't moved the entire time. I didn't know what to do, but thought I'd start with the basics. "Hi, Urien, sir. It's nice to meet you." I mouthed the word, "Dad", unsure if I was allowed to call him that. Morgan didn't like me calling her "Mom".

I don't know why I expected a response, but when nothing came, I was a little disappointed. I picked up his hand, since there were no witnesses. I dusted it off, and studied his pliable skin. Though there were no windows, and he'd not been outside in who knows how long, his skin was a shade darker than mine. Since Morgan was paler, I guessed I got my easy tan from him.

I racked my brain for something to say. "I, um, I grew up alright. That depends on who you ask, I guess, but Lane will tell you I turned out okay. I flossed, was going to school, had friends." I tried to think back to my life up in Common. "I recycled." I grimaced and smacked my hand to my forehead. "Who cares about any of that? I'm sorry. I'm screwing this up. I don't know who you want me to be, or if the things that are important to me even register with you. But I'm here, and I'll try to be here every day so you know the world hasn't forgotten about you."

Sadness gripped me hard around the throat. I raised his palm to my cheek and molded his thick fingers around the curves of my face, wishing he could do that on his own – hoping he'd want to. My plea came out in a whisper I couldn't bring myself to say too loud. "I wish you knew me."

A tear fell from the corner of my eye, and I turned my chin so I could press a kiss to the center of his palm.

"Is someone near me? Is a woman speaking?"

My head whipped around, but no one was there. "Huh? Who said that?"

The voice came back confused. *"Hello? Can you hear me?"*

I dropped his hand and moved to the door, pressing my ear to it.

"Can you hear me?" the man repeated. *"Is it possible?"*

My eyes zeroed in on my father, my mouth going dry. I bolted to his side and scooped up his hand again. "Urien? Is that you?"

His mouth didn't move, but I could hear him clear as day. *"Yes! Have I finally gone mad, or is there someone who can actually hear me?"*

Frantic tears pricked my eyes as my fingers fluttered over his hand. "I can hear you, Da—your majesty. How did this happen? How can I help? What can I do?" I knew it was a cop-out not telling him who I was, now that he could hear me and focus on my voice, but I couldn't handle a second parent hating me before I had a chance to prove myself.

"Morgan!" he roared in his mind, though his body remained motionless. *"Morgan le Fae did this to me! By what miracle can you hear me?"*

"I don't know," I lied. "Just lucky, I guess. Are you in pain?"

"Only the pain of my heart. I've been trapped in my own mind for so long! Tell me, how many moons have passed since I fell into this sleep?"

My neck shrunk into my shoulders. "I'm sorry. I'm new here myself. I don't actually know much about you or Avalon. I'm thinking someone told me you've been out around twenty-one years or so."

Urien let out a strangled cry of grief that was fueled by rage. "*Twenty-one years? Has someone killed Morgan yet? Tell me her reign came to a bloody end.*"

The fury in his voice made sense, but I still flinched. "Uh, no. You're lying on a bed in her castle, actually. I don't know why they didn't at least get you a room with a window. Maybe a little sunshine would help you get better."

Urien scoffed. "*Morgan doesn't want me to get better. She put me here to make sure I remained useless to Avalon.*" His voice changed to dread, and for a second, he sounded scared. "*Tell me Elaine took my Rosalie away. Tell me she escaped with my daughter. Tell me my daughter is safe!*"

His anguished plea wrenched my heart from my chest and threw it across the room in a bloody mess. "She did. That much I do know. Rosalie is safe and well, and so is Lane. She took your daughter up to Common, where they've been living for the past twenty-one years."

Urien exhaled internally with dramatic relief. "*That's good. Just knowing Rosalie is far away from Morgan gives me enough peace not to go insane. To be trapped like this for twenty-one years? I cannot bear it!*"

"Hey, I'm here now." I tried to stuff down my swelling

emotions and keep a calm bedside manner. I squeezed his hand. "Can you feel this?"

"I feel nothing. Are you doing something?"

"I was squeezing your hand. Nothing at all?"

"I'm sorry, but my body deserted me a long time ago."

I sat on the side of his bed, frowning at the dilemma. "I don't know how to fix this. I'm not from around here, so I don't know all the magic and whatnot that went into making you like this. Any ideas?"

"Of course I know what did it. It was the Hemlock she gave me. No doubt small doses over time. I noticed my body weakening, my mind losing control over my limbs, but I couldn't put reason to it all until it was too late. My mouth had stopped being accessible to me, and my hands were useless to write out the problem. Morgan ground up the flowers and distilled them into my wine. She tore the edges of the Hemlock leaves into my salads. Small doses that went unnoticed at first, but weakened me over time. She admitted as much to me when she was sure I could do nothing about it. She confessed her crimes to torment me, knowing I could not make the poison known."

I wanted to say the right thing, but knew there might not be a right thing that existed in this totally wrong scenario. Though he couldn't feel the gesture, I pressed his hand to my cheek to warm it. "I don't know anything about Hemlock. Is there a way to fix it? Something I can do to help?"

"If only there was. No one can help me now. Just staying

here with me, talking to me is the only kindness I can ask you for."

My shoulders slumped. "Well, I can do that, but there's really no other way? Nothing that can bring you back to me?" I cleared my throat. "I mean, back to Avalon?"

"Miracles stopped giving themselves to me long ago. That you're here? It's the greatest gift I could hope for. Tell me, what's become of Province 1?"

10

THE HOT GUY

took my time explaining the little I knew about Avalon to my father, never once slipping up and telling him who I was. It was right on the tip of my tongue, but the secret stayed tucked inside of me. I was afraid of disappointing him, or that he wouldn't like me. By the time Rigby knocked on the door to let me know my time was up, I'd managed to make my dad laugh at one of my lamer jokes. That was present enough for me. I made my dad laugh. Though he didn't know who I was, he got me.

I walked behind Rigby to my bedroom, wishing I could take another tour of the grounds to see if I couldn't fish out that jewel I knew was in the moat. Rigby retightened my corset, in case Morgan came back to check on me. The stays were constricting, but not as punishing as Morgan had ordered. "I promise I'll come up here and loosen them if Demi is detained longer than the usual beating."

I nodded, wishing there was something I could do to save Demi, to save my father, to save myself. I felt impotent, and like Superman was always just out of reach. "Rigs, I need to pick your brain. I want to make something we have up in Common, but I don't know how without, like, a saw or something."

"What is it you require?" Though his words were formal, Rigs' body wasn't so stiff. After our time where he'd held me on the floor, his hand often found its way to my shoulder, brushing my loose hairs back from my face, or holding my hands with my knuckles facing the ceiling, like a gentleman.

"They're called bowling pins, but I can't think of anything you might have that's a similar shape."

"Did you say rolling pins? Because we have those here."

I smacked my forehead at the obvious solution. "Rigs, you're a genius. I was seriously about to try my hand at whittling the stinkin' things. I think a rolling pin would work. I just need to take one of the handles off, and fill in the hole so the other end stays pointy on top." I demonstrated with my hands that the pins would stand upright.

Rigs tried to picture what I was talking about. "I can have that seen to, of course. But for what purpose could you possibly need that?"

"The greatest purpose of all – fun. Any chance I could get my hands on ten of them?"

"I suppose so." He stared at my smile with far off eyes. "My, you're captivating when you light up. Fun. It's been a long time since the castle's seen much of that." He cleared his throat and straightened, as if catching himself in a moment of letting his guard down. "Shall I bring you your supper, your grace?"

"I guess that would be best, yeah. Morgan's in a mood, so I probably should stay out of sight."

"You're learning. Very good, Rosie."

After Rigs left, I expected Demi to come up, but when night fell, I'd been sent my supper to eat alone in my room. The next day was much the same, only Rigs warned me that even walking to see my father might risk her majesty's wrath. I spent the entire day in my bedroom, wondering if this was how Rapunzel was kept locked away. I'd been ostracized in Common because I wasn't pretty enough, but now that I didn't make people cringe? I was holed up in my room with two guards posted outside, to make sure I didn't go anywhere that might cause a dude to lust, or some nonsense.

When evening fell again, I opened the window and let the birds in that were perched on the sill, just waiting for a minute with me. It was a powerful feeling to have them be so excited to see my face. After my mother's clear hatred of me, it was refreshing to listen to them clamber to get near where I stood.

They had much to report, and kept talking over each other. Apparently, Morgan went on a daily walk that encompassed the grounds, stopping for a breath at a few key points along the way. One of those places was the exact spot near the moat that I noticed. They promised to track the times of day Morgan did these walks. They even had birds posted around the grounds to see if there were any guards who circled the marked areas, and at what times the coast was clear.

I yawned, thanking them over and over for how brave they all were, and how much I needed and appreciated their help. The bed beckoned to me, but the knock on the door interrupted my climb up the platform toward the pink satin sheets.

I wasn't expecting Demi, holding a dinner tray, looking down at me with tears in his eyes, but the second I saw him, my heart jumped into my throat. I took the tray from his trembling hands and set it on the table near the center of the room, keeping quiet until the door was shut and locked behind him. The second I was sure we were alone, I threw myself into his arms to make sure he was real, and that he'd been returned to me in one functioning piece.

"I'm sorry I'm late with the tray. The kitchen was a little backed up."

"Are you kidding me with this? I don't care about the food. I care about you! Tell me everything that happened. What did she do to you?"

His face softened into a gentle smile of affectionate

indulgence. "It was the standard whipping, sweet girl. Nothing more. I just... I'm still reeling from what you did to try and save me. Were you really offering yourself up in my stead? Had Morgan consented, would you have allowed yourself to be tied to the post and whipped until you'd spilled enough blood to satisfy her majesty most high's fancy?"

"Of course I would have. It was my fault you got into trouble in the first place. I'm so sorry, Demi. Tell me where it hurts."

He looked down at me, enraptured. Demi had the most expressive eyes I'd ever seen, and I felt like I could understand a thousand of his many conflicting emotions without a word. His arms encircled me, pulling me tight to his chest. He spoke slowly, with throbbing passion in his voice. "I *ache* for you, Juliet. That's where it hurts the most. That you would take my place? No one would do that for me."

I gulped at his declaration, coupled with our close proximity. "I told you; we're friends. Friends take care of each other. What can I do? How can I make it better?"

With his free hand, his fingers traced the curve of my lower lip as if it was made of glass. "If we could finish the kiss you started yesterday, that would make the entire world better – every dark and maddening spot of it. It was a kiss worth savoring, and right now, the world seems like a grim place, in desperate need of true loveliness."

His words were so gallant and swoon-worthy; I couldn't help the intake of breath that stole my words away. I tilted my chin up at him, my lips slightly parted as my eyes zeroed in on the mouth that had only ever been kind to me. "Just one kiss?"

"I would trade worlds for it, Rosie."

Again, with the Romeo-in-action pledges that made me go weak in the knees. I couldn't help myself. I'd gone from being with a guy I couldn't keep in one place to standing in front of a man who looked at me like I was the sun and moon and something altogether precious. I was the dude friend, and wasn't used to being precious, but somehow Demi saw the softness Avalon was trying to stamp out.

My fingers floated up to stroke his jaw and gently beckon him closer. When our lips touched, it wasn't the explosion I felt when Bastien and I went at it, but the fire was still there, slowly kindling into something with actual potential to be lethal.

Of all the things I could've guessed, it was no surprise that Demi was a good kisser. His lips were soft and knew what the crap they were doing, which was a far sight better than me, who'd only just gotten my training wheels off. Demi drove the kiss deeper, sucking on my lower lip between breaths, like I was a piece of candy he needed to savor and treasure and keep in his pocket when the world grew cold and devoid of treats.

I was his treat, and for the moment, he was mine. Demi was sweet, and I indulged in him for probably too long, promising him things with my lips that my mouth would never admit to aloud. It was too soon for such declarations. I'd only known him a few days. He was still mostly a stranger to me, yet here I was, threading my fingers through his hair and tugging on the follicles just to hear him groan into my mouth. I loved the sound of Demi coming undone. He was beautiful, and in real life, I never would've had a chance with someone as pretty as him. It was a heady thing, to be desired by someone so desirable.

When my hands drifted down to wrap around him, gripping his back to force him closer, I jumped when I swallowed one of his gasps that turned into a grimace. "What's wrong?"

"Nothing. Just the cuts from the whip. Don't stop, though." Demi shook his head and went back in for my lips.

"Oh, jeez!" I dropped my hands from around him, fighting the desire to hug him through the pain. "Show me, sweetie. Show me what she did."

"She got you to admit you feel something for me. I'll not hold that against her majesty most high. I'll endure as many lashings as it takes to get a repeat of that."

"Okay, smooth talker. I'm serious, Romeo. Let's take off your shirt."

Demi quirked his eyebrow at me, a playful and charming smirk teasing his features. "If you insist."

He hissed only once when I got his shirt all the way off of him. "What... What... Demi, I..." I couldn't find the words; I was horrified. I guess I had only a passing understanding of what being beaten with a whip would do to a person. The real picture was far more gruesome. "What can I do? Does it sting? Is there something I can put on it?" There were crisscrossing slashes marring the middle and top of his muscular back. The part that made me debate between tears and vomit was that beneath the fresh slices, there were similarly designed scars from years of this kind of brutal abuse. "How can I help?"

Unlike Bastien, Demi didn't turn mean on me when I saw his scars. He merely studied my face over his shoulder, and reached back to squeeze my hand. "You can stay with me while it hurts. You can kiss me until I forget about the pain."

"This can't be your life!" I recalled Lane's wisdom, hoping it might give Demi some solace. "This isn't all there is for you. Avalon isn't your adventure. This awful castle isn't where it ends for you. You are your own adventure, Demi. There's so much more in store for you than this."

His chin lowered. "No, sweet princess. This life is all Avalon has for me. I've accepted it, and one day you must accept it, as well."

My reply came out in a strangled whisper. "Don't break my heart like that. I see you beyond the bowing and the 'her majesty most high's.'"

"I hardly know who that is anymore," he admitted.

Tears dotted my lashes and fell down my cheeks as I tugged him over to the bed, climbed up with him, and gently pushed him down until his stomach was pressed to the mattress. I pulled off his shoes and reached for the oil that was kept on the nightstand. It was supposed to be used for all the raucous sex we were expected to be having, but it worked well enough for massage oil, too. His cuts had been treated with some kind of shiny ointment that kept his white dress shirt from sealing to the wounds, but I couldn't imagine it was comfortable to be wearing material over throbbing marks.

I started on Demi's feet, making him jump when I started massaging his toes. "Rosie, no. You shouldn't be doing this. If someone saw you, I would be punished severely."

I got down off the bed and crossed the room to make sure the door was locked. "There. Now we can be as crazy as we want." I went back to rubbing his feet, taking my time and making sure to drag out each stroke so he knew not everything in this castle would hurt him. I fished around for a change of topic to distract me from staring at Demi's tight backside. He had a baseball player's butt; it was hard not to gawk. "Tell me about your brothers and sisters. I never had any, and always wished for some."

Demi's reply came back weighted as he grew drunk on my touch. "Geraldine was the youngest. I miss her terribly. She always looked at me with hero worship in her eyes, like I was something great. I hold onto that memory when I'm polishing floors and being traded like a toy." His mouth didn't close all the way, and I was pretty sure he started drooling halfway through his response. "I'm not supposed to talk like this."

"Like what? Honest? You can be yourself in here, Demi. Maybe not anywhere else, but with me you don't have to worry."

"I always worry now," he admitted. "I never used to before you came along. I did as I was told and accepted my fate. But you? You treat me like I'm a person."

"You are a person, silly."

"I think I forgot that until you came to live here. Now I worry something will happen to you. Her majesty most high does what she likes, regardless of who gets hurt." He groaned into my pillow, his butt clenching in a way that made me bite my lip to keep the lust tucked away. "Oh, right there."

"Like that?" I reached under his pant leg and dug my knuckles into his tight calf muscle.

He reached under his stomach and rocked his hips. For a second, it looked like he was humping the bed. When his belt came undone and he slid off his pants so I could better massage his legs, I understood.

"I hate to bug you now that you're so relaxed, but would you mind undoing this stupid corset? It's wicked uncomfortable."

Demi sat up, his eyes lidded. He swung his legs off the bed and dropped down with the soundlessness and agility of a jungle cat. He extended his hand to help me off the raised platform, so my feet could plant themselves firmly on the polished wood floor. "Of course. You should never be afraid to ask me for anything. Turn around." His fingers were adept at undressing women, which wasn't a huge shocker. My dress fell to the floor, and the corset was a sweet relief when it hit the ground. My ruffly under-dress came off, leaving me in the dressing gown, which was actually pretty comfortable. The white gauzy material kissed my toes and left my cleavage mildly exposed to the evening air that wafted in through the window. My ribs expanded with the freedom of being able to take in a full breath. "Oh, that's a hundred times better. Thank you."

His hands wrapped around my waist from behind, lingering on my stomach. I couldn't help the butterflies that swarmed around the spot where he touched me. I leaned so my back was pressed to his swelling chest and closed my eyes contentedly. He wore only his boxer briefs, and I knew if I turned around, my eyes would be drawn straight to where I shouldn't be looking. "Are you quite certain you don't need help out of this dressing gown?"

Shivers rolled up my spine at his husky tone. "I'm sure. This whole thing? I'm not great at it. Not a whole lot of practice with gorgeous, almost-naked men."

His face moved to my neck, where his lips lingered, turning my limbs to jelly. "Would you prefer me all the way naked?"

I'm sure there were cooler ways to respond, but the pinched and panicked squeak of, "You're too sexy for that!" was all I could muster. I smacked my forehead at my geeky response. "I'm not used to guys like you paying me any attention. Not like this, anyways. It's... This... I don't know what I'm doing."

"Guys like me?" His tone closed off, and I knew he'd misunderstood me. "Surely I'm not the first man below your station to fancy you."

"Not that, you dork. You're too hot to pay attention to me like this. It feels like all the cool kids are going to laugh at me because the sexy guy is hitting on me as a joke, just to see if he can make me weak-kneed for him. Which, incidentally, has happened to me twice."

Demi's eyebrows furrowed, and then he tilted his head back to let loose a hearty laugh. "I forget that you're a maiden. You really think of me like that?" He ran his hand up my side, tracing the curve of my hip. "Do I make you nervous?"

I turned around and took a step back, giving him the stink eye through my blush. "You know you do. Knock it off. I'm trying to be good to you, and I'm barely keeping it together, here. You can't touch my side like that, or say things that are too sexy. I have no idea what I'm doing, and you're just confusing me, making me think I'm in the hot people ranking. I know my social status, and it's not up where you are." I fixed my eyes on the ceiling to avoid his smirk that beamed out at me. "Oh, shut up. Just lay back down so I can stop thinking about things I shouldn't."

Demi pressed a sweet and simple kiss to my lips, looking very much like a mostly naked man, and nothing like a submissive servant. My stomach did a violent flip when he taunted me with a low rumble of, "You want me."

I covered my face with my hands, hoping to obscure some of the pink in my cheeks. "Yeah, yeah. Shut up about it. I think I mentioned something about a massage you're missing out on by teasing me like this." I waited until he lay face-down on the bed again, and slathered more oil onto my hands. I picked up where I left off, and rubbed further up his leg, pretending his beige boxer briefs were just plain shorts so it wasn't weird. Demi groaned and moaned pornographically, making me wonder when the last time was that someone took the time to be good to him.

"Tell me about the first kiss guy," Demi mumbled, catching me off-guard.

"There's nothing to tell. He never trusted me enough to really give us a shot, and I got tired of his constant mood swings."

"Were you nervous around him, too?"

"I guess not. He was so antagonistic that I guess I forgot to be nervous."

"Do you miss him?"

I swallowed hard, unsure how Demi danced the line between half-naked hot guy to platonic girl-talk friend so seamlessly. "I try not to let myself think about him. Too painful." I was quiet a few beats while I rubbed the outside of Demi's thighs, loving how hard the muscles were. "The way it ended was a bummer. I thought we could've had something real, but he never trusted it. He's a loner, so he wasn't good at leaning on me – on most people, really. We'd get close, then he'd bolt. Kind of sucked being run out on that many times. It's better this way. Now he can be happy being by himself, which he made pretty clear was what he wanted all along."

"I can't imagine him being happy now that he's parted from you. Trust me, no matter what you think, he's suffering."

"You can't know that. You don't even know who he is. He doesn't suffer over me. He pushed me away. I was right there, and he couldn't see me. No matter how much I wanted it to work, after the way it ended, it can't."

"How did it end?"

I moved up to rubbing his forearms, avoiding his perfect glutes. I don't know why I had the overwhelming urge to bite down on the tight, delicious swells. I tried not to look even remotely near them, but my eyes kept ogling as if they were tethered to his sweet can. "Do you really want to hear this? I can't imagine this is interesting conversation. My pathetic excuse for a love life isn't exactly fascinating."

"How did it end?" he repeated, his jaw going slack at the deep pressure.

I swallowed hard, trying to pick the right words. "He's engaged, for one. So there's that. We were traveling here, and one of the people in the party accused me of stealing something. I told him that of course I didn't steal it, but he took me into the woods and told me to strip down so he could make sure I hadn't taken anything. Didn't trust me enough to take my word for it, and humiliated me on top of it."

Demi buried his face in my pillow. "Oh, Rosie. No wonder you don't want my help dressing. I'm sorry, Juliet. There's no excuse for that. Did he..."

"No, he didn't come near me. But he was the first guy to see me naked, and it happened like that. After how it all went down, I can't look at him the same way. He should've trusted me. He was my first kiss, and he knew enough about me to know how far over the line what he made me do was. Broke my heart a little."

"I'm sorry, sweet girl." He reached around and gripped my hand.

I shrugged, like it was no big deal. Like it didn't wake me up in the middle of the night, choking me with sadness. I didn't know how to make peace with it all, and wasn't sure how much closure existed in a situation like this one. "Once I got my clothes back, I punched him for it, so I'm glad I stood up for myself. I'm not all that great with the love stuff. It's fine. I'll never see him again, and I guess that's how it should be. Besides, my adventure wasn't him. My adventure is me, and I'm still very much here."

I worked my way up his toned arms, unsure how to make his back better without being able to massage the muscles. Instead of rubbing his back, I opted for light and gentle kisses placed on the edges of his cuts.

Demi purred and clawed at the sheets like a cat, getting revved up over something so small. It was a powerful feeling, to be able to get such a handsome guy worked up like that.

When I ran out of parts that were kosher to massage on him, I laid down on the bed at his side, closing my eyes while I listened to his even breathing. I knew I couldn't stay here forever with him, but that night, I was grateful for his company. Despite the dark place we were both in, we finally weren't there alone.

11

UNWELCOME GUEST

My bowling pins were a welcome addition to my room, and teaching Demi was a great way to pass our time together as the days passed by. The birds acted as my spies, covertly following Morgan around the grounds to see where she stopped most often, and any other telltale signs that she might be guarding something nearby. This freed me up to stay out of Morgan's eyesight, which served both our interests. In the morning, she would stop by to make sure Demi tightened my corset beyond human standards in order to "retrain my drab figure." She would squeeze my face with the threat to "be beautiful," and then left me alone for the rest of the day, locked (actually locked) in my bedroom with Demi. So far, I hadn't seen the benefit in having a mom like Morgan.

I missed Lane terribly, and as the celebration banquet neared, the anticipation of seeing my girl soulmate again lifted my spirits. I thought about summoning Kerdik, now that my bowling game was complete, but guessed that a better time for houseguests might be after the hoopla of the Avalon-wide party. Besides, Morgan imprisoned me in my bedroom, instructing Demi that I was not to leave.

Demi and I pretty much made out like teenagers most of the time. It was safer, really, than to risk pissing Morgan off yet again. Demi schooled me on the provinces, filling me in on how the different duchesses rose and fell, and who was in charge of what now. We talked about our child-hoods, our dreams for the future, and all sorts of mischief and fun. He read to me, and I swooned at the kindness every time.

Rigby finally interrupted us a week and a half later in the late afternoon with a polite knock. "You've a visitor in the parlor, your grace."

I pulled back, confused. "Oh, me? Seriously? Am I allowed to leave the bedroom?" Hopeful light shone in my eyes. "Is it Lane? Oh, just wait until you meet her, Rigs. She'll love you. Well, this version of you, not the one you have to pretend to be in front of Morgan."

Rigs pampered me with an affectionate smile. He'd been letting his guard down when it was just him, Demi and me, though his perfect posture was never sacrificed. "Well, I'm afraid only you two get to see this side of me, so the duchess will have to tolerate the me the rest of Avalon gets. But it's not her who's come to visit. It's the first of your suitors."

We'd avoided the subject of my impending engagement entirely, until it was shoved in my face. Demi's shoulders fell in time with mine. "Oh. I have to go meet this guy?"

Rigs nodded, trying to give me a buck-up-kiddo smile. "Indeed. Though, of all the potential suitors I would have thought might throw their hat into the mix, I admit I did not anticipate this one. He traveled from another country entirely for this, so do try and be grateful."

"Okay. I can be a team player." I clung to the bedpost, assuming the position for Demi to tighten me back up so I'd be presentable. He made sure I could breathe, but only just, so neither of us got into trouble. Demi fixed my hair, pinning a stray curl so it stayed with the up-do Demi expertly fashioned. I turned around and brushed his cheek, bringing him in for a light kiss. "Just so you know, I don't want to do this. I'd rather stay up here with you and go bowling."

Demi's overly expressive eyes bore into mine, saying things he wouldn't give voice to. Demi always gave me the shivers. His eyes said, "I don't like this," while his mouth gave me a reassuring, "Let's go, now. Perhaps you'll find someone who will make for a suitable companion."

I nodded, not believing him one bit. I followed behind Rigs, and Demi trailed along behind me. I wished I could've held his hand, but knew out and about, we had to be cool. With every step, panic started to well up in my throat.

I stopped halfway to our destination, plastering my back to the stone wall of one of the empty corridors. "I don't want to do this," I admitted, my heart jumping erratically. "I mean, what kind of a screening system is there for this? At least the online dating sites try to match you with similar interest people, and cross potential serial killers off the list. I'm a perfect stranger to pretty much everyone in Avalon! And this guy is waiting to meet me, why? Just because of who my mother is? Because now I'm suddenly some rich girl? That's not a good system!" My breaths were coming in uneven jumps, shallow as they were. "The party isn't until tomorrow, right? I have a whole twenty-four hours I'm supposed to be able to pretend this whole thing isn't happening."

Rigs looked around to make sure we were alone, and then took my hand in his like a gentleman, my knuckles pointing toward the ceiling. "Your suitors are here because they want to see if you would be an asset to their land. It's a high honor, your grace." He kept his words formal, in case there were any eavesdroppers nearby. "Most of the other courtiers are spoken for. Since birth, for some of them. Think of that arrangement. Betrothed before your first birthday. You have choices in this, your grace. Down in the parlor is merely one of your many options."

I pulled Rigs in for a hug, leaning my forehead on his chest to center myself. It didn't really work, because he couldn't get me off him fast enough. He leaned down and whispered, "I cannot comfort you here, my sweet. If her majesty most high should see me showing affection to you in such a way, there would be no end to her jealousy."

I pulled back, embarrassed. "Sorry. I forgot. Can I hug Demi in public?"

Rigs brought Demi closer. "You can do whatever you like to Demi. He's your *soumettre*. You can parade him around naked, for all her majesty most high cares. He's your attendant to do with as you wish. But I belong to her majesty most high, and she does not wish to share my affections."

I sunk into Demi's arms, taking as deep a breath as I could manage, while the two men exchanged worried glances that I was going to royally screw up and get them both beaten. "You're all worked up. Take a minute to calm yourself. It won't do for your suitor to see you looking like you're afraid he'll murder you in your sleep."

"I wasn't even thinking about that! Are you kidding me? Could that really happen?"

Demi and Rigs exchanged another weighted look. "No, of course not," Demi lied. "Not to worry. Would you prefer I stayed with you?"

"Yes." I gusted out my relief, clinging to him. His handsomeness still made me nervous, but my fear of the unknown man waiting for me in the parlor trumped the shyness that came with such swirling attraction. "Really? You'd do that?"

His eyes held a promise in them that I clung to as

solace. "I'll do anything you ask of me, even watch while another man takes your hand in marriage."

My heart dropped to the floor. I leaned up on my toes to kiss his cheek, hating that I'd finally found someone who was good to me, who seemed to genuinely like me, but I was being pushed in the opposite direction. Part of me wanted to ask if I could just marry Demi to be done with the whole suitor business, but I didn't think asking a dude to marry me after we'd only started kissing a few days ago would go over all that well.

I nodded into Demi's chest. "Okay. If you're there too, I can be cool." I stood straighter and rolled my shoulders back, trying to appear in control. "Sorry for freaking out. I can be good now. Or be beautiful. Or less of a baby. Whatever I'm supposed to be, I can be that thing." It dawned on me that with this marriage set-up, I was very much a thing, and not a person.

Rigs looked both ways down the empty hall before touching under my chin to lift my face. Something about that simple motion reminded me to be brave. "There's that spark," he said with a soft smile. "Come, now."

I wasn't expecting the parlor to be so opulent – bedecked in red tapestries with gold end tables and matching upholstered couches with tall, upright backs. The seats all looked impervious to bending, and I guessed it was to reinforce the regal status even in a casual setting. I wasn't expecting a gold tray of exotic fruit to be waiting for us. I wasn't expecting a whole lot of things – least of all the men who rose from their straight-backed seats to greet me.

My jaw hit the floor when I saw who occupied the fancy room. I took a step backward into Demi, who impeded my flight with a brush of his hand on my back.

12

MADIGAN'S BRIGHT IDEA

"Don't go, honey! Please hear me out." Bastien took a few steps toward me, reaching for my arm. The simple contact sizzled with too much heat and memories where he touched me, so I jerked backward.

"No! I told you we were done. I told you I never wanted to see you again."

Bastien flinched, like my words were sharp enough to cut him, thick-skinned as he always tried to be in matters of the heart.

Rigs and Demi exchanged confused glances, unsure of what to do. On the one hand, I was a princess, so there were certain rules about the riffraff coming to call and putting their paws on the good furniture. On the other hand, Bastien was an Untouchable, and short of murdering a royal, could pretty much get away with whatever he wanted. I think both my mansion buddies were a little taken aback that I was on a first name basis with an Untouchable, and that we had enough of a history to be knee-deep in a feud, new as I was to this land. Rigs stood near the door like a sentry, and Demi kept his arm around me, leading me slowly toward the couch, where he sat me down and stood at attention behind me, where I couldn't see him.

My voice was quieter now, but my temper was still shooting off sparks like a wonky firecracker when Bastien resumed his seat next to Madigan across from me. There was a table with the bowl of fruit between us, but it wasn't enough space. I needed an ocean of distance between us. "I can only assume you need something if you're here, pretending to be a suitor just to get in the door. What you're looking for? I don't have it." I held Madigan's eye with meaning, letting him know I wasn't in possession of the jewels yet.

"Aye. I told him it was too soon, but the mule won't listen to me." Madigan tried to lean back in his chair, but the darn thing was so unforgivingly rigid that he settled for crossing his left ankle over his right knee, scowling. He was too tall for the furniture, poor thing.

"I'll reach out to Reyn if anything changes. You don't need to ever come here again." My words were spoken to Madigan, but directed at Bastien. They both seemed to get it. Madigan didn't take offense, and Bastien leaned over, his elbows on his knees while he cradled his forehead in his large hand.

"You can't contact Reyn right now. I'm not even supposed to be here, for more than the obvious reasons." Bastien kept his eyes down while he spoke to me. "Rachelle died a week ago. Never woke up, and just sort of faded away in her sleep. Reyn's family is in mourning. I'm supposed to be with them, since Rachelle was my fiancée. It's six months of mourning, Rosie. Six months I have to stay respectful of my promise to marry Rachelle. Six months I can't take a wife without shaming her family."

When his eyes climbed up to meet mine, I tried to keep my banging heartbeat inaudible, but it rang throughout the room like a gong of just plain too much. It was hard enough to be in the same room with Bastien, much less try to decipher subtext. I stood and made my way to the door. "I'll go see Reyn, then. Rigby, can I get my hands on a horse and a guide? I need to go visit the judge's son from Province 2 to pay my respects to Rachelle. Reyn is a friend of mine."

Rigs held up his hands and stood in front of the closed door. "I'm sorry, your grace. Her majesty most high wishes for you to stay on the grounds. She won't hear of you leaving, what with the celebration coming tomorrow."

I backed up, like a dog learning the hard way to steer clear of an electric fence. My eyes darted around while I hugged myself. I didn't like the trapped feeling this cold, stony place always seemed to give me. Though it was massive, it felt cramped with too many failed expectations and dark intentions.

Demi met me halfway and took my elbow, escorting me back to the couch and sitting me down with care. He traced his middle finger discreetly from the tender inside of my wrist to the center of my palm – a thing he sometimes did to flirt with me when we were alone. Then he moved back to stand behind my chair, where I couldn't see him.

I cleared my throat a few times before mustering up what I hoped were the right words. "I'll see what I can do about going out to visit Reyn after the party tomorrow. If Morgan won't let me out, please tell him I'm so very sorry. Really, Bastien. I'm so sorry to both of you for your loss." The words felt hollow, but it was the best I could do. I couldn't imagine what Reyn and his dad must be going through. To keep that hope alive for so long, only to have it stolen soundlessly in the dead of night was terrible.

Bastien clutched his chest like my bland words hurt him deeper than my sharp ones had. His voice came out uncertain and rough. "You can't say my name like that."

I shifted on the couch, smoothing out my dress. "Like what? I said it like normal."

"Just don't say my name at all. I want to hear it too much, but not like this. Not when you can barely stand to look at me."

I wasn't sure what to call him, since he didn't want me

using his name, so I made Judah proud and stuck with the meanest bad guy name I could think of. "I don't know why you're here, Voldemort," I stated frankly, unwilling to smile and make it all okay. It wasn't okay. He hadn't trusted me. He'd told me to take my clothes off to appease his buddy's suspicions. He'd pushed me away too many times, and was now acting like he was hurt that I finally took the hint and stayed gone. "You've got a long journey ahead of you, but it's not with me. I'm not your great adventure."

"You know why I'm here."

Right, the jewels. "Well, I can't help you yet. I'm working on it, but you came too soon."

Bastien lifted his head to address Rigs and Demi. "Could you guys give us a minute? I need to talk to the princess in private."

They made to leave, but I stood. "No need. We're done here."

"Rosie, wait!" Bastien reached out and touched my arm, and I fought the urge to punch him as I wrenched myself from his grip.

"No! You had nothing but chances, and you let it go down how it did. Go be there for Reyn and his dad. That's where you should be right now. Go make it with all the girls who think being Untouchable is something cool and mysterious. Let them feel special when they think they're getting close to that rock you call a heart. I've got enough on my plate without you adding to the mix." My breath came in pants because of stupid Bastien getting me all worked up. I stomped my foot to the ground, my palm pressed to my stomach when my lips started to feel fuzzy. "Doggone this corset! It's too tight, Demi. I can barely get in a full breath."

"Allow me to take you back to your chambers, your grace. I'll adjust it. Apologies."

Bastien's face scrunched. "Why are you wearing a corset? You're a tiny little thing."

I shot him a look with too much emotion in it, which was my first mistake. Bastien didn't need to know how I felt about anything. "Morgan thinks I'm fat, apparently." I waved off his protest. "Whatever. It's fine. I'm doing my job, being the Lost Princess everyone needs me to be. Now I'm the rich girl, with corsets I can't breathe in, and a castle I can't walk around in. Lucky freaking me."

Bastien's eyes begged me in earnest to forgive him, until his gaze fell on Demi. "Wait. This guy's going to adjust your corset? Who is he?"

I stood straighter, trying to find a little breathing room in the immovable material. "Sorry. Demi, this is Voldemort. Voldemort, Demi. Madigan. Rigby. Rigby is the *soumettre* for Morgan, and Demi's my *soumettre*."

Bastien's chest puffed, his eyebrows pulled downward and his fists clenched in sudden anger. "This guy's your *what*?" he thundered.

"My *soumettre*." I wondered if I'd pronounced it wrong. "What?"

"Rip my heart out, why don't you!" Bastien yelled out of

nowhere.

"Jeez! Calm it down, Anger Management. Morgan assigned him to me. What's the big deal?"

"I screwed up, what? Two weeks ago, and you're hooking up with another guy like it's nothing? I thought I meant something to you, but apparently you'll just throw yourself at anyone."

My nose crinkled in distaste. "Ugh. Would you listen to yourself, you snob? What, just because Demi's not an almighty Untouchable, he's not good enough for me?" I turned to Demi, whose face was the only one that was composed, other than Rigby's. "Demi, this fight isn't about you, so you don't need to hear it. Why don't you and Rigby go on out, so I can deal with him. I'll meet you upstairs."

Demi nodded curtly, his smile nowhere in sight. "As you wish it."

I waited until the two exited the room before I barked at Bastien. "Are you insane? What was that about?"

"I'm not allowed to be mad you're having sex with someone after you built up how big of a deal your first kiss was? What, you started up with me, but decided to finish off with him? Do you even know who he's been with? Your mother, Rosie. He slept with your mother, and who knows how many of your aunts. And now you're giving it up to him?"

I was standing in my princess gown with my fists

clenched, feeling anything but royal in that moment. I wanted to slap Bastien. I wanted to scream at him. There were so many things I wanted in that moment, none of which were all that princess-like. "Get. Out."

Madigan stood and clamped his hand down on Bastien's shoulder. "Aye. This was a bad idea. It's too heated for the two of ye to make sense of yet. We came here to see if ye needed help with the jewels."

I breathed in and out through my nose, trying to remember that I wasn't furious with Madigan, and he didn't deserve a full blast of my anger. I kept my voice quiet to avoid being overheard, in case anyone was lurking outside the doors of the long room. "I convinced Morgan that my Compass ability doesn't exist anymore, that it disappeared because I spent too much time up in Common. I'm using the birds to scout out the area because Morgan doesn't like to look at me. She keeps me locked in my room most of the time, but I've got a good idea where at least one of them is hidden."

Bastien was fuming. "You stay in your room all day and night with your *soumettre*. Nice."

I lowered my chin and moved it slowly from left to right. "You are without a doubt the most selfish man I know. I just told you that my own mother locks me in my room because she doesn't like the look of me, and all you can think about is whether or not I'm having sex with someone other than you? Man, did I ever get you wrong."

Bastien's mouth opened and closed through his unintelligible spluttered response, and finally Madigan cut him off. "Give us a mo, Bastien. I need to talk to Rosie, and ye aren't helping."

Bastien's face was red as he stormed out, taking about fifty percent of the tension out with him. I leaned against a gold end table, trying to catch my breath that was still coming in short pants. "What can I do for you?" I asked, though my tone was none too congenial.

"Ye can sit down, for one. I'll never understand women and the lengths ye go to for no good reason."

I was grateful for the uncomfortable couch, and tried not to fidget when I sat across from the chair he claimed. "You're preaching to the choir, dude. This wasn't my idea. This is my punishment for wearing jeans outside of the castle like a peasant. Morgan's making a point. Even had Demi beaten for it. Things are a little tense here, so if you're thinking of complaining that I'm not finding the jewels quick enough, maybe pick a different tune. I'm not exactly living my best life these days."

"Aye. Just so ye know, Roland tracked down Duchess Avril and took back the three gems she stole. He's got his, and he gave the other two to Lane. We came here to check on the remaining jewels, but word of ye choosing a suitor reached us, too. Bastien's been driving himself mad, trying to find a way to offer his hand without turning disrespect on Reyn's family. Unless ye can push back your wedding six months, I don't see a way."

My mouth fell open that this was what he wanted to talk about. I rubbed the stress from my forehead, trying to fish out the right words from the crapfest I wanted to spew. "First off, Bastien could barely kiss me without running away like a scared little boy. You misunderstood him. He doesn't want to marry me."

"Aye, he does. He's been mad for ye ever since ye left, and for however long before that. I've known Bastien a long time, and never seen him like this over a lass. But since there's nothing he can do about it, and ye don't have the jewels yet, I don't see a way out of getting married to appease Morgan. The second ye find the jewels, we'll bust ye out of here in the next breath."

I wanted to toss him a sarcastic "great," but knew it wouldn't be all that helpful. "Yup. Awesome."

"We were thinking how helpful it would be to have one of us on the inside to help ye get the jewels and smuggle them out. Since Bastien can't do it for six months, and you're due to choose a bloke this month, we were thinking of me."

"Thinking of you for what?"

"For ye."

My nose scrunched. "Huh? I don't get it."

Madigan gripped the back of his neck and rubbed, looking off to the side uncomfortably. "I thought I'd throw my hand into the mix. I wouldn't bother ye, unlike the other lads who would want an heir right away. It would be a business arrangement so we could get the job done and get out.

Plus, it bodes well for ye to choose an Untouchable. Morgan can't kill us, and she won't try to marry ye off to take our land, since I don't own nothing but a plot in Éireland."

I thought I'd hit my maximum capacity for shock that day, but apparently there was a whole new roof for me to jump through. "I don't know what to say."

"Ye don't have to. I know this isn't what ye dreamed of. And if ye get an offer ye actually want, ye can go off with him and I'll never say another word about it. All I know is tha Bastien wants to marry ye, but he can't. If he can't keep ye safe, I'm your best bet."

I stood up and sat down three times in my debate to either run for the door or stay to hash out the weirdest offer I'd ever been given. My hand pressed flat to my lips while I thought through the arrangement I never expected. "What happens after we do the job?"

"Ye had plans to go back to your life up in Common, aye? Fine with me. I'll go back to Éireland, the son of Morgan le Fae. Grand. I don't care. I care that Bastien's lady's being sold off to the highest bidder. Some of the lads putting their names into the mix are... I may not be your best option, but I know for certain I'm far above the worst. Tha's all this is – trying to save ye from the worst."

I gaped at Mad. "Did Bastien like, save your life in Vietnam or something? It's a heck of a bond you two have, that you'd do this for him."

"Aye. He brought me out of the Forgotten Forest and

never once made me tell him why I was there. He did save my life, but the Brotherhood of Untouchables does that without a blink. We don't have many people we can trust, so we take care of each other." His voice changed to a grim note when he continued. "Bastien put my Meara up in his cabin for a few months while I was sorting out threats in my homeland. He stayed with her morning, noon and night, not laying a hand on her until I came back. It's a rare man who doesn't go after a beauty like tha. Bastien did tha for me, so I can do this for him."

"Is Meara your girlfriend? I have a feeling she won't be too thrilled with this arrangement."

Madigan kept his eyes to the side and held up his left hand to show me a gold band that had scuffs on it from too many dirty fights. "She was my wife. Meara's dead now, so I don't think she'll mind me helping out one of the brothers."

I let out a shallow breath. "Oh, jeez. I'm sorry, Mad. I didn't know."

"Aye. Think on it, and I'll see ye tomorrow when I offer my hand." He looked up at the ceiling, as if he was trying to avoid eye contact at all costs. I could see his throat fully exposed, his Untouchable neck tattoo, and the scars that littered his body and crept up his skin like vines. "And I know Bastien's not your favorite person right now, but he just lost a family friend. He's not thinking straight. Took me a few days just to get him sober after we left ye. Then to see ye cozy with your *soumettre*? Well, there's only so much a lad can take."

I held up my hand to stop his bros before hos code. "I get it, and I can be cool, but I don't really think I need to put up with his issues anymore. If he would've wanted it to work, he had every opportunity. He didn't trust me, Mad. And on top of that, he humiliated me. You might feel like you owe him, but I don't. He brought me into this messy world, but pushed me away every chance he got. I'm here to square away Avalon, and that's it."

"I saw ye gazing at him when things were right, and I've put up with his obsession to find a way to get ye back. Ye can say 'tha's it' all ye want, but I know the real thing when I see it. Ye were happy with him."

"I was. I was happy, and then he broke it." I waved my hand between us to stop the stupid and pointless conversation. "I don't need to hash this out." I cleared my throat. "About the marriage thing? That's way cool of you, Mad. I mean it. I've been keeping myself up at night, scared of who I might end up with. Morgan wants me to choose someone tomorrow."

"Grand," he said flatly. No doubt this wasn't the way he'd seen himself settling down, either. "I'll see ye at the celebration for Avalon, and offer my hand officially to your mammy. Do what ye want with it."

I didn't know how to say goodbye to him. After the marriage proposal, it felt weird to high-five the guy. But I didn't feel comfortable hugging him, either. He seemed to have a strict don't-anyone-friggin'-touch-me rule. "Okay. Thanks, Mad." A wave of exhaustion swept over me, so I leaned on the arm of the hard, red couch. I like to think it was from chatting with the birds while they'd cheered me and Demi on while we bowled in my bedroom all afternoon, but really it was the gravity of my life these days that weighed me down and made me wish for a bed.

13

THE DANGER OF A SOUMETTRE

Bastien burst through the door, his sleeves rolled and his I've-got-this face on, like he was going to war or something. "I'm not waiting in the hall like a dog for you. I'm a part of this whole thing, too, you know."

Madigan waved off Bastien's bluster. "We've already reached an understanding. I'll offer my hand officially tomorrow at the celebration."

Bastien glanced my way like an animal afraid to get beaten on the snout with a rolled-up newspaper. "And what about my offer?"

Madigan blew out a raspberry toward the ceiling, exasperated at the scene. "I told ye it weren't the right time for tha."

Bastien dragged his chair across the divide between us and parked his beautiful backside down on it. His shoulders were hunched forward, like he was gearing up to tell me a secret. I didn't want to see Bastien up close. I didn't want to memorize his barbed wire tattoos. I didn't want to inhale his cinnamon and Christmas tree scent. None of that mattered, though, because there he was, forcing me to deal with him. "Rosie, I'm sure Mad explained why I can't marry you yet. But there's something I can do that might help. I can't stand the thought of you in here without me. It's killing me to be wandering around Avalon away from you. There's no point to being here anymore if I have to be without you."

I kept my words short and concise. "Spare me your dramatic love sonnets. I wouldn't want you to say anything you'll have to take back just because you friggin' feel like it. I mean, what would Roland say if he heard you spouting such lovely things to a thieving witch?"

Bastien narrowed his eyes at my attitude, but said nothing to spar with it. "I could sign on as your *Guardien* if you give me your *lueur*. Then I could stay here with you."

I closed my eyes and pinched the bridge of my nose, doing everything in my power to remember to be kind and compassionate. Mercy had to be somewhere rattling around inside of me. This was Bastien at his most raw, and I didn't want to bite him too hard when he was so exposed. It was the nicest offer he could give me, about a month too late. My response was barely louder than a whisper. "You ran away when I accidentally tried to give you my *lueur* before I knew what any of that was. You, me, and the entire

Backstreet Boys crew are singing the same, tired song. Quit playing games with my heart."

He pried my hand from my face and mashed it between his, warming my chilly skin and pressing my fingertips to his lips. Oh, how I missed the feel of Bastien. I couldn't bring myself to look into his caramel eyes and see all the swirling emotions we brought out in each other. "I was stupid to ever run from us. I was stupid to listen to Roland when he accused you of stealing the jewels. I've been stupid every day since then, trying to give you your space and stay away. I should've followed you here the day you walked away from me. You don't belong here." He reached out and gripped the back of my neck, forcing me to look in his eyes. "You belong with me. Don't you feel it?"

It would be too easy to kiss him and throw my well-earned distance out the window. Just a few inches separated us, so I knew I had to add more depth to the wall I had built up to keep him from getting inside again. "It doesn't matter what I feel. You can't build a relationship without trust, and I don't trust you anymore, Bastien. And you clearly never trusted me, taking me into the woods like you did. I'm with Demi now, so as much as I appreciate the personal growth leaps you're taking to offer yourself up to be my *Guardien*, it just wouldn't work." I carefully slid my hand from his and placed it in my lap. "But thank you for the apology. I'm sure one day I won't be this hurt by it all."

Bastien followed my example of keeping voices low so we didn't shout at each other. "Rosie, Demi isn't your boyfriend. He's not in this for you. He's not even with you by choice. A *soumettre* is ordered to serve you, to give you his body at your request. That's not love. It's a dinner order."

I couldn't help the upset that welled in my chest. I inched away until my back was pressed to the furthest corner of the couch. My words came out in a pained whisper. "Why are you trying to hurt me?"

To his credit, Bastien kept his temper. We were going on four whole minutes, which had to be some kind of record for the guy. He kept his voice gentle, pleading with me to understand. "I'm not trying to hurt you, honey. I'm trying to explain Avalon to you so you *don't* get hurt. Demi is your sexual slave, just as he was to your mother, and to a few of your aunts. Everyone in the kingdom knows the purpose of a *soumettre.* He's supposed to make the crown easier to handle. He's a professional, babe. He's fitting into the mold you need your perfect guy to be." Bastien reached out and took my hand again, just to feel my skin on his, however small that contact might be. "I'd be willing to bet that he's kept his clothes on for the most part, that he hasn't tried much beyond kissing you. If he's as good as advertised, I'd be willing to bet that he plays sports with you, gave up eating meat for you, and holds you while you sleep." His eyes closed on the last part, his plea dropping to an agonized whisper. "Tell me he doesn't hold you while you sleep. Lie to me, Daisy. I'm dying over here without you."

I shook my head, my disconcerted frown announcing that his words were hurting me deeper than I could take. "You're trying to wreck it because I'm happy with him. You're putting things in my head so I'll break it off. You're wrong, Bastien. Demi cares about me."

"Oh, honey. That's the danger of a *soumettre*. It's his job to care about you. Your mother's forcing him to pretend you two belong together, so you'll be pacified and distracted from life and stay here with her. That's not the same thing as real love."

Tears moistened my eyes, but I refused to let them fall in front of Bastien. "You don't know. He looks at me like... like I'm amazing. He likes me, even though I have a hump and a lazy eye. Even though I look like this." I knew I wasn't making any sense, but to me, that's what our connection was like. In my heart, I still felt like the ugly girl people grimaced at, so each glance from Demi was a new thrill I cherished.

"Everyone who's met you for more than two seconds looks at you like you're amazing. He's playing a part. I'm not saying he's a bad guy; I'm saying you're his job."

I shook my head, and I knew my nose was turning red from the unshed tears that were collecting. "He's nice to me. I need someone to be nice to me here, and I hate you for trying to ruin this! Why won't you just let me be happy for once? You took me away from my regular life in Common, and now you're trying to take this away, too?"

Bastien blew out a steadying gust, holding tight to my

hand. "Honey, you can stay with Demi for as long as you want. I can't control that, even though it breaks me to think of another man kissing you." He pressed my palm to his chest to remind me that yes, Bastien did have a heart, and it was capable of rupture. "Just make sure not to tell Demi about the jewels, or anything that's a secret. Morgan owns him, and everything else in this mansion. Never forget that. Please, Daisy. I'm trying to be straight with you. For the good of all we're working for, Demi can't be in on this."

I nodded slowly, waiting a few beats so that when I opened my mouth, a giant sob didn't come out and let him know he'd hit me where it hurt. "I haven't told him, and I won't. I don't want to risk him like that. If Morgan finds out what we're up to, I don't want him involved. Rigby, either." I let a bit of my raw emotion shine through. "Morgan had Demi beaten because I wore jeans outside the castle. Whipped, Bastien!"

He closed his eyes at the sound of his name on my lips, inhaling deeply before he spoke. "I could've put money on that happening. Morgan's smart, and doesn't trust anyone. Of course she would play on your thing for wounded animals. Of course she would hurt Demi to bond you two closer together. She wants you to trust him, to tell him your secrets so he can report them back to her. I'm guessing you two really stuck close after that?"

I was stunned, but managed to nod wordlessly. "Well, yeah. She locked me in my bedroom with him. This is the first time I've been allowed out in over a week."

Bastien's nostrils flared, but I could see him talking his temper off the ledge. "After this jewel business is over, I'll bust you out of here, honey."

"Demi cares about me. You're wrong," I said, but the conviction wasn't there as it had been before. Bastien had stolen my conviction. He'd stolen a great many things from me.

"I just want you to be careful. If you won't give me your *lueur*, I can't move in with you here. I can't keep you safe. You have to be careful, more careful than falling for a guy whose job it is to make you fall for him." He closed his eyes and leaned closer to press his forehead to mine. His hand was still holding my palm to his chest. His thumb traced over the ring Kerdik had given me. "Man, I wish I could go back to the day when another guy's ring on your finger was the worst thing."

14

WHAT YOU GET FOR BEING A DOUCHE

I managed to make it out of the room without kissing Bastien or crying in front of him, which I would like some kind of cookie or cash prize for. The guys left, and I rounded the corner of the giant castle, trying to remember where exactly my room was in the maze. My gut led me left, so I followed that hallway until I heard footsteps echoing behind me. I looked over my shoulder, casting up a wan smile to the soldier with rust-colored hair. "Hey, man. I'm thinking my bedroom's this way, but I'm still kind of new here." I wasn't supposed to have a Compass ability, so it played in my favor to pretend I was lost every now and then.

"Actually, it's this way, your highness." He motioned for me to turn around, which was the opposite of what my gut was telling me to do.

The guy looked kind of familiar, though I wasn't sure

where I could know him from. It's not as if I'd met a whole lot of Avalonians. He had a roundish face with a few freckles dotting his forehead. "Oh, thanks. You're sure it's not this way?"

"I'm sure. Allow me." He popped his elbow out and led me through the wrong corridor downward, not upward. I knew my bedroom was on the eighth floor, and we were definitely going below ground.

I pulled my hand from his arm with an apologetic smile. "Sorry. I think I forgot something in the parlor. I'll figure it out. Thanks, though."

His professional demeanor melted into a sneer. "You think you can get Talbot killed and just strut around the mansion, tempting every man in sight?"

"Huh? What are you talking about? Who's Talbot?"

The soldier let out a cruel laugh and jerked me forward by my arm. "Priceless. A royal if I ever saw one. You don't even know the name of the man you had killed."

"Killed?"

"Yes, killed! Talbot didn't know you were the Lost Princess. None of us did. He wanted to have a go at you in the stocks, and you dragged him inside to her majesty most high and got him killed for insulting the Lost Princess!"

I remembered dragging a dude in with more rage in my veins than reason. "Oh, that guy. I didn't ask Morgan to kill him. I just reported his behavior, which I had every right to do. So what if I looked like a peasant. Is that how the rest of the women of Avalon are supposed to be treated? Because I'm a princess, it's suddenly not okay to harass me, but if I wasn't, it'd be fine?"

"If you were a peasant, we'd have you bent over a barrel so we could take turns going at your fine little backside." He reached around with his free hand and grabbed my butt through my skirts. He couldn't actually get at anything beneath all the layers, but still. Not cool. "I may not be able to lock you up in the stocks, but I can take you down to the dungeon and make you scream easily enough."

I snarled at him, horrified. "Get off of me!" I ripped my arm from his grip and let an angry punch fly out, smashing him hard in the nose. I both felt and heard a satisfying crunch, which gave me just enough time to make my escape.

Let me tell you a little something about running in a corset and a long, poofy dress. It's about exactly as challenging as it sounds. "Help!" I cried, my voice echoing through the castle off the stone walls. I ran as fast as I could, listening to my gut that tugged me up steps and through hallways. I prayed my frantic footfalls would lead me somewhere good.

I didn't stop until my gut led me into the kitchen, smacking me straight into Rigby. I tried to catch my breath, but my lips felt fuzzy. "Rigs, thank God! A dude back there... Trying to... And he grabbed my butt!"

Rigby broke from his conversation with a tall gym rat in a white apron, who had flour smudges all over his beefy forearms. "Someone put their hands on you? Who?" Rigs set his tasting spoon down on the vast marble counter, wiping his hands off on a towel. The whole kitchen was all stone and marble with gold fixtures. The gilded chandelier we stood beneath had hundreds of thin arms that stretched out from the center and crawled along the ceiling like arms from an overzealous spider. The whole place smelled of freshly baked bread, but I couldn't even enjoy that, because I was so worked up.

"I don't know his name, but just look for the dude with a broken nose. Red hair, a few inches shorter than you. Soldier. Blood all over his face for being a douche."

"Broken nose?"

"Yeah, I broke his nose."

Rigby looked at me like I'd just told him I wanted a unicorn for Christmas. "You broke his nose? How?"

I shouted incredulously. "With my fist! You wanted me to just let him rape me?"

"No, of course not. I just didn't expect a princess to be able to... Well done, your majesty." He turned toward the cook guy. "Carry on, Fabrice. Allow me to escort you back to your chambers, Princess."

"Thanks, Rigby."

Fabrice lifted his finger in the air. "I'll go with you, Rigby. If it's Earl she's talking about, he won't take the defeat and walk away."

We walked out of the kitchen that had come to a stand-still at my dramatic entrance, and made our way down the hall. I'm not sure if it was the adrenaline, the almost being raped thing, Bastien, Madigan's proposal, Demi or the stinkin' corset, but with every step, oxygen grew harder and harder to find. Rigby was leading the way, with Fabrice keep watch behind. Rigs didn't see my stumble, or my crash to the stone floor.

15

DEMI'S LOVE

I felt my body being jostled in strong arms I didn't recognize. I burrowed into the warmth of the man who carried me with gentle hands, seeking shelter and a firm place to rest my head. I blinked up at him, the world shifting into focus to reveal Fabrice's clenched jaw and worried eyes. "Almost there, Princess."

I was so turned around and woebegone that I nearly burst into embarrassing tears when Rigs opened my bedroom door to let Fabrice inside. His cheeks turned red when he climbed the steps up the platform and laid me down in my bed, as if I was naked and he was a peeping tom. "Thanks, man. Sorry about that. Long day, I guess."

"What happened to her?" Demi demanded, livid.

Fabrice kept his eyes trained on my no doubt pale face. "I'll send up some fruit to liven you. And I know you insist on not eating meat, but perhaps just this once a little pheasant might help you feel stronger."

"You're the one who's been making my meals?"

Fabrice nodded while Rigby opened my window. A flock of birds raced inside, making all three men cry out in shock. The birds alighted on me, chirping songs of love and I'm-here-for-you-girl sentiments that I desperately needed.

"She needs mint to rouse her senses!"

"I'll get the Voix *some flowers!"*

The birds kept suggesting things, some flying back out in search of whatever they deemed to be nature's cure for me. Gotta love them.

Fabrice tried to shoo them off of me, but I caught his hand. The beefy arm turned surprisingly gentle under my touch. "It's alright, Fabrice. These guys are my friends. That's why I can't eat meat." My fingers were shaking, and dropped to the mattress. "You're a really good cook, by the way. That soup inside the gourd you did last week? Blew my mind."

"Thank you, your grace." Fabrice's eyes widened, like he'd never been paid a compliment before in his life.

I wanted to ask if I could go down to his kitchen sometime so he could teach me how to make the potatoes I liked, but another swoon hit me, knocking my head back onto my pillow. "Oh, man. I don't feel so good."

Rigby all but shoved Fabrice out the door and latched it. He whirled around and ran to the bed, scooping my torso up in his arms and pressing my chest to his, so Demi could untie the stranglehold that was my dress. As soon as I could take in a full breath, the tears I'd had on standby bubbled to the surface, spilling down my cheeks and all over Rigs' shoulder. I hated that I was breaking down, and hated even more that Bastien had put doubts in my head of whether or not I could trust them. "I don't like it here!"

Rigs threw away his stiff butler demeanor and hugged me tight, his hand holding my head to his shoulder so I didn't have to support myself at all. "I know, my sweet. This place kills the light in people. I've seen it time and time again. I'd hoped it wouldn't happen to you."

"My mom doesn't like me!" I confessed, the fainting making me feel slightly tipsy. "She thinks I'm fat and doesn't want to be around me because I don't have any Compass powers."

Rigs said nothing to this, not daring to step so far out of bounds as to insult the queen. "You are lovely, and you don't need power to keep kindness in your heart. That's all the magic you need, and you have it in spades."

His words were too sincere to brush under the rug. I clung to Rigby, wishing I could trust the shoulder I wept on. I felt Demi's hand on my back, and my body instinctually leaned toward his touch. I exhaled when Demi's arms banded around me from behind, giving me strength to calm myself enough so I didn't hyperventilate. "Can I go visit Lane? I'm not doing so hot here."

"I'm sorry, your grace. Her majesty most high has requested you stay inside until your unveiling tomorrow."

I suspected as much, but it did nothing to assuage the trapped feeling that choked me around the throat. "Okay. I'm sure you've got things to do, Rigs. Thanks for making sure I made it back up here safely."

"What happened to her?" Demi asked, unable to be patient anymore. Rigs explained it all to him, turning Demi's docile embrace into a protective hold. "I want two guards you trust posted outside her bedroom at all hours, Rigby. I mean it. If Earl had it in his head it was possible to attack Rosie, others will try their luck."

"I'll see to it. I'll select the guards myself, and see to Earl's hanging."

I sucked in my surprise, unsure if I should protest or not. Rigby left, and Demi tried to coax me to eat something, but I had no appetite. When Demi left to take my tray down, I tore off the layers of royalty that confined me and shoved my fist into a drawer in the wardrobe, fishing out the nearest thing I could dress myself in without assistance. It was white, strappy and silky, and hung to my knees like a sundress. I'd been sleeping in my dressing gown for the most part, but I didn't want to be wearing anything Earl had touched or breathed on. I'd not worn such a beautiful and sexy nightgown before, and had never felt so disgusting and awful. I hoped the silk would balance out the dismal mood I was stuck in.

I sat on the platform between my bed and the window,

hiding and hugging my knees to my chest. The tears poured more freely, now that I was alone and the corset was on the floor. I looked out at the early evening sky, wondering if the blue moon that was peaking over the horizon had anything better in store for me. My adventure with myself wasn't going so well these days. The desire to cut loose and run was strong, but I knew the hundreds of thousands of displaced Avalonians needed me to find the Jewels of Good Fortune, so they could set their land right again. Someone had to take Morgan down, though I wished that job fell to anyone besides me.

When Demi came back in, he set a tea tray on the table and moved to my side, staring down at me in faux disappointment. "I'm sure you know this already, but princesses don't sit on the floor."

"Well, I guess the jig is up. I'm not a real princess. Wouldn't that just solve it all?" I kept my eyes on the blue hue of the moon, again willing it to give me a better night than the crummy day the sun had shoved down my throat.

Demi latched the door, and then came to sit by my side on the tall platform, leaning against the bedframe. He tilted his head back, his chin jutting up toward the sky. "You never mentioned his name."

"Who's name?"

"Bastien the Bold. I didn't realize the man you still loved was him."

Alarms went off in my head. "Whoa, I never said anything about love."

Demi cast a soft smile up at the moon, patiently waiting for the same thing I was – for the moon to give us some good news. "You may not know it, but you do love him. You can't feel betrayal or hurt as deeply as you do concerning what he did, unless you're in love. It's one of the things I'm good at spotting."

I didn't want to argue with Demi, so I switched the spotlight over to him. "Have you ever been in love?"

"Oh, yes. Many times. It's hard not to get attached when you're in my position. Some of the women make it easy to hate them, but I've learned that hate is often just the other side of the coin from love. I loved Tyronoe for a time, your aunt from Province 2. Duke Henri was wretched to her, so she sought comfort from me. I loved her very much, toy as I was to her. I was younger then, more easily swayed, perhaps."

I swallowed hard, unsure what to do with that information.

"Rigby mentioned to me that Duke Henri was one of your potential suitors, and that's when I knew I was falling in love with you. All sorts of murderous thoughts crossed my mind at the idea of him taking you into his bed. He is... Duke Henri is a vile man with many unusual tastes. I could not watch you endure what Duchess Tyronoe had to."

I let the silence settle between us, stunned that he could proclaim his feelings so easily. "I'm getting engaged tomorrow, I guess." I grimaced, knowing that when I finally spoke, I would choose all the wrong words.

Demi didn't seem crushed by this, but there was a tightness to his nod that mirrored the tension in my chest. His hand moved to rest on mine in the space between us. "I still belong to you, you know. You can have me as often as your husband allows."

I let out a humorless snort, knowing Madigan wouldn't care about sharing me.

But *I* cared. I cared if I kissed one guy while another one put his ring on my finger, even if it was all for a show. I cared if I made a joke out of marriage, and if I could only give part of myself to Demi behind closed doors.

I stared at my knees, pulling them up so I could focus my gaze on them and avoid Demi's eyes altogether. I hated the embarrassing words that came out of my mouth, but my strangled whisper was the bravest voice I could muster. "Maybe I could marry you. Then I could kiss my husband as often as I felt like, because it would be you." I had to know. I had to try. Part of me wanted to prove Bastien wrong and show us both that Demi cared about me, and that he wasn't just using me to feed information to Morgan.

The other part of me was still a girl who just wanted a simpler life than all this, and someone fun and caring to share my journey with.

My face flushed red when Demi's hand stiffened atop mine. I spluttered about a dozen apologies, wishing I could stuff the awkward words back into my mouth. I'd just proposed to a man I'd known less than a month. I wasn't sure which way was up anymore.

I didn't know what to do, so I hid. With frightened eyes, I ducked down and rolled my body under the tall bed, wishing I could be a child and hide from the things that were too big for me to handle gracefully. I laced my fingers behind my head and burrowed my nose into the wood, hoping that closing my eyes would make what I just did disappear. "Forget I said anything! I shouldn't have put you on the spot like that. I'm sorry, Demi. Please don't freak out on me. I take it back!"

Demi's movements were careful and slow as he got down on all fours to peer at me under the bedframe. "Are you hiding from me?"

"I think so."

He gently fished me out, dusting off my hair when my chagrin was exposed to the moonlight. He stood and lifted me up by my elbows, squaring his shoulders to mine. His irises burned with that glowing passion he seemed to have on tap. "You wish to marry me? Of all the suitors out there, you wish to be mine? Bastien the Bold came to win your hand, but you would choose me?"

"I don't want to talk about Bastien. I'm sorry I made it weird. We barely know each other. I just know I'd rather be with you than anyone else right now. I don't want to marry a stranger! I want to laugh and go bowling with you. I want to listen to you read every night!"

Demi's kiss was so powerful and so enthusiastic that he lifted me up off the ground, cleared the steps and dumped me back onto the mattress. I let out a squeak of surprise, not expecting my impromptu proposal to go over this well. He tugged at my hair, bending my chin skyward so he could kiss a heated trail of gratitude down my neck.

"Yes," he breathed into my skin, tasting the dip in my clavicle just to make me squirm. "Yes, I would marry you. If I could, I would make you mine forever." His experienced hands hiked my nightgown up, exposing my entire bottom half to him. He traced his favorite parts, lighting my nerves on fire and making my body writhe without me telling it to.

"If you could? What do you mean?" I asked between kisses, tasting his tongue. I let out an audible noise that was both passion, trepidation and borderline anxiety when his body pressed down on mine.

"I'm a *soumettre*, and you're a princess. You can't marry so far below your station. But that you would? That you would choose me over all the others? Over an Untouchable? I love you, Juliet." He dragged the silk up my torso. "You're so kind, and good, and beautiful. I was alone before I met you. I don't like being alone." His voice was seductive and nearly a purr. "Let's not be alone tonight."

It was when the silk threatened to hike over my breasts that I put a quick stop to the emotional chaos. "Wait! Wait, Demi. This is too fast."

I could tell this wasn't a popular decision, but Demi

consented without protest, relenting his passion and lowering my nightgown while he slowed his frantic kisses to luscious, languid ones that seemed to pour over my entire body like melted wax. I felt beautiful and precious under his care, and like it mattered that I was actually breakable. I took a chance and looked into his eyes, and saw the truth in them. Demi wasn't using me, or trying to get close so he could report back to Morgan. He wasn't faking his feelings for me.

His whisper in my ear was pained with his audible heartbreak. "I will stand in the shadows and curse my life the day you marry Bastien the Bold, but I'll be with you. I'll bring you warm towels after he makes love to you. I'll get your breakfast ready and serve him as faithfully as I've served you, because that is my lot. I told you, my journey ends here, in this wretched place." He paused to kiss my lips, drinking me in like I was the last gulp of water. This castle was a desert for us both, so we clung to the respite we found in each other. "But know that every day I watch you love another man, my soul dies and my heart shrivels in my chest." He brought my fingers to his pecs, so I could feel the solid, lean muscles that rose and fell for me.

For the third time that day, tears brimmed in my eyes. I didn't have it in me to correct him at his assumption that I'd be marrying Bastien. "You're too good to me. I don't want to hurt you with this. I don't want to get married! I'm only twenty-two! Would it help if I requested a different *soumettre*? I don't want you to have to wait on me and my new husband. That's horrible! I wouldn't be able to do that."

"If you sent me away, then I wouldn't be able to see your face every morning. I'll take light where I can find it, even if it shines for another man."

"Jeez!" I wiped the tears away, frustrated. "Stop saying perfect things like that! Just be horrible to me, and make this easier."

Demi's gentle smile fell down over my body, taking me in and sheltering me as best he could. "Take my love and let it make you stronger. Let it focus you so you can endure what you need to. I will always be here, as long as you'll have me." He twined his fingers through mine and kissed my knuckles. "You're not alone on your journey, Juliet."

Yup. That did it. Tears flowed down the sides of my face, pooling on my pillow and making any response unintelligible, and not worth the effort.

Then Demi did the sweetest thing I didn't even have to ask for, but we both knew I needed. Demi tucked us both under the covers, rolled me onto my side and held me until I cried myself to sleep.

Bastien was wrong about Demi. You can't fake kindness like that. As I drifted off to sleep in his safe and corded arms, I hoped this night together wouldn't be our last.

16

KING URIEN'S PLAN

'd gone to prom with Judah and Jill, tagging along and feeling like a loser who couldn't get a date. Lane had gone as my date, not caring that she was in her thirties and attending a high school dance. I love Lane for many reasons, and her unswerving loyalty to our friendship was only one of them. I'd missed her sorely, and as the birds brought Demi flowers to braid in my hair, I wondered if she was already on her way to the castle.

"Do you think she's here yet?" I asked for the fourth time that morning.

"Duchess Elaine will be here with the rest of the guests. I've told the guards to send up word the second she's seen."

I chewed on my lower lip. "That Earl guy, he's..."

"Dead," Demi confirmed. "Rigby had him hanged within the hour of your attack. You're safe now."

"Safe" seemed like a foreign concept these days. "Thank you. I'm having a hard time finding my center. Between Earl and the whole coronation thing, my mind's all over the place."

"Take a breath, Rosie. Everything will be alright."

"Easy for you to say. You're not being sold off to the highest bidder."

"You do have some say, you know. You can choose your suitor before her majesty most high chooses for you." Demi looked over his shoulder to confirm my bedroom door was still locked. "I overheard her say again this morning that you would go to Duke Henri so she could expand her territory. His land borders hers, so it's the most fertile of the other provinces. To acquire it would be most advantageous for her." He tugged a stubborn curl up into the braid that wrapped around the top of my head like a crown. Demi always impressed me with how adept he was at doing hair. "Duke Lancelot of Province 5 is a worthy candidate. From what I know, he's good man."

My palms were sweating as I tried to remember I already had a backup plan. Madigan was definitely the lesser of all the evils. While Lot was a great guy, for sure, he deserved to have a wife who wanted to be married to him. Mad didn't want to marry me any more than I wanted to go through with the charade, so I knew there wouldn't be any feelings crushed when I split and ran back to my life up in Common. Lot was sweet, which meant he should be far away from Morgan. He should have a wife who would stay with him until the end, and I knew I couldn't give him that. To take Lot's offer for marriage if he tossed his name in the mix would be selfish on my part.

When Demi turned me around to do my makeup (among his many talents, the makeup thing always caught me off-guard), I saw moisture sparkling in his bright green eyes. "After I put on your lip stain, I won't be able to kiss you."

I reached forward and pulled him down by his collar so I could taste his tongue again. He took the opportunity to sit on my lap, straddling me like a stripper as he cupped my face. Demi smelled of peppermint oil and felt like a dream I never wanted to wake from. Part of me knew I was attaching so hard and fast to him because of the danger of my current situation, but I didn't care. I wanted him near me. After I chose my husband, I wouldn't be able to reconcile kissing one man with another's ring on my finger.

"I'm sorry. I'm so sorry."

"If I could marry you, I would take you away from all of this. I would build us a cabin and till the soil so we could have our own food, our own land, our own home far from this castle. I want nothing more than to be yours, Rosie."

I pulled back, taking a deep breath and wringing my hands while I tried to get a grip on myself. "Okay. No more nice words. You have to be meaner to me, or I'll never be able to stop kissing you. Say something mean."

"Your mother," Demi replied without missing a beat. "She's the meanest thing I can think of." His eyes darted to the door again, and he covered his mouth with wide eyes, shocked at his own daring. "Oh, I should not have said that. I apologize."

I balked at his bravery, proud of him for speaking his mind. "For what? She's crazy. You can be yourself around me."

He pressed his forehead to mine, crouching to meet the height of my seated position. "I hardly know who that is anymore. I've had to be so many things for so many women. I don't think I'd know what to do with actual freedom."

"You'd run away with me," I suggested with a broad smile. "I'd take you to Common and dress you in ripped jeans and faded t-shirts. We'd get an apartment together next to Judah and Jill, with Lane and Draper and maybe even Reyn down the hall. We'd play soccer on the weekends and watch bad TV together. You could read to me while I rubbed your feet."

The corner of Demi's mouth twitched upward, and he gazed at me with that adoring expression he wore when he was falling in love with me. "Could we play bowling, like we do here?"

"Oh, Commoner bowling is way better than the game I rigged here. There's a machine that resets the pins for you automatically."

"My, that is inventive. Could we be married, and make love all night long in your world?"

I gulped, picturing what I'd been trying to scrub from

my mind. I nodded, unable to look at him anymore, lest he see the lust that threatened to burn me alive from the inside out. "There might be some of that going on, yeah."

Demi closed the gap between us and kissed me one more time. He drew out my lower lip, sucking on it like it was a piece of candy. "You can still have me, you know. The men expect it of the duchesses by now."

I stiffened, rolling back my shoulders and remembering who I was. "I am not my mother's daughter. I'm Lane's daughter, and she would freak out on me if I did what you're suggesting. Once I'm engaged, you and I have to be over. It's not right to marry one guy and keep another on the side. It's not who I am." I hugged myself while Demi silently finished rubbing delicate shades of pink and peach onto my cheeks, eyelids and lips. "Romeo and Juliet don't end up together."

Demi paused, pressing his forehead to mine to steady us both through our simultaneous heartbreak at my declaration.

I cleared my throat and straightened. "Can I go see my dad before it all starts?"

"Of course, but we'll have to be quick about it. Her majesty most high wants you downstairs in an hour."

Demi led the way through the winding stone castle, silent and professional with a straight posture. He walked slowly so I didn't trip over the dusky rose-colored dress that had gold trim on the edges and too much cleavage to be considered ladylike. Yick. If the guys on the soccer team could see me now, they wouldn't believe it was me. The dank stone air that hit my bosom now gave me goosebumps, reminding me that not only could Demi see the tops of my breasts, but so could strangers, the guys I'd gone traveling with if they showed up, and my potential suitors.

I needed to find those gems and get the crap out of here.

When we reached the guarded room, I kissed Demi and asked him to wait outside for me. I didn't like sending him away, even a few feet, but Urien didn't know he was my father, and no one knew I could hear him. I wanted to keep it that way.

With careful steps in the empty room, I made my way to my father's side. My heart led me to him, but also my gut tugged me closer, which was a first. I didn't understand why my Compass was pushing me to his bedside, but I went and situated my bell-like skirts so I could sit on the edge of the bed, facing him. "King Urien?" I asked quietly, hoping the magic we shared wasn't gone. Of all the mojo I needed, the whole unknown languages thing was the one I clung to. I wanted to know my dad more than anything. I needed to know that he was truly Superman.

"Is it you? You came back for me?" The hope in his voice made my heart rise in my chest.

I squeezed his hand in mine, though I knew he couldn't feel it. "It's me. I wanted to see you before the day got away from me. How are you feeling? Any change?"

He let out a humorless chortle in my mind that didn't touch his deadened facial muscles. *"Nothing changes in here, except that I now look forward to you coming to break me from my endless silence. I'm so grateful you returned."*

"Sorry I can't stay here all the time. I'm not allowed to wander around. It's a little tense in the castle. There's a big party happening today, and Morgan's extra on edge. It's better for everyone if she doesn't see me. Just the look of me seems to make her angry."

"You must be very beautiful, then. Morgan knows the difference between true loveliness and women who aren't a threat."

My father called me beautiful. I swallowed the lump of shyness in my throat, knowing that he couldn't see me to verify that with his own eyes. "Well, I don't know about that, but I do know she doesn't like the look of me."

"Yes, you're beautiful, then. She doesn't bother lifting her finger for anything less than the steepest competition."

"Oh, jeez. You with the compliments." I batted my hand in a "knock it off, but don't ever stop" kind of way. "Now that I've met Morgan, and seen what she's done to you, I want to stop her. Can I tell you a secret?"

Urien chuckled like Santa Claus, and I half-expected his stomach to shake like bowl full of jelly. *"I don't have any other choice, dear. Tell me, what is your name? I was too shocked to ask last time."*

I fished around for a quick lie. "I'm Britney. Britney Spears." I flinched at the first name that popped into my head. Why hadn't I picked Eleanor Roosevelt or someone with political feminine prowess? I rolled my shoulders back and owned the lie. "I'm trying to find a way to take down Morgan. I've been searching for the Jewels of Good Fortune she stole from her sisters. I'm going to find them and give them back to the duchesses." He was the first outsider I'd told the plan to, and the admission felt liberating.

He was quiet while he mulled over my plan. *"That's admirable – especially that you don't want to keep the Jewels of Good Fortune for yourself, but plan on giving them back to the Daughters of Avalon. It's one of the only good things about my Rosalie being gone. Elaine was always a good judge of what's important. Rosalie won't have to suffer the greed that seemed inescapable with Morgan and her other sisters."*

I digested the compliment as my heart swelled. There was no misinterpreting that one – my father had a little respect for me. "Thank you, sir. My only problem is that I don't totally know where they're all hidden. I found three so far, and gave them back. Avril has one. Lane should have the other one, I'm hoping. Heloise's made it back to her province, plus the extra one Lane is in charge of until we can figure out our next move. Avril's got a serious case of sticky fingers."

"That's four down, five to go."

"Four, actually. Morgan's jewel would stay in Province 1 with her." I measured the distance around my father's fingers using my own, examining the lined skin that looked like it had seen hard work before his life in the mansion. "One has to stay in Province 1, of course. I'm not set on punishing the people here because Morgan's a jerk. I just want the jewels to go back where they came from."

"Very good. That was a test, by the way. If I'm to help you, I need to know you're of good quality."

I smiled down at his lifeless form, wishing there was a way he could help me. "You're a sneaky king, Urien. But seriously, what would I need with a jewel? Especially one that could help bajillions of people." I looked down at my finger, examining the gorgeous aquamarine ring Kerdik had given me. "Besides, I already have a ring. It's not magic or anything, but it makes me feel like *I'm* magic when I wear it. Pretty. The nine jewels might as well be nine lumps of pretty coal that need to go back to where they came from. The sooner that gets straightened out, the better."

"Ah, but you're not thinking it all the way through. As soon as the stones leave Province 1, Morgan will notice. You must sneak them out one at a time, so the plants don't wither overnight. Send them to the furthest provinces in need first, so she can't immediately see their prosperity grow."

"Huh. I didn't think about that. Good plan. Thanks, man."

"It will only buy you a little time. Morgan will put it together and go after the duchesses again. It will be just like it was before I fell into my sleep. War until the other provinces surrender. You must make sure that doesn't happen again."

I frowned, bummed that my plan wasn't foolproof. "Maybe I should find some dummy jewels or something to replace the ones I steal. That way she won't immediately know which one is gone. Maybe she'll just think the magic in the jewels is fading."

"*That's definitely worth a try. But something must be done about Morgan, otherwise she'll send her army to war again, and more devastation will occur, all over shiny rocks.*"

"Crap. You're right." I closed my eyes. "I'm not willing to murder her, if that's what you're hinting at."

"*I was, but I won't anymore if you're opposed to it.*"

"I couldn't kill another person, Urien. It's just not in me. I want to help Avalon get back on its feet. I don't know how Morgan fits into all of it."

"*I'll give this Morgan business some thought. In the meantime, we should get started on our plan.*"

My lips curved into a smile that my dad and I were in cahoots, hatching up schemes. "Okay. I think I know where one of the stones is. There's a spot in the moat she stops by once a day on her walks. It's not much to go on, but it's better than nothing."

"*I think we can do better than a hunch. Yes, she hid one in the moat fifteen years ago, but you'll never find it. She's a witch, Britney. She's put it in a pouch that has an invisibility charm in it. She sliced open the throat of a Brownie to get the blood for the spell before Kerdik took the higher magic from the land. You could search the moat forever and never see what's right in front of your face. You have to feel around for it. It was in a leather pouch, and then placed in a hollowed-out stone before she laid it to rest in the moat. Assuming it's still there, you'll want to look for a rock that's about half the size of my head."*

"Whoa! I wasn't expecting you to have actual intel. That's way cool, Urien. I mean, seriously. If it's still there? That would be the first one, done and over with. Thank you. How did you know that?"

"Morgan likes to come here to gloat on occasion, since I'm the only one who can keep her secrets. I don't know where they all are, unfortunately."

"Oh, that's terrible. You've been stuck with this information for this long? That sucks!"

"Indeed. The gem in the moat will be your second one. The first one is here."

My mouth fell open. "Here? Like, in this room, or somewhere in the mansion?"

"Inside my mouth. She sealed my body so I wouldn't need food or drink. The Hemlock paralyzed me, and her spell sealed my body from needing sustenance. She said it all under the guise of keeping me safe while she searched for a cure for me, but as she's the one who poisoned me in the first place, I hardly think that's the case."

"Sheesh. And I thought I had relationship drama. Dude, that's serious."

"Indeed. Since there's no need for my mouth to open, it's the perfect hiding space for one of the jewels. If you pry open my jaws, you'll find it in a similar invisible pouch."

I let out a string of spluttery expletives. "Are you serious? It's been right here this entire time?"

"I needed to know I could trust you with it before handing it over. You'll return it to one of the further provinces?"

"You have my word, sir. I can have it sneaked out today, actually. I know the jewels have to be moved quickly once they're taken from their hiding place."

"Keep it secret, Britney. The Daughters of Avalon weren't always so greedy. The gems turned their darker sides loose. If it's known you have one, you'll be a target, for certain."

"Yes, sir." I stood and leaned over his mouth. "I'm sorry. I feel like a jerk opening your mouth for you like this. It's totally intrusive. Forgive me?"

"Think nothing of it. Only promise me you'll take it far away from Morgan. Promise me you'll avenge me, and pay her back for all she's done."

I stood at his bedside and smoothed back his brown hair that had wisps of gray on the temples. Then I leaned over and kissed my father's forehead. "I promise to do all I can to get you back, and get this jewel safely to a province that needs it." I felt awful prying my father's jaw open, but I did what needed to be done. I fished around in his mouth with a swiping finger, latching onto a small, damp velvet pouch I couldn't see. My eyes were wide as saucers when I pulled it out. "I've got it!" I fumbled with the invisible thing, finally finding the opening and peering inside. Glittering out at me was an amethyst as wide as a silver dollar. Clear and pure lavender-colored, it shone at me, finally getting its chance to show off after decades of hiding. "Wow. It's pretty."

"The deadliest things always are. Quick, now. Hide it some-where out of sight, but never let it out of your reach."

"Well, what the crap? Where is out of sight but not out of reach? I'm sort of going to a giant party today." I cast around for an option, but of course the giant ball gown didn't have pockets. I sighed and turned away from my father (though his eyes were shut and he couldn't open them if he wanted to), and stuffed the pouch down the front of my dress, tucking it between my breasts. The corset was so tight, I knew it would hold the treasure in place and not let it slip down. But just in case, I tied the pouch's string at the opening onto a gold ribbon that laced through the front of my gown. I waved my arms around to make sure it stayed in place. "Okay, it's secure now." I moved back to his side and scooped up his hand, wishing my touch could warm him. "Any chance you've got a cure that might wake you up?"

"Sadly, I can only solve Avalon's problems, not my own. My duty is to my country, so it comforts me to know that no matter what my state, I am still the man I set out to be."

"'Know who you are,'" I quoted Lane sagely. "I think it's heroic, what you're doing. Helping me figure this out. Thank you."

"Thank you, fair maiden."

I kissed his hand and laid it back down, resolving that I would not give up on my father – even if the rest of the world had.

17

FORMAL AND FAKE

I thought college life had prepared me for loud music, but all the hard rock-blasting dorms, football games and pep rallies were nothing compared to the trumpets that never seemed to tire of announcing each new royal and important official who rode through the decorated stone-lined paths. The super cool officials entered on horses, some in carriages, waving to the peasants who had come from far and wide. Their chins were high and they all wore nicer, pressed clothing. Each blast made me jump in my chair. Well, to call what I sat on a chair would be doing it a gross injustice. I sat next to Morgan on a... well, let's just call a spade a throne and be done with it. It was pure gold, encrusted with rubies. The stones caught the sun's rays to shine pure, unadulterated light out on the hundreds of thousands of people, who milled about on the grass in various states of wonder.

I'd been instructed by Demi and Rigby to stare straight ahead with a bland expression on my face. Apparently smiling would upset Morgan, and was thought to be a weakness on the part of the royal in these grand public situations. It was just as well. I was too nervous to smile anyways. My hands gripped the golden armrests, my fingers clutching the claw-like grooves that had been engraved to look both menacing and regal.

Morgan wore a crown so thick, tall and heavy, it was a wonder her neck could hold it up. The spires jutted out nearly an entire foot, and were crusted with diamonds and jewels of every color. Her usual stone of preference was the ruby, hence the signature red color of her banner, the guards' uniforms, and our dresses. Her crown made a statement, wearing the jewels of all the provinces to declare herself without having to come out and say it. She was the Queen of Avalon, a notch above the sisters she'd stolen land and power from. Her expression was fierce, ignoring the civilians who whispered beyond the row of emotionless guards lining the platform we were positioned atop. On Morgan's other side was an empty throne meant to represent my father, who was gone, but not.

The other royals led their people, and the throngs of civilians grew by the minute. There had been plenty of space that morning in the vast prairie, but now I wondered what might happen if someone sneezed wrong.

On the sides of the wide expanse of green were smaller platforms – eight of them – one to represent the rest of the provinces. Though some had been completely absorbed by Province 1, the illusion that their failed regions were somewhat represented was an offering to the people who clung to their heritage. Really, it served as a grim reminder that Provinces 4, 6, 7, and 8 were no more, and had been absorbed by Morgan. Lot was standing proudly at the fifth platform, his blue cape gently flapping behind him, making him look like Duke Ken Doll in the flesh. He shot me a sweet little smirk, which I nodded at, since I wasn't allowed to smile. He seemed to understand, and turned his attention out to the crowd, who genuinely seemed to love him.

My gaze kept shooting towards Province 9's platform, my exhale audible when Lane finally rode in with Draper and Reyn, and took her seat on her smaller, but still beautiful golden throne. I wanted to run to her, to throw my arms around my best girlfriend and beg her to run away with me. I wanted to make cookies with her, paint each other's toenails and talk about nothing and everything until we had no more words left – a thing we had not yet attained, though not for lack of trying.

The whispers gave way to rude pointing and a mixture of jeers and cheers at Lane defying Morgan so openly, making off with her daughter in the dead of night. Though Lane had been pardoned when the letter bearing my dad's seal surfaced, stating that he'd given permission for Lane to take me away, the scandal was still a stench in the air. She moved up onto the platform nearest our grand stage, on the left side. The provinces seemed to start at us, and moved counterclockwise from the lowest number to the last. At least that meant Lane was closer to me.

The third scandal of the day (behind me being alive and well, and then Lane reclaiming her throne) was when Roland rode in on a horse, his chin in the air and a look of "come and friggin' get it" on his face. He didn't bother with a smile to the people, but rode his horse right to the platform, dismounting on the raised spot earmarked for the fallen Province 4.

Roland didn't wait for Morgan to permit him to speak, but raised his arms high in triumph. "People of Avalon, I've come back to you this day, ready to reclaim the throne of Province 4. All you who are proud of where you came from, return to me this day! I've come to bring you back to a land that is bursting with life, waiting for its sons and daughters to return to its hills." He had an unadorned gold crown on his head and his fist in the air. "Province 4, today I've come to call you home!"

Morgan was a live wire beside me, her face composed but taut with fury she'd learned to control. She stood, and the people who had been flocking to Roland paused at her impending speech. "How is it you've come back from the Forgotten Forest, Duke Roland? You abandoned your people long ago, but now you show up, eager to take them to a devastated land? I've cared for your people – took them under my wing when you abandoned them. How is it you expect them to return to a shepherd who walked out on his sheep?"

"You ran me out of Avalon once, Morgan, but never again. My people know my quality. They know I would not abandon them unless I was forced out."

"What you're suggesting requires proof, of which you have none. Clearly you were hiding like a coward elsewhere in Avalon. Clearly you didn't get on the Cheval Mallet, or you wouldn't be returned to us."

I prayed Roland wouldn't rat me out, my fervent worry interrupted by a commotion coming from the empty platform from Province 8. There, amid gasps and shouts of confusion was Aunt Avril, stepping up onto the rise from her horse so she could glare out at her sister. Lane's platform was positioned between her two sisters, and her head whipped between the two, clear concern marring her proper smile.

Aunt Avril wasted no time backing up Roland. "I can confirm that Duke Roland was driven into the Forgotten Forest by Morgan le Fae, because she did the same thing to me!"

The crowd turned to her, gasping and pointing, afraid and amazed, as if they were seeing a ghost. Avril was thought to be dead, but there she stood, soaking in the scandal of being brought back to her people.

Roland was a jaggoff, for sure, but on his platform, he looked regal and ready to rule the province he'd inherited. His dimpled chin creased when he scowled. "Duchess

Avril and I have come back to reclaim our thrones. Morgan le Fae chased us away from you all, but we've returned, ready to welcome you all home." His face broke into a smile of triumph. "Duchess Avril, Duchess Elaine and I are in possession of three of the lost Jewels of Good Fortune, so do not be afraid to return to the land of your childhood. It will always be there to welcome you with the open arms Avalon was once known for."

"Province 8, return to your duchess!" Avril stood tall, her face fierce with pride at the scandal of going to the Forgotten Forest, and returning with a crown. My fingers itched with the desire to knock her flat out for stealing the jewels I'd rescued; I didn't like her platform being so close to Lane's. Birds flew overhead, circling and asking me if they should attack. I held my tongue, but was tempted to let my minions loose.

Lane carried herself as she always had – with poise, a "deal with it" attitude, and her chin raised to fend off whatever came her way. She was glorious in her flowing emerald gown, a tasteful silver crown on her head.

Of all the people I'd ever known, Lane deserved a crown most of all. She lifted her arms high and called to the crowd. "People of Province 9, I come to you today with my gemstone and all the love in my heart. If you wish it, my land is open to you. In fact..." She turned and met Morgan's eyes, a calm smile firmly affixed in place. "Province 9 is open to anyone who is tired of living under the thumb of Morgan le Fae. All you who are troubled from the long years of waiting for King Urien to rise up and remind Avalon what was once great about Province 1 can come to my land until your beloved king is returned to you."

Morgan's nostrils flared. "I cared for you all when your rulers abandoned you. I took you in and gave you food to eat and a place to water your flocks. Would you abandon your queen so easily?"

My mouth fell open when Rousseau charged to the front, his fist high and a sneer on his hairy lips. "You taxed us until we had less than what we came to you with! Your soldiers pilfer our crops and take our daughters for themselves. You didn't protect us, you corralled us, lining us up for the slaughter!" Spittle flew from his lips. "Well, not me! I'm going home!"

The thick crowd didn't really have room to shuffle around, but that's exactly what they started to do. People tried to make room for each other, beelining toward the platforms for districts 4, 8 and 9.

I remained motionless, suddenly scared that they might start rioting. I was positioned right next to Patient Zero for all the drama. Morgan was fuming, but quickly plastered a benevolent expression on her face as the sea of people shifted below us. "You are all free to go wherever you wish. You were never my prisoners. I had hoped you would love Province 1 as I love her, but if you have grown ungrateful to the hand that fed you, I see no reason why I should sway you to stay. Province 1 deserves the best –

those who truly love her and would fight for her. Do as you must. As your queen, I wish the newly reinstated provinces nothing but the best as you rebuild. I do not envy the long journey that lies ahead of you all."

She motioned for the trumpets to play a tune while the crowd reconfigured, everyone clambering to get to their lost ruler with gleeful grins and new hope in their eyes. It was a thing of pure beauty to watch those who had been resigned to living under Morgan light up and reclaim their lives.

As the trumpets droned on, the whispers and pointing didn't stop. I realized that some of the attention was directed at Draper, with furtive glances en masse cast over shoulders toward Duke Henri, who was stony-faced and fuming. It was then it dawned on me that Draper was wearing a silver crown on his head, his clothes regal, and an emerald cape to match Lane's dress flowing off his shoulders. He was Duke Henri's son that had been cast out. If anything, he should have been on Henri's platform with his brother and sister, Damond and Gwen. Damond was staring at his older brother longingly next to his father, wearing the orange sash of Province 2.

Lane didn't wait for the assembly to be called to order, and stood in front of her throne, commanding a crowd as easily as she always had. The trumpets ceased as one, trained perfectly to obey any royal who had something to say. Her brown curls were spilling loose down her back, and her dainty features that matched mine shone out with rebellion only the youngest of nine daughters could get away with. "Draper of Province 2 was cast out long ago by his ungrateful father, Duke Henri. But since I've resumed my post as the Duchess of Province 9, Draper has been adopted into my family as my son." Her voice rang out in triumph at the scandal.

Despite the instructions I'd been given to remain stoic, I couldn't stop the grin that spread across my face. Draper had a parent who loved him again. My heart leaped in my chest at the wonderful news. In the sea of so many wrongs, that one shining moment was purely right.

Lane stood next to her new son, with Reyn positioned behind her throne as a display of unity. "All of Avalon will recognize Draper's new title as the proud and noble Prince of Province 9."

At least half the crowd bowed their heads in respect to Lane's ruling, shocked but following procedure. The other half shot cagey glances over at Duke Henri, who said nothing, but turned red as a beet.

I wanted to go to them, to place my familial allegiances where they belonged. Lane was my mother, and Draper was my brother. I didn't belong next to Morgan, who sighed disparagingly whenever she looked at me. I belonged with the woman who'd held my hair back when I puked my guts out after we found out the hard way that Chen Li's Best American Good Food Yum-Yum is the absolute worst place to acquire food poisoning.

Demi seemed to sense my dilemma from where he

stood at attention behind my throne. He whispered a calming, "Steady, now. The royals will stay after the ceremony to visit with each other. You'll see Duchess Elaine soon enough."

Demi was my rock today, keeping calm while the introvert in me had a mini panic attack at being so thoroughly on display in such a ridiculous getup. Luckily I didn't have to do or say anything (yet). Rigs broke it down for me when I'd been freaking out in my bedroom earlier that morning. The only thing I would have to do is collect the pledges from the eligible suitors, and then later I would have to swear my allegiance to Avalon when Morgan crowned me in front of the whole country.

In front of the whole country.

I took as deep a breath as my corset allowed when Morgan deemed that Avalon could withstand no more surprises. She stood and stepped forward, her mere presence quieting the entire country without a word necessary to make them fall in line.

My eyes scanned the crowd for people I knew, while Morgan started her welcome speech. I'd heard her practicing it yesterday morning over breakfast; it was your standard politician-speak, so I didn't feel any guilt tuning out. My gaze fell on Rousseau, who nodded serenely at me with a stony expression. He stood at the foot of the platform for Province 8. I'd never seen him dressed in his military gear, and tried not to stare rudely at the man who was so hairy, he could give Chewbacca a run for his shaving cream.

Morgan's speech started to gain passion, her volume building when she spoke of the joy she felt over me coming home to her. That was sure news to me. "My poor husband, your beloved King Urien, was growing weak of mind before his sickness took him. He convinced Duchess Elaine to take our Rosalie away to escape the wars that went on decades ago between our provinces. He did it to save me the heartbreak of watching one of my now deceased sisters slaughter my only daughter. Duchess Elaine kept your princess safe, and for that, she's to be welcomed back with opened arms."

I met Lane's eyes across the way and wished with everything in me that I could run to her, and away from Morgan's lies.

Morgan's voice boomed out as she motioned to me. "And now, may I present to you, my daughter, the Lost Princess, Rosalie of the First and Greatest Province, returned to her people at last!"

18

MY VERY OWN HUSBAND

I jolted in my seat when the crowd cheered as one, erupting in joyous shouts and loud "Huzzahs!" that made my heart bang in my panicked chest.

Demi was offering his hand to me – for what? I couldn't tell you. I took his hand and stood, moving to Morgan's side. It was all I could do to keep my chin raised, as Lane had taught me to do when I wanted to hide. I caught Draper's eye, who disregarded the "no smiling" rule and shot me a dimpled grin, knowing, as I did, that we'd both won the lottery being taken in by Lane.

I felt a low seething directed at me, and it wasn't from Duke Henri. I'd been avoiding the area I could feel Bastien was in (near the front of the crowd a stone's throw from my throne. Not that I was keeping track). I hated that I knew where he was – that I could sense him without looking to verify he was watching me. I could feel his frown locked in place that Demi had touched my hand.

Morgan went on about securing her kingdom through an heir, and that I was the one who could keep the legacy of Province 1 safe and untouched. I nearly choked on my heartbeat when she made the announcement I'd been warned was coming. "And now, eligible suitors can come and lay their pledges at her feet."

Instinctively, I backed away, letting out a miniscule noise of distress when several men with regal capes hanging off their shoulders moved out from the crowd and made their way to me. Each one wore a look of purpose, determined to either make a good impression, or to get the offering over and done with.

As I looked around, I noticed that the only other princess was Gwen, and she was still young, only sixteen or so. I remembered someone mentioning that she couldn't sit on the throne, because she'd been adopted into the family, and not born into it. It was just me who was a female heir. Many were in search of someone in my position, each man determined not to marry below their station.

My mouth fell open when I counted a dozen men making their way to me. The crowd was pointing at the candidates as they stalked to the main stage, and I heard a crier taking bets on who I'd pick.

Me.

Rosie Avalon, who couldn't get a date to senior prom.

The Humpback Whale, who'd been one of the guys for as long as I could remember. Remedial Rosie, who couldn't read for crap, who was a joke to elementary schoolers everywhere. It would have been flattering, if the balance of the entire world didn't feel completely off. It might have been thrilling, had I earned a lick of it. This was all due to a blip of genetics that tied me to the woman who couldn't stand the sight of my face.

Men I didn't know approached Demi, who stood at attention on the edge of the stage, a shoebox-sized gold coffer outstretched. One by one, each man rested something inside – a ring, a gold bracelet, a jeweled necklace. It was their pledge that, if chosen, a wedding ring and a life of luxury would be provided.

I didn't know the first five men who put their tokens in Demi's box. Like, had never seen them before in my life. The ages ranged from maybe eighteen to late fifties. After they dropped their token in the box, they made their way across the stage to kiss my hand. I could tell which province each segment of the crowd was loyal to when the people cheered at the potential their hometown heroes had of bringing me back to their land.

The next man was a familiar face, but not one I wanted to see in this parade. Duke Lot had always been kind to me, and once upon another time, I'd considered giving him my first kiss for a fleeting minute. He was kind in that dashing gentleman way I knew I didn't deserve. He dropped a shimmering necklace in the box and strolled across the stage, his shoulders back and a pleasant fondness on his face when our eyes met. He bowed his head in front of me, shooting me a charming grin when his back was turned to the crowd. "It's a delight to see you again, Rosie. Do consider my offer. I would be good to you."

I met his eyes with gratitude that at least there was one friendly face. I didn't have to marry a stranger, if worse came to worst. A shadow fell over my heart as I took in his kind eyes, his blond hair that fell slightly over his forehead, and the gentle smile he wore for me. Lot deserved better than me. He deserved a woman who wanted to marry him because she had buckets of adoration in her heart for him, and chose his smile above all others. I cared about his happiness, so I knew that I couldn't be selfish with him. "You're a good man, Lot. Please always be this way. Always be the best man in the crowd."

"If a princess commands it, how can I say no?" he teased with a sweetness to him I hoped he saved for the woman he would someday marry.

Morgan was irritated, her acerbic exhales picking up speed enough to be grouped into the derisive snort category. "Duke Lancelot is of Province 5, dear. He hardly has a fortune to offer you," she sniped quietly, though just loud enough for Lot to hear.

I was shocked that Morgan would cut him down when he was offering himself so generously. Lot's eyes hardened, but he said nothing in his defense. I straightened and squeezed his hand. "Thank you for your kind offer, your grace." That was code for, "Peace out, dude. Run before my mom turns crazy axe lady on you." As he dropped my hand, I whispered, "I know exactly how valuable you are, Lot. It's a true honor to have an offer from someone as noble as you. Thank you."

Lot brushed his fingers to mine once more, and Morgan caught it. She noticed that I relaxed around Lot, and probably looked less like I might fling myself off the back end of this platform and run away.

"No. Don't even consider it. I'll not align my kingdom with a land as plain as Province 5." Morgan's grumbled rule was firm when Lot moved off the platform and down into the crowd. His people cheered him on, and I noticed a few other provinces chanted his name as the clear frontrunner favorite. Morgan cringed, her fists clenching at her sides.

Five more men I'd never met nor heard of gave expensive tokens and kissed the back of my hand. The crowd was getting more riled up by the minute, placing bets and cheering on their favorite picks. I could feel Bastien was near, though I still hadn't looked in his direction to verify that the unbreakable stare of longing and frustration was radiating from him.

The crowd went from excited to a wave of concern. It was Avalon-style celebrity gossip in action, and I was friggin' Britney Spears, smack in the middle of it.

The man strutting his way across the stage to me was none other than the man who'd slapped Lane across the face and cast out Draper from his perfect family. Duke

Henri was easily in his mid-fifties, but his confidence was still in the full swagger of youth that came when one had too much power and money. Henri bent his head to me after exchanging a knowing look with Morgan. "Princess."

"*Uncle* Henri." I laid on the familial term to remind him that what he was doing was sick, and that I was younger than one of his children.

"I trust you understand what's best for your kingdom, and that I'm the only one here who can secure the great legacy your parents built for Province I."

I knew he despised Morgan, so to see them in cahoots over the proposal churned bile in my stomach like a taffy-pulling machine. Morgan had the power, and with me in his kingdom, she would be forced to share resources so that I didn't live in a failing province, which would ulti-mately reflect poorly on her. I was a tool, and nothing more.

Morgan inhaled like she was smelling the sweetest perfume. She lifted her voice and let it carry to the people, making a grand announcement. "People of Avalon, I think my daughter's finally chosen a worthy suitor."

Lane's voice was heard above the din, shouting out an angry, "No, Morgan!" Draper was next to her, standing from his throne, holding his stomach like he might be sick.

My head whipped to her, frantic in my fear that I would be married off to such a mean man. A mixture of uproar and praise rose up, but above it all, I heard a heavy clang of gold hitting the bottom of Demi's box. I nearly cried out in relief when my eyes fell on Madigan, freshly bathed and wearing soldier's clothes, though this uniform didn't match any of the provinces represented here. His pressed jacket was light green with four-leaf clovers on the shoulder, draped over his black military garb. His light brown hair was neatly cut, giving everyone a full glimpse of his permanent scowl. He was tall and muscular like a pro wrestler, and looked ready to pull limbs off the bodies of his enemies.

"Madigan!" I shouted, throwing my princessly demeanor out the window, and running to greet him. That break from protocol stole everyone's attention from Morgan's grand pronouncement that Duke Henri was a worthy candidate. It gave me the floor before Morgan could choose a life of misery for me.

Before I crashed into him in a desperate hug, Madigan fished his token out of the coffer and presented it to me – his gold wedding band from Meara that looked just about as beaten as he did. Though I was now a very rich girl, it was the most wonderful piece of jewelry to me in that moment.

Mad got down on one knee, forgoing the formal kiss to the back of the hand, and going straight into public proposal mode. "Princess Rosalie, will ye have me as your husband?" Madigan was scarred all over his tall and broad, toned body. The slashes and beatings that had gotten him to where he was today only made him look more rugged. The tattoos crawling out of his shirt seemed to hiss at the naysayers, who were too stunned to voice an opinion. The entire crowd went from shouting their exuberance, to completely silent with shock. Like, silent. Hundreds of thousands of people, and not a peep. Madigan was the motorcycle tough guy equivalent to Avalon, when I was surrounded by Ken dolls (and one very old uncle).

Madigan was acting like this marriage was what he wanted, but no grand thespian feats were necessary for me. In that moment, I wanted nothing more than for someone to get me out of this sinkhole I felt utterly stuck in. I decided to ignore protocol and give the people a good show. Instead of a demure nod, I knelt down and threw my arms around Madigan's midsection, holding him so tight, his eyes bugged. My thighs were pressed to his, my face gazing up at him with a crazed expression I hoped looked grateful. "Yes, Madigan! Yes, I'll marry you."

The crowd went bonkers, screaming and hollering their shock. Not only had Duke Henri been rejected after what seemed like a sure thing, but I'd gone and taken up with an Untouchable – the bad boys of Faîte. Add the dramatic embrace on top of it, and it was a day for the books, no doubt making it into all the bar gossip and bedtime tales for years to come.

I was afraid to let go of Madigan, who was still stunned at the very public display of my affection. The people only cheered louder when his rigid body exhaled, and his arm snaked around my waist, holding me to him. "There, there,

Rosie. You've no need to fret. I told ye I would do right by Bastien."

I only clung tighter to his neck. "Don't let go yet. Don't leave me up here by myself. She almost married me off to my uncle, Mad! If you're in plain sight, she won't try anything. Please, Mad. Please stay with me."

Madigan's voice was surprisingly gentle. "Aye, Rosie. I'll stay with ye. Bastien even called the rest of the Brotherhood here, in case Morgan had a problem with me. They're all ready to offer ye their hand, so if Morgan objects, take up with one of the lads Bastien sends ye. Look for the neck tattoo, and you're safe." He took one hand off of me and dipped into his pocket, tugging out a gold chain he threaded his ring through and fastened around my neck. "Thought my ring might be too big to wear around your wee finger." He waited a few beats while the people worked themselves into a frenzy, each touch magnified by the scandal of celebrity. No doubt it would be rumored I grabbed his crotch by the end of it. He awkwardly patted my back, which only encouraged the chaos that raged below us. "Ye can let go now, lass."

My grip around his waist tightened like a boa constrictor. "Just ten more seconds. I'm not ready yet."

A low chuckle echoed from Madigan's chest. "Aye, take as long as ye need. It's alright, Rosie. Morgan won't get ye now."

I nodded, my eyes accidentally locking in on the ones I could feel in a crowd of hundreds of thousands. Bastien's gaze was fierce, and I noticed two similarly scarred men with neck tattoos had their hands on his shoulders, holding him in place. He pressed his hand to his heart and mouthed, *I love you.*

Every move I made was watched, so the most I could give him was a subtle nod of deep gratitude, putting our feud aside for the moment. I owed Bastien and Madigan my sanity, thanks to the high premium they put on my safety. Even after I'd turned Bastien away, he was still there, watching out for me and making sure nothing happened that wasn't fixable by his capable hands.

"That's enough!" Morgan hissed through gritted teeth.

I squeezed Madigan once more before he rose, taking me with him. I heard so many things, but one man's voice shouted Madigan's name over and over, so much that I tore my gaze away from my fiancé to investigate.

A man with bulk to match Bastien's, and tattoos crawling all over his arms and neck, called out in desperation to Madigan. "Mad! Mad!" He had short, honey-colored hair, a square jaw, both arms in the air, and a neck tattoo declaring his Untouchable status. His wild desire to get closer to Madigan tugged at my heart.

Madigan's inhale was sharp, and his eyes softened in that brotherly way when he recognized the man waving his arms like a lunatic. "Link's here?" He jerked his head at Bastien, who flagged down the straggler and brought the man into the group of ruffians.

I knew Madigan wanted to go to the guy, but chicken

that I was, I couldn't risk my safety net disappearing on me. I reached out and clung tight to his hand, earning a collective "aw" that the princess couldn't be parted from her soon-to-be prince.

"The entire Brotherhood's here now, and they'll be needing to meet up after this is over," he informed me. "The lads will want a word with us."

"Okay. Please don't leave me, though. I'll come with you."

Madigan tore his gaze away from his buddy and looked down at me, taking in my fear I didn't bother concealing. "Aye. If you're tha afraid, I won't leave ye. I've not known ye to be one to throw shite over nothing."

I clung to his hand and all but dragged him over to the center of the stage. I didn't address Morgan, but spoke to the people, who'd already given me their wildly shouted approval. "I've chosen my husband. Join me in welcoming Madigan..." It dawned on me that I didn't even know his last name. "Please welcome Madigan the Untouchable to Province I."

The people roared anew, throwing hats and handkerchiefs up into the air. I heard none of it. I felt none of it. The only thing I could feel was Morgan's fiery gaze, burning into my back.

19

MY GUEST OF HONOR

To her credit, Morgan's face never cracked. Her serene expression remained in place even after I defied her wishes that I marry Duke Henri. Rigby announced to the crowd that it was time for my coronation, but no one really heard him. The celebration seemed never-ending. It was only when shrieks of terror and cries of oh-holy-crap-get-me-out-of-here started splintering through the merriment that the partiers quieted.

The crowd parted like the Red Sea, falling back and making room for a figure I couldn't quite make out. Madigan stiffened and brought me to stand behind him, his chest puffing out territorially. I now belonged to the Untouchables, and it showed. The rest of the Brotherhood followed suit, forming a line in front of the guards to add an extra layer of protection between me and whatever foe was stalking our way.

I blinked a few more times, the sun making the figure difficult to pick out at first. When my vision became clear, a much-needed smile leapt onto my face. "Kerdik!"

Madigan nodded. "Go on. It's dangerous, but I can't wait to see the look on your mammy's face when she sees ye talking with Master Kerdik."

I let go of Madigan's hand, whatever I'd salvaged of my princessly demeanor, and my nerves, and ran down the steps of the platform.

"Stop her!" Morgan ordered her guards, horrified. I wasn't sure if she was more scandalized by my display, or if she was scared of me being so near her own personal monster. When the guards moved to wall me off from my goal, I spun to frown up at Morgan. It was then I could see clearly that she was scared for me, and didn't want me near someone who had let such grief and war come to Avalon. It was refreshing, however frustrated I was at not being allowed to say hi to my friend, to see that Morgan had a glimmer of motherhood in her. In her own way, she cared about me (or her legacy, at least).

"It's really fine," I assured her. "That's just Kerdik. He's my friend."

Kerdik was unperturbed, but I knew the gasps directed at his skin cut him in the vulnerable spots he didn't like to leave open for public perusal. His green skin clashed with his sky-blue, perfectly combed hair, making him look handsome and totally unique. He was a sweetheart.

Kerdik waved his hand at the guards, who scattered as

he neared with terror etched in their faces. Only the Brotherhood didn't back down, though I could tell they wanted to. He paused when he reached Bastien, who stepped forward to take the brunt of whatever Kerdik had for them.

I ran around the members of the Brotherhood I'd not met, and grinned like a giddy goofball when I crashed into Kerdik with a rough hug befitting a soccer game win, and not a royal affair. In my heart, I was a Commoner, and not even a corset could change that. "I missed you! What are you doing here?"

Kerdik let out a surprised "oof!" when I crashed into him, his smile stretching wide across his chartreuse face. "Miss your coronation? I wouldn't dream of it."

"You came for me?" I was touched, since I didn't have all that many friends. Madigan and Bastien stood on either side of me, unsure what to do, but unwilling to be parted from me. My birds squawked for me to run from Kerdik, but I shot them a frown to scold them for being rude to my friend.

"Of course, *Fleur*. You look lovely, as usual."

"Thank you." Color heated my cheeks at being doted on by someone so stunning. "I know you don't like coming around here. You really came out of hiding for me?"

His eyes narrowed at me in mild scolding, but Madigan and Bastien both backed away, as if Kerdik might melt me with his laser beam eyes or something. "I wasn't in hiding. I don't need to hide from insects."

I rolled my eyes and released him, chucking him on the

shoulder. "You know what I mean. I know you don't like being around people all that much, and this is like, the most people ever. That you came here just so I'd have a friendly face? Thanks, K. I really needed it today."

That broad smile came back, but the crowd only grew more afraid of him, smooshing into each other and giving us as wide a berth as possible. "I wouldn't have missed this for the world." He picked up my hand and examined his ring on my finger. "You haven't taken this off, have you?"

"Of course not. It's so pretty. Why would I?"

"Good girl." His eyes grew intense again, and several women nearby actually burst into tears. "You never called for me."

I lowered my voice, though I'm not sure what good that did. We were the focus of every eye and ear in the entire nation. Everyone seemed tense, stretched tight like a guitar string and ready to snap into painful oblivion. "I know you don't like Morgan, and I've been staying at her place. It's not been the best, K. I didn't want to make you come to a place *I* didn't even want to be. I haven't been allowed out of my bedroom all that often, so I couldn't exactly invite you over." My face lit up all over again when I remembered what waited in my bedroom. "I made you something, though."

He took my hand and looped it through his arm, turning me to lead me like a gentleman back to the stage. "You did, eh? Tell me all about my surprise." He wore the same chocolate-colored pressed slacks, wrinkle-free white dress shirt, and charcoal vest.

When I turned, I came face to face with Lane and Draper, who'd left their platform to rush to back me up, should I need it. Morgan was still standing, white-faced and afraid on her stage, clinging to Rigby. I saw very clearly which one was my mother. Lane didn't see her own fear when she thought I was in trouble; she only saw me. I dropped Kerdik's arm and wrapped Lane in the hug I'd needed to survive. "I missed you, Mom."

Lane softened in my embrace. "Oh, kid. You have no idea. Are you alright?" Her voice was taut with fear.

"That's a question for another time." I kissed her cheek and squeezed her once more before releasing her. "I think we might have an audience."

Lane snorted, but held tight to my hand, facing Kerdik with the air of a little girl staring down a raging bull. What can I say? Lane's always been heroic. "Master Kerdik. I see you've met my Rosie."

Kerdik nodded. "I have, and I mean her no harm. Nor you, if you go back to your throne and let me help her. You raised her quite well. I wouldn't dream of undoing a masterpiece like your daughter. Run along, now. Always good to see you, Little Lane."

Lane bowed her head, but only moved aside when I gave her the "it's cool" nod. Kerdik tucked my arm in the crook of his elbow once more, not even bothering to address Draper or Madigan, who fell in line behind us like soldiers. He glanced back at Bastien appraisingly as we strolled slowly toward the stage. "I see you haven't given him your *lueur*. And marrying a man from the Brotherhood? Just what sort of tricks are you up to, darling?"

"Tricks are for kids," I quoted a cereal from my childhood, "and I haven't had time to be a kid in a while. I'll tell you everything when we're not being watched by a bajillion people. After you've been blown away by your surprise, that is."

"As you wish it, sweet *Fleur*." He reached his free hand over and gave my fingers an affectionate squeeze. Each little tease of fondness felt like a gift we both needed, isolated as we were. "I brought you a little present, as well."

I gazed up at him, a bashful smirk playing on my lips. "You already got me a present. You gave me the most beautiful ring in the world, and your hat. Give a girl a second to catch up to you. My present for you is not nearly as impressive, but I think you'll like it."

"Is it from you?"

"Of course."

"Then I'll love it, darling."

"Oh, you." I batted my other hand at him.

When we reached the foot of the main stage, Kerdik held my hands in his, and leaned in to kiss both of my cheeks. Dozens of people screamed – actually screamed – in terror. Like two sweet little cheek smooches from Kerdik were a potential knife in the chest. He ignored the crowd and gazed at me lovingly. Lost as I was, I basked in the glow of something incredible being beamed at me. "I haven't been greeted so beautifully in ages. *In ages*, Rosie. Thank you."

"That's how I greet my friends, but I couldn't risk it with anyone else. You're the only one who can break the stuffy royalty rules, so you got the giant hug. Lucky duck."

"Yes, well, speaking of stuffy royalty rules, you've a coronation to attend. I daresay I've bought myself a front row seat to the festivities."

Having Kerdik there gave me a little of my personality back. "I guess if we're here and all, I might as well." I gripped his fingers when he made to drop them. "Stick around until I'm finished?"

He looked at me as if I'd told him he was handsome. A tender expression touched his features and softened him with the simple request. "As you wish it, darling."

20

CORONATION GONE WRONG

I straightened my dress and rolled my shoulders back, though that was all a wasted effort. The people had seen me giddy and unpolished at this point. Still, Morgan seemed to need me to try harder. Her mouth was drawn in a tight line, and I noticed she was sweating and breathing in shallow pants. Her in-control demeanor faltered under Kerdik's icy stare.

I could tell she'd had a speech prepared, but raced through it in light of the unwelcomed guest. There was something in the address about serving the great country of Avalon, giving my heart to the good of the people, and ruling the province for Avalon's best collective interest. There was no secret clause of signing away my soul or anything, so I decided I was cool with it.

Demi placed a red crushed velvet pillow on the floor of the stage, and held his trembling hand out for me to take.

He didn't even have a forced smile of reassurance for me, so I knew he was freaking out.

When terrified horror-movie-style screaming broke out in the crowd, I turned and saw Kerdik at my other side, offering his hand for me to steady myself. I didn't fall or wobble when I knelt on the pillow, and squeezed Demi's clammy and shaking fingers in thanks for not letting me have a clumsy moment onstage.

"I'm watching, Morgan," Kerdik threatened, squeezing my fingers protectively. "Choose carefully."

Morgan nearly dropped the tall, golden tiara with rubies as large as dimes that she held outstretched above my head. She was frozen, unsure what her next move should be. "I'm to crown my daughter, Master Kerdik. Surely I have that right."

Kerdik leaned forward and sniffed the crown. "Put it on your head first."

Morgan blinked at him in shock. "What? This is a crown for a princess, not a queen. This is for Rosalie only. Surely you don't think..."

Kerdik's voice was controlled, his tone merely that of a professor reproving a wayward student. "I don't need to tell you what I think. Put it on your head, in front of your entire country, or three breaths from now will be your last."

A dozen emotions flickered across Morgan's face, worrying me that I'd missed something crucial. I blinked up at Kerdik, but he saw only Morgan's conflict. "K? What's going on?"

"Just something I suspected might happen. Not to worry, darling. I'm here." He patted my hand, but didn't look at me. His gaze pierced Morgan so deeply that she shook where she stood, showing weakness in front of the entire nation. "I'll not ask again, Morgan."

Rigby nearly dropped Morgan's enormous crown when he lifted it from her head and placed it on the pillow. A solitary tear rolled down Morgan's cheek, and her clenched jaw shook with trepidation and rage. I was confused as to why there was so much drama over her wearing my crown for a second. Finally my crown rested on her hair, her chin raised in defiance.

I don't know what I was expecting to happen, but when nothing did, I wondered what layers of deception and politics I'd missed. "Is everything alright now? I don't understand." I was still on my knees, and couldn't bend my torso enough to stand on my own without potentially toppling over in my heavy dress.

A small twitch of a smile lifted the edge of Kerdik's mouth when Morgan clutched her chest and suddenly stumbled backward. Rigby cried out in fear when Morgan's eyes drifted shut, and she collapsed into his arms.

I didn't care about decorum. I scrambled forward and pressed my hand to her cheek, horrified that Morgan fainted on her important day in front of the entire nation. Lane and Draper were by my side in the next second, and out of nowhere, Remy made his way up the steps. He'd been lost in the sea of faces, but suddenly, he was there. "Remy, help! What happened to her? Morgan!"

Kerdik permitted Remy near Morgan, but held Lane back with his arm around her slender waist. Reyn charged up the steps – another face lost to me in the hubbub of the day. Reyn stood in front of Lane to block her from whatever harm was going down.

Kerdik motioned for Draper to scoop me away from Morgan, putting a healthy several feet between myself and my birth mother. "Don't let my *Fleur* touch that crown. It's got a sleeping spell on it. Morgan's fine, Rosie. She bewitched your crown so that you would fall into a deep slumber when it rested on your head. Take it off, and she'll come back to you within the day."

Lane touched her forehead, not fighting Kerdik's hold, or Reyn's protection. "This circus is over." She motioned for the nearest uncertain guards to come up on the stage. "Take this crown and melt it down. The fire should purify the magic from it. Then you two take Morgan into the castle and lay her in her bedchambers." When they hesitated at the prospect of being so near Kerdik, she barked in that you'd-better-clean-your-room voice I knew all too well. "Now, soldiers!"

Several men carefully and respectfully lifted my mother's body, with Rigby following sadly behind. He shot me a look of utter loss – not for the fate Morgan had steered herself into, but for the trust he assumed I wouldn't have in him anymore. Guilty by association, he assumed, but that's not how I roll. I didn't break his gaze, but gave him a slight nod of "I get it" before he disappeared off the back end of the stage to go with Morgan into the castle.

Draper was hesitant to surrender me to Kerdik when my green friend waved me to come to his side, but my brother knew he didn't have a choice. Kerdik kissed my forehead when I returned to him. My arms banded around his waist, confused. "She was trying to knock me out? But why? I don't understand."

Kerdik rocked me gently from side to side, as if I was a wounded animal in need of shelter. I heard fearful weeping from women in the crowd at the sight of me in their monster's arms. They were more concerned about that than their queen fainting onstage.

Kerdik was unperturbed, apparently used to being the leper. I clung tight to him, making sure that people knew he wasn't a monster; Kerdik was my friend. "Now, now. We'll have time to investigate later, darling. We still have your coronation to tend to."

"I may be missing a crown. And I don't think the crowd can handle much more excitement."

Bastien met my gaze, and I could tell he was holding himself back from scooping me up in his arms. Madigan was by his side, unsure what to do. The rest of the Brotherhood were at the foot of the stage, surrounding it like the fearless rogue soldiers they were. There were five

Untouchables – each man built like a brick house, and scarred too deeply to enjoy the gift of their elevated status.

I tried to be brave and not let anyone see that I was shaking inside. Had Morgan really meant to put me into a sleep, like she'd done to my dad?

Kerdik gave me an affectionate squeeze. "Darling, we're causing quite the scandal, embracing as we are. Oh, the rumors. What will the neighbors say? Next there'll be talk of little green children running about the castle."

I cringed at the insinuation. "You're my friend. They're just going to have to get used to you being around."

"You want me around?" A note of insecurity poked through.

Bastien and Madigan shot me silent looks of warning over Kerdik's shoulder.

I frowned. "Of course I do. Why wouldn't I? But let's call this whole thing done. I don't care about being crowned. That was all for Morgan, anyways."

"Humor me. You are their princess, but you're my queen." Kerdik lifted my hand to kiss the finger he'd put his ring on, and then gently lowered me down to the kneeling pillow once more. His voice boomed out at the crowd, and I guessed there was magic used to amplify the sound, since his cadence carried farther than Morgan's had. "People of Avalon, your queen is resting from her ill-used magic. May I present to you, your princess, Rosalie of Avalon."

Lane held my left hand, and Draper clung to my right,

steadying me and showing the three of us as a united front to the people. Of all the things that had gone wrong that day, the two of them standing beside me felt right.

Too many people were screaming; I couldn't escape being nervous. I couldn't see what Kerdik was doing, but when a crown rested on my braided hair, I waited for whatever it was that they were afraid of to happen. Kerdik's voice finally broke me out of my worry. "Rise, Princess Rosalie of Province 1." Then he addressed the crowd again. "Everyone, look on the beauty of your nation. You may now welcome your future queen, the Avalon Rose!"

There was no applause, only swift kneeling, the sea of hundreds of thousands hitting the ground in a giant wave that stretched from front to back.

"Now can this be done?" I asked out of the corner of my mouth to Lane.

"Oh, babe," she replied, scared and upset as she squeezed my hand. "This whole mess has only just begun."

21

THE JEWEL AND THE ANTIDOTE

I didn't speak until I'd been shunted into my bedroom by Kerdik. He slammed the door after barking that we were to be left alone, leaving the others in the parlor to wait it out. "Wait a second, Kerdik. I need Bastien here for a second before all of Avalon goes back to their homes."

Kerdik sent Demi to grab Bastien, who appeared in under two minutes. His eyes met mine, and I knew he wanted to say a million things, but kept them on hold, due to the company. There were always too many things separating us, and still sometimes, not enough.

Demi was clearly scared, his hands trembling as he awaited my instructions. I needed to give Bastien the jewel I'd found in my dad's mouth, but I knew I'd never get it wedged out from between my boobs unless my corset was loosened. I was embarrassed when I jerked my chin toward the partition. "Demi, could you help me with my stupid corset? It's too tight."

Kerdik raised his eyebrow at me, but said nothing when Demi and I disappeared behind the divider. He removed my crown and carefully moved to set it on the table in the center of my bedroom. When he came back, his shaking hands made a few missteps unlacing me, but he managed the task, and I thanked him with a grateful gust that filled my now fully-expandable lungs. "You're amazing, you know that?"

He gave me a curt nod, but was too anxious to say anything. He helped me step out of my dress, the corset and the skirts underneath. I tucked the pouch with the jewel in the palm of my hand to keep Demi safely away from our master plan. He kissed my lips only once as he helped me into a simpler dress that wasn't so regal, heavy and pretentious. I could breathe in the rose-colored gown with green vine embellishments on the cap sleeves. It didn't require a corset or the ruffly under-dress thing. The hem brushed my bare toes after I kicked my shoes off. Even though it showed off my breasts more than I normally cared to, the simpler gown was a welcome relief. The style was sort of like Wendy's dress in *Peter Pan* – comfy yet feminine.

"Thanks, Demi. Would you mind giving us a minute? Just some business to catch up on."

"Of course." Demi excused himself, practically fleeing the room to get away from Kerdik. It gave us the privacy we needed for me to hand over the treasure that had been stolen back, fair and square. "Here, Bastien. I found one of the jewels. You need to get it out of the castle before Morgan wakes up."

Bastien's jaw dropped. "Where did you find it?"

Kerdik watched me dump the enormous amethyst out of the invisibility pouch and into Bastien's palm. He examined my face for signs of panic, like I was going to change my mind and beg for it back. "You give away the treasure as if it's a mere trinket."

I flashed my aquamarine ring at him to show off my bling. "I've already got a ring. What would I need this jewel for? It's not mine."

Kerdik stared at me as if I was a beautiful bug he wanted to get closer to, so he could study my habits. "If I hadn't blessed you myself, I would never guess you were a Daughter of Avalon. Only Elaine has ever seemed to be able to resist the lure of the gems, though she was always the strange one."

"Like mother, like daughter," I joked, but the levity fell flat. Lane wasn't my biological mother, though I wished my very best wish that she was. I turned my attention back to Bastien. "She hid it inside my dad's mouth. I um, I sort of had a conversation with my dad about it. He's not all that thrilled with Morgan. Apparently she poisoned him with Hemlock?" I said the name of the poison like a question because I had no idea what it was or where it came from. "Said the paralysis is irreversible, but he'll do what he can to help me find the other jewels. I've got a decent idea where the next one is."

Kerdik stiffened. "Urien's mind is still sharp?"

"Yeah. Sucks that he can't get up and move around, though."

Bastien shook his head. "Man, what a cruel joke. He finally gets his daughter back, but he can't get up to take you out of this mess."

I rubbed the nape of my neck. "I sort of didn't tell him who I was. He thinks my name is Britney."

"Why wouldn't you tell him?"

I didn't want to defend my actions to Bastien, but the response tumbled out of me anyway. "Because Morgan hates me. One look at me, and she cringes. I told her I didn't have my Compass ability anymore, and she lost all interest. I've been locked in this bedroom for most of the time I've been here because she can't stand the look of me. I know everyone likes to think I'm bulletproof, but I couldn't handle letting my dad down, too. I want him to get to know me and like me. Then I'll tell him who I am."

Bastien shook his head at me, his eyes filled with pity. "Honey. You should tell him."

"I will when I'm ready."

Kerdik was impatient. "Did he say how the Hemlock poisoned him? Did he breathe in burning leaves of it? Was it ground up? Distilled?"

I shrugged. "I think he ate some of it in a salad. He said

the flowers were distilled in his wine, too. He has a few theories, but nothing for sure."

Apparently, that was all Kerdik needed to hear. "Take me to him now."

I noted his lack of a "please" but said nothing about it. "Okay. No problem. Bastien, could you do what you need to do with the jewel? It should probably be gone before Morgan wakes up."

My mind started kicking into high gear, now that I had a few minutes to separate myself from all the drama. "Wait, on second thought, this is the perfect time to scour the grounds for the jewels. I'm guessing only Morgan knows where they are, so the soldiers wouldn't care if I go snooping, since they wouldn't put together what I'm snooping for."

Bastien's eyes widened at the possibility of knocking several items off our list. "Well, let's do it, then." He slapped his hands together and leaned his shoulders forward, readying for the race. "You lead the way, Daisy."

My jaw clenched. "My name is Rosie. I'm not your Daisy," I reminded him, running for the door.

Kerdik caught my arm. "But, Urien. I need to speak with him."

I leaned up and pressed my lips to Kerdik's cheek. "I know, sweetie. I'll go as quick as I can with this. Then I'll take you to see my dad." I grinned up at him. "Oh, he'll love you."

Kerdik let out a soundless chuckle. "He already knows

me, darling. I thought his brain dead, so I gave up trying to resurrect him. I also admit I thought the Hemlock leaves extinct. How Morgan got her hands on them, I'll never know. You're certain it was Morgan?"

"Dad is, yeah. I mean, all I know is what he's telling me."

"If it's Hemlock poisoning, I'm not sure what to do about that. It's not a total lost cause, I don't think, but it'll take some time. Summon me when you're finished playing with the Jewels of Good Fortune, darling. I'll go to the more obscure parts of Faîte to see what antidotes I might be able to find for Hemlock poisoning." He shook his head at himself. "I can't believe he's been trapped in there this whole time. Had I known, I wouldn't have..." His gaze turned steely. "I'll fix it. I'll get him back."

Bastien was getting anxious, but he didn't dare rush Kerdik and risk his wrath. He ran his thumbs along the tips of his fingers impatiently, raring to go.

I cleared my throat to steer the conversation back on track. "Do your thing, K. I'll meet you in a couple hours, hopefully with more gemstones."

"Okay, darling." We leaned in to kiss each other on the cheek at the same time, the cuteness in the familiarity catching us both off-guard. "Do be careful while I'm out," he warned.

"Where's the fun in being careful?" I turned to leave with Bastien, but paused to reach out and squeeze Kerdik's fingers. "Hey, I'm sorry today turned funky. I got you a present, and I want to actually hang with you without all the drama. Can we be boring together tomorrow?"

"I can't imagine a lovelier offer." Kerdik's grin warmed me from the inside out. It was like watching a baby deer take his first steps. Awkward and unpracticed, Kerdik's smile was just introducing itself into the world, and it was a beautiful thing to watch.

22

THE LINK IN THE PLAN

After Kerdik tucked my modest, and dare I say tasteful, diamond-encrusted white gold crown in a safe place in my bedroom, Bastien tore me away and all but ran down the hall toward the steps, our feet echoing off the stone. "I don't want you hanging around him," Bastien ordered as we ran. "He's deadly, Rosie."

"Hello, so are you." I had to hold up the front of my dress so I didn't trip. "You don't get to tell me what to do. You're not my guide, my *Guardien*, or my boyfriend. Let's just do the job without fighting." That was probably too much to ask, but I had to try. "I have an idea where one of the stones is."

"Good. Let's stop at the parlor, and you can send one of the guys to it, while we look for the next one."

It was the most solid plan we had, so I went with it. "Mad!" I called when we burst into the parlor. I was a little taken aback by the additional person I didn't know, but I wasn't sure we had time for introductions.

Madigan stood, his relaxed demeanor fading as he went into soldier mode. Rousseau stood at my entrance, too, as well as Draper, who all but ran to scoop me in his arms. Draper's hug was purely loving, and forced emotion to rise up in me. My sweet older brother had been worried about my well-being. He didn't care about the jewels; he cared about me. Lane smashed me in on my other side, the two of them holding me together to make sure I stayed theirs. It was a heady feeling, to be loved so wholly.

"I only have a minute," Lane apologized. "I have to go out and deal with my sister. Avril's causing a scene about your crown and your ring."

"Jeez. I can't believe she's making such a fuss over something so small."

"It's not small, Ro." Lane couldn't stop squeezing me, and it warmed me to know that she'd needed me as much as I'd needed her. "Since when are you friends with Master Kerdik? Roland mentioned that he saved you all from the *tonnerre* storm, but you actually hugged him. Did he really give you this ring?" Lane held up my finger to examine the sparkling beauty.

"Yeah. He's a nice guy. Just needed a friend."

Lane shook her head slowly, her expression torn between alarm and trepidation. "A gem from Master Kerdik is a big deal, babe. Be careful with this. Sheesh, I thought Avril was being dramatic. And honestly, I wouldn't have believed it if I hadn't seen Master Kerdik doting on you with my own two eyes. Be careful. I mean, like, more than careful."

"I'll wear seven seatbelts. But I've got more important things to deal with first." I rushed through my plan to Lane, Draper, Madigan, Rousseau, and the dude who'd shouted Mad's name through the crowd earlier. He had tattoos of zippers all over his body to cover some of his scars, and he wore a mischievous grin that split his roguish features. "New guy's cool?" I asked Bastien, who nodded. I offered up a quick two-fingered wave to the new tattooed Untouchable. "Hey, man."

He sniggered at my informal address, and offered up a charming grin. "Hallo, wee princess. Link of Éireland, at your service."

Link had the same brogue as Madigan, but an entirely different demeanor. Madigan was rigid and standoffish. Link seemed like the guy who pulled your hair in class and grinned at you like you started the whole thing. I couldn't fathom how the two of them became friends, other than being in the Brotherhood together.

I slapped my hands together to focus the group. "So we have to find the last two Jewels of Good Fortune before Morgan wakes up, and get them out of here."

Lane held up her finger. "Roland gave my jewel to me, and I know Avril has hers in Province 8. She's been bragging about it nonstop. Roland's got Heloise's, and I'm sharing the extra jewel with Province 3 to get them back on their feet. The rumor we're spreading on that is the jewel was found with Bayard's body, so he'll get the credit for bringing Gliten's Jewel of Good Fortune back to his people. The Dukes and Avril are outside. I can stall them from leaving, if you like. Avril might be hard, though. She's pretty upset about Master Kerdik giving you a crown."

Bastien spoke up. "Stall them without telling them what we're doing. We'll send out the jewels as we find each one."

Lane nodded. "Of course."

Though I was the smallest person in the room, the heavy hitters had no problem deferring to me. "Alright guys, the jewels might be in a box or a pouch or something with a vanishing charm on it. So don't rule out the area just because you don't see it. Remember, Morgan's kept some of these jewels hidden for two decades." I reached across the huddle and put my hand on Rousseau's hairy arm. My gut was being all confusing, telling me the gem that I'd thought was for sure in the moat was now somehow not. "Rousseau, why don't you go after the first one. I'm not sure if it's been moved, but at one point, I could tell you exactly where it was." I explained where I knew it had been hidden, and the landmarks nearby so he could locate the area easily. "It's in the moat, though, so be quick and quiet about it. Though, if it's been moved, it won't be there, obviously. Still, that area should be ruled out. Maybe you should take Bastien, just in case you run into trouble."

"No," Bastien ruled, resolute. "I'm not leaving your side. Morgan made an attempt on your life today. Keeping you safe is higher priority than finding the jewels."

I stared up at him, flabbergasted that he could be so magnanimous after I'd given him the very clear cold shoulder up in my bedroom. "Okay, then just be careful, Rousseau. But don't leave that area until you either find it, or you're sure it's not there. As soon as you have it, bring it straight to Lane. Only Lane."

Lane nodded. "I'll be out in the courtyard, stalling the royals." She squeezed me once more. "Be safe, babe."

"I've got her," Bastien assured Lane, who seemed to accept this as some sort of apology for the idiocy he'd inflicted on my life.

She didn't need to tell Draper to follow her, he simply went, kissing both my cheeks before going with his new mother.

Link jerked his head toward the entrance to the castle. "The other Untouchables are outside, so if we need more bodies, we've got them waiting."

I rubbed my forehead, trying to concentrate on which way my gut was leading me. It was hard to get a hold on my jumping nerves, now that real progress was being made.

"Which way, Rosie?" Bastien prodded, as if that would make things move faster.

"I'm not sure. Hold on a second. It's not an exact science."

Link eyed me curiously. "Is she really trying to find the missing Jewels of Good Fortune with her mind? This is the lass ye found?"

"Aye," Madigan replied. "I've seen her Compass in action. I've learned not to question it."

"I lost my mammy's kerchief in grade school. Think she could find tha? Earned myself a wallop over tha thing."

I glowered at Link, who grinned at me like an incorrigible boy. "How about let's concentrate on the jewels first, Lucky Charms. The Compass thing is harder than it looks."

Bastien tugged me away from the group so I could get a little distance. "Just breathe, honey." He rubbed my shoulders, centering me as his arms fell around my waist.

The dance was too easy, and the moves too familiar. My eyes closed when I inhaled his comforting scent I'd tried to scrub from my memory. Pine and cinnamon, mixed with something deeply masculine flooded my senses, jerking me right back to a place I swore we wouldn't go again. He brought my head to his shoulder, my forehead nuzzling his chest like it belonged there – like *we* belonged *here* – in this moment, with each other. His head leaned down as his large hand spidered the back of my head to massage my scalp. My skin erupted in goosebumps when he whispered, "Feel it all now. Listen to your gut. I've got you."

Again, with his simple promise that comforted me every time.

I reached my hand up with the intention of gripping

his bicep, but hesitated to make contact of my own accord. I didn't know what it would mean if I held onto him – if he would vanish, or if I would get sucked into his vortex. I'd barely made it out alive the last time. I decided against clinging to him, but permitted him to hold me while I breathed through the confusion. I banded my arms around my stomach to keep my hands from taking me down a road I might never return from unscathed. "I haven't been able to find them so far," I admitted. "The one in the moat was there, but I can't feel it outside of the castle anymore. My dad told me where the second one was. I haven't been able to feel my gut much in this place." I squinched my eyes shut. "What if I can't find them?"

"You didn't have me here before, but you do now. We've got this. Deep breaths, baby." His chest made a show of expanding and contracting, so I'd mimic the motion.

I breathed in Bastien's scent, pulling my focus to my gut and asking it to take me to the jewels Morgan had stolen from her sisters. When nothing happened, I started to worry. "I can't feel it."

Bastien's hand trailed from the back of my head down to my tailbone, relaxing me from my fear that I would let everyone down so close to the finish line. "Stop worrying," he urged quietly. "Don't you know that I've always got you?"

His signature reassurance resonated in my chest, spreading out the inner peace like molasses through my body. His warmth chased away the scattered sensation I hadn't been able to master to properly listen to my gut. "There you go," he said as he felt me relax in his arms. "That's how we do it."

Slowly, and without warning, something clicked in my brain. "Upstairs." I straightened in Bastien's arms, now sure of where the next one would be. My eyes met his, and that familiar spark of connection, intrigue and oh-holy-crap-it's-on crackled between us. "Let's go."

23

THE TALLEST TOWER

Bastien threaded his fingers through mine when I turned to open the doors to the parlor, but I retracted my hand. "Rosie, please." He was hurt, but that wasn't why I'd dropped his hand.

"I'm engaged to Madigan. In public, I'm not going to hold another man's hand. I won't make Mad look like he can't keep a woman faithful the day he gets engaged. I care about your friend, and so should you."

Bastien swallowed as he shoved his hands into his pockets. "Okay. That makes sense."

Madigan said nothing, but trotted along behind me with Link while I led the way up the stone steps. We moved quickly, slowing only when we came across soldiers in the hallways. We passed the eighth floor my room was on, my gut tugging me higher still. I could hear Madigan breathing loudly behind me, but none of the guys wanted to be the first to admit that nonstop stairs were no one's favorite thing. "You guys want to take a break? We can if you need to lie down." I worded the offer just sweet enough so they didn't hear the dig, but only resonated with the challenge. It was a great way to keep a steady pace. My high school basketball coach used to play that trick on us all the time.

I lost count after ten flights of stairs, my sturdy thighs burning and my heart racing with the adrenaline of a kingdom on the brink of change. The few guards we ran by in the hallways didn't even try to stop us, though I could tell they didn't have a clue why we were climbing up to the more obscure parts of the castle.

When we reached the end of the road, my gut was telling me to go higher still. "This isn't high enough. Are there more stairs somewhere?"

Bastien nodded. "There's got to be a way to get to the tallest tower. Of course she'd hide it there. No one could get in and get it out without coming across dozens of guards. Lucky we have you, really."

Link grabbed a stitch in his side and keeled over at the waist. "Aye. They're all afraid to stop ye. Magic ticket, ye are. Is tha part of the bewitching Master Kerdik put on ye?"

Madigan answered for me. "They're all afraid Morgan might not wake up. That would make Rosie Queen of Avalon, so no one's going to cross her. Quick, now. Where next?"

I cast around, but the hallway seemed like a dead end.

I frowned at the stones at the end of the short walkway that formed a door shape with rounded top edges. "Huh. We still have to go up, but I don't see how if that door's walled off."

Madigan moved toward the stones, feeling their commitment to the rest of the wall. "I can break this down. Someone go get me a sledgehammer."

I shook my head. "No. The trick is to get as many jewels out as possible without letting Morgan know we took them right away. I still have to live here until the last one's gone. I think a giant hole in the wall might clue her in."

Madigan waved off my concern. "So she finds out you're after the jewels. I'll move in here to watch ye. She won't be able to hurt ye if I'm here." He jerked his finger to Bastien. "And if Bastien moves in, too, she'll have even less reign over ye. Might want to consider having the whole Brotherhood move in until this is settled."

I shook my head to stop that right quick. "No. She was pissed I wore jeans outside, so she had Demi beaten. She'll find a way to punish me. Plus, she might move them again, and make them harder to find. Stealth, Mad." I trusted a hunch and jerked my chin toward the stairs we'd just hiked up. "This way. I'm feeling something."

Link groaned dramatically. "How sure are we tha this Compass thing is real? I mean, the lass might just be jerking our chains to see us running up and down for nothing. I've got a fine arse. She just wants to stare at it, I'm certain."

I guffawed, but then caught Link's grin that told me he was joking. "Yes, that's exactly it. Nothing gives me more joy than to watch a bunch of men go for a run, and then whine about it."

"Aye, I knew ye were a saucy one. Bastien's lady and Mad's fiancée? Where do I fit in?"

I started back down the hallway. "You can be my puppy. Dog's don't talk, though, so best fall into the role without a fuss." I couldn't help my smile when Link didn't fight back, but let out a bark. "And I'm not Bastien's lady. Stop spreading that around. It'll look bad for Mad, besides the fact that it's not true."

I didn't look over my shoulder to see if the others followed, or if I'd hurt Bastien; I just went back down the first flight of stairs, stopping at the floor below to glance around. "I can't put my finger on it, but something on this floor can get us up to the jewel." I took a step forward, trying not to judge the likelihood of victory by the first uncertain step. I kept my pace measured, going where my gut led without questioning the "why" I couldn't see quite yet. I rubbed my temples when Link's whispering started to distract me.

"Is she always so intense, Mad?"

"No. She's usually one ridiculous joke away from being shoved in the ocean."

Link mimicked my tensed body language. "If I massaged my temples, do ye think I could be the Compass? Or is tha something tha only helps her, like a spell of some sort?" He kept rubbing his temples with his eyes closed. "Lead me to a giant pot of beef stew."

I whirled on the guys and yanked Link down by his collar, keeping my voice quiet. "Look, Lucky Charms. I can't concentrate when you're yapping like that. Be a good little doggy and let me do my thing. You can lead the search party on the next mission. Then I'll be sure to crack jokes and talk nonstop when you're trying to concentrate and get the job done."

It was as if I hadn't spoken. "You're a wee little thing. Mad's going to have to pick ye up for your wedding kiss."

"I'm five-foot-six-inches. That's not 'wee'. You're all just overgrown football players." I rolled my eyes and released him, guessing he was incapable of being serious or focusing. "Don't talk about wedding stuff. Job first, yapping second."

I moved forward, ignoring the others, who kept whispering about how it was going to work with me being Bastien's lady, and marrying Mad. Link seemed to have been filled in on the broad strokes, but didn't have the details colored in on his playmat yet. "Your mammy's going to be Morgan le Fae, Mad. If that don't get ye labeled a badass, nothing will."

I geared up to spit out an acerbic retort, but Bastien closed the gap between us, cupping the back of my head and bringing it to his shoulder again. "Close your eyes, honey. Focus on the jewel." He shot Link a disparaging look when the grinning leprechaun asked which one of my two suitors was allowed to knock me up. Bastien's free hand rubbed slowly up and down my back to center me. "Just breathe. Ignore everything else. What do you feel?"

What a loaded question. I couldn't get near Bastien without feeling a thousand too many things that each warred with each other, and tried to take top billing in my brain. "I can't feel my gut, but I know the way up is here."

Bastien turned me around so my back was pressed to his chest. His hand spidered out and palmed my stomach possessively while he leaned over my shoulder to speak in my ear. "Tell me what you feel now."

I closed my eyes and placed my hand over his, willing the jewels to call me to them. Bastien's free hand pressed against my forehead, anchoring the back of my head to his chest. We breathed in unison, and I hated that he knew exactly how to center me. I resented the fact that he knew what I needed, and that it was actually working.

Bastien moved with my feet as I stepped forward, his hand slipping from my forehead to lace his fingers between mine. There were no soldiers around, or anyone else on this floor, it seemed. We moved quietly, still, making sure to keep our foot-steps light through the stone hallway. There were too many cobwebs stretching from the narrow stained-glass windows, letting me know that this floor didn't see a lot of action.

My gut led us to a small doorway that only came up to my waist. "Huh. I think this is how we get up there." I shifted the sliding door to the right, so I could peer inside.

"It's the dumbwaiter. Of course. You did it, babe." Bastien squeezed my hand, and I was too relieved I hadn't led us to a dead end to pull out of his grip. He took a knife from his belt and handed it to Madigan. "Take this, so it doesn't drop."

My nose scrunched. "You're not going. That door's barely big enough for me."

"You're not going," he scoffed. "It's a drop you'd never survive."

"And you would? I said I'm going."

Bastien shrugged. "Fine. But where you go, I go."

I blinked at him, unsure where this stubborn loyalty came from. When I wanted to be close to him, he pushed me away, but now that I was keeping him at a distance for his own good, I couldn't shake his shadow. "You can't be serious. You'll never fit."

"Then I'll break the wall!" he retorted, raising his voice. His eyes weren't angry, but worried. "I'm serious, Daisy. I'm not leaving you to shimmy up a dark shaft alone. I'm supposed to keep you safe."

I let out a long breath and placed my hand on his chest to calm his anxiety. "I appreciate the offer. Really. It's very sweet. But it's not your job to keep me safe. You're not my *Guardien*."

It was like I'd slapped him just by stating the obvious. I had a hard time getting a read on the guy.

Link flinched, like the verbal chastising stung him, too.

"Jays, you're a cold one. Do ye think it's every day an Untouchable offers to chain himself to another person?"

I tried not to get distracted by the way the two Untouchables said "jeez", and focused on the matter at hand. "He didn't want the job before. Nothing's changed. I'm looking out for him, Link. This is a big step he doesn't even know that he wants to take. We can barely be in the same room for five minutes without fighting. Do you want your brother chained to someone he fights with all the livelong day? I make him miserable, and I don't think you want that for Bastien." I grew frustrated and stomped my foot on the ground. "This is all beside the point. I'm the only one who can fit up the shaft, so deal with it. Mad, could you keep watch by the stairs, and send away any soldiers that might come up here?"

"Aye. Can ye go up without falling to your death? It's a steep drop, Rosie."

I gulped, never having been a fan of heights. "I probably can."

Bastien groaned. "Oh, that makes me feel much better."

I ducked my head into the chamber, leaned forward and tugged on the cord to see if I could manually move the elevator box, so I could just hop on in. "Crap. It's not moving."

"Dumbwaiters are controlled by the kitchen in our castles in Éireland. Keeps people from doing what we're about to do, sneaking onto other floors." Link crouched down to peer over my shoulder. "Jays, tha's a long fall."

I gulped and willed myself not to look down a second time. I could feel the stale air wafting up at me, reminding me that one slip would equal a swift death. My hand trembled on the thick cord, but before I could freak out, Bastien's arm wrapped around my waist, reeling me back in to rest against his firm body on the stone floor where we sat. "No," he ruled. "I know you don't like heights. It's not worth it. We'll find another jewel. This can be the gem Morgan keeps for Province I."

I steadied myself against him, indulging in the manly scent that soothed me when I was on the verge of freaking out. I meant to reach up and pat his cheek to calm his jumping heartbeats, but his lips caught my hand and planted a kiss in the center of my palm. My skin warmed around his affection. My fingers curled down his cheek, moving as slow as dripping candlewax, tracing lines like water droplets through his quarter-inch scruff.

When my pulse finally calmed, I patted his arm and stood, hefting him up and motioning to the stairs where Link stood next to Madigan, gaping at us. "I've never seen Bastien with a lady before. I thought ye might die alone."

"Ah, Link. I *know* you'll die alone, because you've already gone through all the women in Éireland." Bastien moved toward his buddies to give Link a playful jab, and I took my opportunity. I moved quietly toward the small doorway and grabbed hold of the thick cord. I summoned all the courage I had in my bones as I leaned forward and let my feet leave the floor. I ignored Bastien's cry, Mad's anger and Link's astonishment, and did my best to put one fist over the other.

This wasn't Bastien's adventure; it was mine.

I gripped the rope with my feet, kicking my shoes into the hallway I'd just abandoned so I could use my toes like a gorilla. I'm pretty sure one of them hit Bastien in the face, which only made him more furious. My dress was problematic, but I tried not to think about it while I climbed as high as I could. Focusing on the things that could pull you down to your death is never a good thing, I've found. Words to live by.

I tried not to worry about the long drop. I pushed out of my head the echoes my movements and the guys made; they told me I was too high up for someone who didn't so much love heights. I kept my lips pressed shut, muffling the noises of fear I couldn't cut off completely. The shaft was dark, with a solitary light shining above me, beckoning me upward. My heart rose up in my throat, threatening to strangle me with anxiety I was unprepared for. This had seemed like such a solid idea at the time.

I stuffed another whimper back down and tried to pep-talk myself through the climb with logic. I couldn't abandon the jewel for another day. The coast was finally clear for a small window of time; I couldn't pass on that.

Bastien's curt whispers echoed up at me, switching from ranting to offering up succinct words of encouragement. I could tell he was still pissed, but knew there was nothing for it now. My forearms shook as I hiked my body up the cord, my hands burning and my toes and fingers slickening with sweat. I recognized the patched dumb-waiter entrance in the wall, and knew I only had one more floor to go. I didn't care anymore that I was letting out quiet whimpers of trepidation; I was doing it. I was actu-ally facing my fear all by myself. *Suck it, heights. I own you.*

When the light touched my arms, I nearly cried. My gut was screaming at me that this was the way, and that the jewel was near. When the light flooded my face, warming my icy panic, I realized I had no way to clear the two feet of space between the rope and the dumbwaiter entrance. The cord had no give, and I wasn't about to risk a jump.

I let out an audible sob when I saw a little lip jutting out from the top, no doubt to serve as the final stop when the dumbwaiter ventured up to the tallest tower. Morgan probably had the floor below's entrance sealed after she stowed the gem in the tower, keeping it hidden and unreachable.

My arm shook when I reached out to grab onto the lip, letting out terrified noises each time I missed. I heard Bastien whisper-shouting up to me. "It's alright, Daisy. You've got this. Take a breath. I'm right here. I've got you."

I don't know why I allowed his words to calm me. It's not like he actually *had* me in any way that would be useful in keeping me from plummeting to my death. I don't know how my fledgling feelings for him swelled beyond my control. Someone powerful and strong believed in my strength, and thought it was enough. Maybe, just maybe, it was.

I let out a growl of distress and victory when I detached one hand from the cord and gripped the steel lip. Before I could calculate my fear, the rest of my body followed, and I swung my lower half into the small room that served as the tallest tower of my mother's castle.

24

BABY PICTURES

I was expecting an empty hallway with maybe a jewelry box sitting in the floor for me to scoop up. I nearly lost my shiz when there was nothing there, until I remembered that the containers had been imbibed with an invisibility charm. My arms were trembling, and I tried not to lose myself to the adrenaline crash I knew would come after facing my fear of heights without a safety net.

I wasted no time dropping to my knees and feeling around like a blind person. The room was lit only by the sun's rays filtering through the narrow window, which didn't help me all that much when searching for invisible things. My hands felt along the floor, seeking out every inch of the cold stone surface until my fingers lighted on a container the size of a shoebox. I giggled nervously to keep myself from bursting into tears of relief.

I felt like Indiana Jones, awaiting wonder and doom as I opened the wooden box. I gasped as a yellow citrine the size of a golf ball glittered out at me. It was circle cut, with the point sharp enough to slice a line down the stone wall. It was too breathtaking to be called gorgeous, too brilliant to be called merely a "precious" stone. It was in a class all its own, daring other jewels to live up to its decadence.

My face pulled into a curious frown when I noticed there were other items in the box. There was a cursive script written across the inside of the lid, with a letter carefully scribed in the same penmanship tucked in the box. My heart pounded at being confronted with a letter I wanted to read, but couldn't. Cursive was the worst. It was a totally useless skill, and a waste of the second grade. Cursive was impossible for me to decipher. I could usually make out enough letters of regular typeface to puzzle together a sentence or two, but if it was written in cursive? Forget about it. I battled with my nerves not to freak out. I didn't know if the letter was important, but I knew I'd never get another chance to read it.

With trembling hands, I folded the note and shoved it down the bust of my dress, judging it to be the best hands-free hiding place. I still had to shimmy back down the cord. I went to close the box, knowing I couldn't take it with me without risk of falling.

My gaze shifted when I noticed another piece of paper resting in the bottom of the box, sticking out beneath the black felt lining. Lips parted, I examined a detailed sketch of the woman who most certainly was Morgan, holding a baby next to Urien. Their shoulders were rolled back, looking regal and proud in the hand-drawn portrait. The black ink had browned in spots over time, but there we were – a family. My dad had shorter hair, like Bastien's, and his eyes were equal parts kind and authoritative. He had broad shoulders and a raised chin that told me everything was going to be okay. He stood beside his wife, who looked... It was strange to see a slight smile on Morgan's face as she held me, gazing out at the person who drew the portrait with poise and unmistakable perfection in her every feature. She looked like... me. Me, with a husband and a baby.

I was captivated, unsure how much time passed while I gaped at the family moment I couldn't remember. They no doubt assumed they'd have many more like this.

I had no baby pictures. Not a one. Judah's mom had whole albums of his first year of life – true story. I'd always wondered what I looked like as a baby, and there I was, round and smiley, trusting and innocent.

I didn't realize I'd started crying, but I knew I couldn't sully the portrait with something as useless as tears. My fingers quaked as I folded the piece of perfection and pressed it to my heart inside my dress. The citrine was nudged uncomfortably between my breasts, which was turning out to be my go-to hiding place. The pointy end of the gem stabbed my sensitive flesh, detracting from its amazingness a little.

It only dawned on me then that Bastien and Madigan were whisper-shouting at me, afraid that something bad had happened, now that I'd gone quiet. "I'm coming, I'm coming. Hold on a second," I whispered down at them.

I wasn't expecting my foot to snag on something and make me trip, almost falling through the gaping cavity of the dumbwaiter's path. My heart raced as I braced myself, my hands gripping the ledge. I pushed my body up to enough to kneel, my fingers fluttering over my forehead as I tried to collect myself. I frowned as I looked over my shoulder at the empty room. Carefully this time, I felt around the spot where I'd tripped, gasping when I flipped back the cover of a book.

Of course it would be a book. Only I would stumble across a clue to... something that I couldn't read, and definitely couldn't take with me when I shimmied back down the cable.

The cover was invisible, but the pages were handwritten in red ink. It wasn't a diary, but what looked like a medical journal of some sort, complete with diagrams and measurements that didn't compute in my brain. I bit down on my lower lip, knowing that I was supposed to be the Indiana Jones in the great adventure of my life.

But Indiana Jones was brilliant, and I was the girl who'd failed Algebra twice.

I pep-talked my way through a few lines, knowing I was getting all sorts of things wrong, due to the bad combination of scrolly handwriting plus dyslexia. After much painful study, I made out, "to bend the wills of the umsmbilting... unmlitlting." *No.* I shook my head at myself. "Unwilling. To bend the wills of the unwilling."

Then what came next looked like a recipe of some sort, followed by a drawing of a soldier standing at attention, and then that same soldier disfigured in the same way I'd seen Silvain scarred (the soldier who had attacked us back in Common, before I'd set foot in Avalon).

A shudder ran through me, and I wished for a lighter to make quick work of turning this book to ash. I decided the best place for it was up here, where no one could make further use of it. Hopefully Morgan had shoved it up here because she realized what a horrible thing it was to control someone's will, as she'd done with a few of her choice soldiers. I quickly shut the book and shoved it away from me, as if the evilness of such a thing might leap into me through osmosis.

I shook my hands and blew out a long breath, turning to the cable and willing my grip to hold steady. I was proud of my legs that didn't punk out on me as they wrapped around the sturdy cord. My thick thigh muscles built on the soccer field assured me that they wouldn't fail me now. I slowly crept my way down, my dress hiking up with every inch I lowered myself, until my thighs were completely exposed to the dank air inside the shaft. The cord burned a line up the tender inner flesh of my thighs, but it was worth the pain of the moment not to fall to my death. When my chest pressed to the cord, the citrine sliced my tender breast, drawing blood from my cleavage that made me gasp.

When Bastien and Madigan reached out and grabbed onto my waist, I almost let go as instant relief flooded me. Luckily, I remembered to grip the cord until they dragged my lower half onto the stone floor.

I let out a triumphant cry of elation, collapsing on the floor with Bastien when it dawned on me that I hadn't died. "I did it! I made it all the way there, and didn't fall once."

"Well, once is all it'd take, ye daft girl. I thought ye were supposed to be a princess or something. I've never seen a Daughter of Avalon do something tha insane." Link scratched his head, staring up the shaft to judge the distance to the light. "I could probably make it up there." He spoke the words like he was challenging himself.

My mouth popped open, letting loose a giddy, crazy giggle that sounded more unhinged than joyful. "I did it, Bastien," I declared, breathing in jumpy gasps, my sweaty back cooling on the cold stone of the floor.

Bastien's eyes were hard, his mouth in a tight line as he laid next to me, our eyes on the ceiling as I fought to calm my breathing. "You did. You shouldn't have, but you did."

Pain came back to me as my adrenaline subsided. "Oh, man. That stings. Rope burn on my hands, feet and thighs." I sat up, hiking my dress so I could rest the back of my hand to the inside of my left thigh in hopes of cooling the heated spot.

Bastien's breath quickened as he sat up next to me. His thumb moved to the angry red mark on my right thigh to soothe what ailed me. "You scared me, honey. You can't do stuff like that." He squeezed my sensitive inner thigh, turning my brain to mush.

My legs shouldn't have parted. My face should've turned away when his lips moved closer to mine. My mind should've had control over my body, but it didn't. Bastien's touch was lightning and feathers on my skin. His hand swept up and down over the heat, riling me up and making my breath come out in scared hiccups. I should've tugged my dress down to a decent level and crawled away from the temptation, but I gave in and fell for the seduction that set me on fire. His cool touch lit every nerve in my body, tearing the castle, Faîte, and the entire world with all of its problems away from me, so that I only saw and felt him – us.

When Bastien's trembling lips captured mine, I could taste every crazy thing about him. I could feel his fear that he'd almost lost me, and his hope that I would find my way back to his side. I tasted how lost he'd been without me to spar with and keep him on his toes. His massage on my thigh turned rough when I let his tongue into my mouth, brushing over mine in a light tease I knew I would never tire of.

"We weren't meant to be apart," he said, his voice husky and earnest. "You shouldn't have kept us apart for so long."

I kissed him again, vaguely catching an inkling that Mad and Link were moving silently past our hideously inappropriate display to give us a little privacy. "You shouldn't have pushed me away," I countered.

"I'm done being stupid, and you're done being angry." He lowered me back to the cold stone floor, my hands falling limp on either side of my head in total surrender to the force of nature that was us. Bastien pressed his body down on mine, parting my aching and shaking thighs, and looping my left leg over his hip to claim as much of me as I made available to him. His caramel eyes burned into mine with passion and authority as he growled out a firm command. "Mine." He sucked on my lower lip when I wanted him to crash his lips to mine and take away my higher brain functions. I didn't want to think it through. I didn't want to think at all. I wanted to feel. Bastien tore his lips away and whispered low in my ear, "Say it. Tell me that you're mine." He teased my neck with fire-laced kisses, knowing I wanted him to claim my mouth, but teasing me just to prove a point.

I was his, or at least my body was convinced he was calling the shots.

My pride couldn't give Bastien the promise he needed,

so instead I snatched at his collar, fisting the material to try and reclaim some of the control in the exchange. "Just kiss me, you jerk!"

Bastien gave up on coaxing an admission out of me and crashed his lips to mine, taking us higher than the tallest tower in the largest castle in all of Avalon.

Our kiss was interrupted in the weirdest way possible. My fake fiancé cleared his throat, while Link gave Bastien a wedgie, and then smacked his butt. "Come now, kids. I thought we were trying to get as many jewels out as possible. There'll be plenty of time for putting a baby in her later, Bastien."

That was the bucket of ice water I needed. "Ho! Yeah, no. Not cool. Sorry, guys. I don't know what I was thinking."

The corner of Mad's mouth curled upward slightly. "It's okay not to think every now and then. Just maybe put tha on hold until ye have the time to make a proper mess of each other." He snapped his fingers at Bastien to wake him from his stupor. He hoisted us both up, but cried out, pointing to my breasts. "What happened to your bosom, Rosie? You're bleeding like ye got attacked by Abhartach himself."

My cheeks were already crimson, but when I looked down, I forgot my embarrassment. "Oh, crap. Yeah, that's all me." I dug my hand down into my cleavage, smirking at Bastien's gratuitous moan of lust. When I fished out the citrine, the whole bottom half was coated in my blood. I grimaced, pulling up the hem of my dress to wipe off the smears of red on the inside of my skirt. "Sorry about that. Careful, Mad. It's pretty sharp." I plopped the heavy stone into his palm, chucking him in the shoulder as I smirked at his astonishment. "Why don't you take that to Lane out in the courtyard? That's one down, and one to go. Link and Bastien, let's see if we can't find another."

25

THE LAST MISSING JEWEL

Turns out, boobs are total gushers when they get sliced, and the perfect gem can be just as sharp as a knife. Things you needed to know, right? The front of my dress looked like I'd been stabbed in the chest. The blood stained the fabric and made it the best Halloween costume ever.

Bastien didn't let go of my hand, but gripped it tight, as if he was afraid I'd forget our reconnection and run from it. He wasn't far off with that assumption, but I was too wiped from the adrenaline rush to push him away with any real conviction.

"Where are we going, Daisy?"

Link chuckled. "It's never going to get old, seeing ye with your lady. Never thought it would happen for ye, Bastien. Thought you'd be alone in your cabin in the woods forever."

"You and me both, Link."

"It's nice you've stopped fantasizing about me, and finally took up with a lady. I told ye before, I just don't fancy ye like that, Bastien."

"Sure, you do," Bastien kidded with a genuine smile. It was good to see him happy, however fleeting that might be.

My gut led me down too many flights of stairs to count, steering us off on a floor that was several stories below the one my room was on. We raced through the castle, whipping through hallway after hallway toward the other end, the soldiers getting thicker and more menacing.

I dropped Bastien's hand, and he seemed to understand that we couldn't be all over each other, since I was going to marry his buddy. The soldiers stood at attention, lining the hallway that ended at the room my gut was screaming at me to enter. I gulped and tried to appear as if I belonged here, like I had any kind of authority with which to command them. Bastien and Link fell in line behind me, playing the part of letting me be the princess I'd been marketed as.

When I reached the room, four guards were standing in front of the door. "Excuse me, guys. I need to get inside."

They looked at each other with grim faces before the one in charge spoke. "I'm sorry, Princess, but her majesty most high is still ill, and requires her rest."

I sucked in a tremulous breath with manufactured emotion that wasn't all that far from reality. "Please move aside, so I can be with my mother while she's sick."

Bastien cleared his throat when the guards didn't move. "Your majesty, maybe you should call Master Kerdik to see if he thinks it's okay for you to visit your sick mom."

I tried not to grin at the name-drop that forced the guards to step aside with no further argument. The one in charge even opened the door for me. "Apologies, your highness. There's no need for you to summon Master Kerdik. We'll stand guard to make sure no one interrupts your visit with her majesty most high."

I'd never been inside my mom's room, which was strange to me. Morgan's was twice the size of my gargantuan room in the castle. It was bedecked in so much gold, it looked like a rap star had decorated it. There were gold frames on the windows, and useless gold trinkets filling tables and littering every surface. Her body was even laid out on a mattress that rested on a massive gold bedframe. Like, a solid gold bedframe.

Lane and I had shared a one-bedroom apartment for many years when I was younger. There wasn't anything better than snuggling up with her and watching cheesy eighties movies while eating popcorn in bed together. On nights where it stormed, I woke up to her holding me. I'd always thought she assumed I was scared of the rain, but after experiencing Avalon's storms, I knew she was the one who had been afraid. We had no space for gold trinkets, which also meant there was no space between us – sisters at our core. Looking at the opulence that surrounded me, I knew I wouldn't have it any other way, not for all the shiny treasures in Avalon.

Rigby and Remy were the only ones in the massive room, hovering over Morgan, who lay motionless on the bed. She looked just like my father, whom she'd sucked the life from.

Remy stood to greet me, grateful that I'd come to relieve him of his post. *"Thank goodness. I need to get out of here. There's nothing I can do, and I'm inches away from strangling her, just to be done with the evil she's brought into Avalon. They ordered me to tend to her."*

"Sorry, Remy. Just a little bit longer." I cleared my throat, making an executive decision. "Actually, I was hoping for a minute alone with my mom. Would that be possible?"

Rigby looked up at me, as if just seeing me for the first time. His long nose was red from crying, and he looked lost without Morgan to order him around. I felt for the guy, but I knew he wouldn't like for me to hug him in front of people who might tattle. "Your majesty, what happened to your dress? Is that blood? Are you hurt?" His mourning turned to panic.

I glanced down and worked up a convincing scoff at the sizeable crimson stain. "Nah. I spilled tomato soup on my dress. Total klutz."

"That's a relief. Are you well? Master Kerdik's crown didn't hurt you?"

My nose scrunched. "Of course not. Kerdik would never hurt me. He's my friend."

Rigby mustered a bitter laugh. "Master Kerdik has no friends, only subjects. If I live a thousand years, I'll never believe the sight I saw today. That you tamed such a vindictive and evil creature? Your magic runs deep, your grace." His words sounded like a compliment, but they felt like caution.

"Thanks, Rigby. Why don't you go get Morgan some soup? That way she'll have something soothing in her belly when she wakes up."

"As you wish it, your grace." He lifted Morgan's hand and kissed it. "I shall return to your side," he promised her. Though I'd hoped I could flip Rigby, the slave-master psychology ran deep in this one. While sometimes he despised her, it was clear there was part of him that loved her, even though she was flawed. Half of me was grateful that my mother was loved, dysfunctional as that affection might be.

I waited until Rigby left before whispering commands to the others. "Link, man the door and make sure no one comes in. Remy, make sure if Morgan wakes up, that she doesn't see me in here. Knock her back out if you have to."

"What are you doing, Princess?"

"I'll tell you later." I ran in the direction my gut pulled me, darting toward her closet in the far corner. Well, I thought it would be a closet, but when I opened it, it was a whole other room she used to store her clothes. It was bigger than our entire apartment, but contained only dresses. Yards and yards of thick, luxurious fabric hung from satin-covered hangers. There were shoes of every color, enough to make even Jill jealous. I tried to picture Jill in here, trying on the "costumes" and donning a high class British accent or something while she pretended to be the princess she always imagined herself.

I blinked twice to rid myself of the distractions, and kept going in the direction my gut pulled me. I opened one of the doors that had gold embellishments framing it, and found a wide closet filled with hair clips and fancy combs. They had all sorts of jewels secured in the ivory settings. I frowned as Bastien swore behind me when he took in the wealth. "I thought it would be in here, but it still feels like we're a few feet off."

"Maybe there's a secret compartment or something? You're sure it's not one of these jewels in the clips?"

"I'm sure. Help me find it." I felt around the different platters and pedestals the hair clips were laid out on, looking like decadent treats at a party. I wished for a noticeable candlestick lever or something that could bend down, like in a Batman movie, revealing a whole other part of the house. There was nothing quite so obvious, so I felt around and tried my hand at finding secret passageways. "Try not to move her jewels around all that much. She'll know if something's totally off."

"You're kidding. She has so many things. How could she possibly keep track of them all?"

"They're her treasure. Best not risk it."

My hands searched until my brain yelled at me that my gut would know how to get where I needed to be. "Hold up, let me try something." I closed my eyes and blew out my air, trying to push out the glittering wealth, Bastien, and the urgency of the moment so I could listen to the small voice that led me here in the first place. I sunk to my knees and felt around on the floor for something that might guide me to where I needed to be.

Bastien sucked in an astonished breath as my hands reached out and felt the wall underneath a doorless cabinet off to the side stretching from the floor to the ceiling. My fingers pressed on the ledge of it, but I kept my eyes closed, so I didn't get distracted. I didn't trust my eyes to lead the way, so I kept feeling around like I was blind, and hoped for the best.

I let out a noise of surprise when my fingertips lighted on a small latch on the bottom edge a few inches from the floor, and hooked on the indentation I never would have seen. I gave the latch a slight tug, pulling out a drawer that couldn't have been more than three inches deep.

Bastien and I both swore in unison when the treasure screamed out at us. Large gems almost as big as the citrine glittered up at us by the dozens. Bastien dropped to his knees beside me, his eyes as wide as saucers. "Which one is it?"

I closed my eyes and placed my hands flat above the jewels like a five-dollar psychic, biting my lower lip to see what my gut had to say about it. "None of them," I ruled, my shoulders deflating. "It's here, but it's not these."

I took a chance and pulled the drawer completely out, guessing that the blessed gem wasn't in the hidden drawer at all, but perhaps resting in the shallow cavity below the doorless cabinet. I laid down flat, hoping my blood didn't stain through my dress on to the fancy red and gold rug beneath my bosom. My arm stretched out, finally hitting the back as I strained with all my reach. I desperately felt around the far wall of the hollow, gasping when my fingers brushed against a velvet pouch I couldn't see. My stomach churned with a scream that this was the one I'd been searching for. Though I couldn't see it to verify, I knew I had the treasure in my hand.

Bastien tugged on the rug to slide me out, and helped me up like a gentleman. "Is that it? Let's see."

I didn't bother opening the pouch. "This is it. We've got to get out of here, though. We can't have Morgan seeing us in her closet. I've got to get this to Lane before she realizes it's gone missing."

Bastien looked like he wanted to argue, but nodded his assent instead. "Okay. Let's grab some of these other jewels and give them to the duchesses and dukes who are just getting their land back. They could use something to restart their rule."

I shook my head as I bent down to push the drawer

back in, cringing at the squeaky noise it made. "First off, we're not thieves. Stealing from my mother is still stealing. Secondly, Morgan will know if anything goes missing. It's her way. We need time, and that's not the way to buy it."

Bastien's eyebrows furrowed. "Are you sure? It's all sitting right there. I can't imagine she'd notice if a handful of those rocks goes missing."

"*I'll* notice if I'm a thief. Right now, I'm only stealing jewels from her to give them back to the people she originally took them from. Righting a wrong. I won't turn into my mother, Bastien. Don't make me into a woman who steals."

Bastien shifted a few of the combs around so they didn't look so disheveled on the pedestal. He shot me a furtive look out of the corner of his eye and said quietly, "Did I ever tell you that I love you?"

It was like being punched in the stomach; all the air flooded out of me in a gust of surprise. There were too many responses to choose from to select the right one. "No."

"Well, I do."

I blew out a gust of air. "Then don't ask me to be less than I am. Stealing is less."

"I get it now. I'm sorry. I love the way you are. I shouldn't have tried to change that."

I didn't address his liberal use of the "L" word, but instead tried to tuck the jewel into my bosom again.

Bastien held his palm out to me expectantly. "You're

bleeding, honey. I can hold onto it for you, and send it off with Link."

"You trust him with something like this? Remember, we trusted Duke Henri at the beginning of this whole mess."

Bastien blew out a raspberry. "I don't trust the Council like I trust the Brotherhood. Link's not even from here, so he's not caught up in the drama of Avalon like the rest of us. He doesn't care about the jewels. He cares about loyalty."

"Rosie! Rosie, your mother is stirring. Hurry back out!"

Bastien's word had to be good enough to clear Link, since we were out of time. "Morgan's waking up right now. Remy needs us back." As we ran back out through the closet, our footsteps tried to stay silent, so our transgressions wouldn't be found out. Bastien held onto my hand as we closed doors as quietly as we could. Then we bolted out of the place no one was allowed.

When we reached the main bedroom, Remy was standing on the opposite side of the bed, prying at Morgan's face to keep it angled away from us. *"She's still in and out of it. Drop down and crawl towards the door, so she doesn't know you were in here. I'll distract her so you can escape. The other Untouchable is waiting for you just outside the door with the soldiers. Go!*

I gave Remy a thumbs-up, and dropped to the carpet, pulling Bastien down with me. We army-crawled to the door as silently as we could manage, rising up on our knees when Remy rubbed salve onto Morgan's face, her eyes automatically closing. He cleared his throat to cover over the sound of the door opening. All three of our hearts pounded erratically as Bastien and I stood up and slipped out of my mother's bedroom.

26

OLD FRIENDS

As much as I wanted to doubt Link's ability to play errand boy without mucking it up, the hard look in his eyes settled a small amount of uncertainty inside of me. "Straight to Lane, okay? Do you remember who Lane is?" We had only just managed to find a hallway where no guards were waiting for Morgan's next command.

Link's mouth drew to the side in thought. "Lane... Lane... Tight arse, double handful-sized tits like yours, and pink, pouty lips?"

I rolled my eyes at him. "Just make sure it's her before you deliver this to the wrong person."

Link made me jump when he kissed my cheek. "I gotcha, wee Rose. I was only joshing."

I shoved at him and scrubbed the affection off my cheek. "Dude, I don't know you."

"If you're Bastien's lady, then we've got nothing but time to remedy that."

"Oh, joy."

Bastien's arm coiled around my waist, not in a territorial way, but to focus me on the task at hand. "Go on, Link. Rally the Brotherhood and find a place out of earshot. Rosie's got a few things to take care of still, and then we'll meet you there."

I touched my forehead, a wave of exhaustion sweeping over me. "I can't believe we pulled it off before Morgan woke up."

Bastien let loose a gust of relief. "Let's go back to Master Kerdik. He said for you to call him when we were finished."

"Sounds good. Water first, though. I'm super thirsty. Let's stop by the kitchen."

"Whatever you say, hun." He held my hand as we walked, and I was too turned around by the day's events to separate myself from him. "I want you out of here as quick as possible."

I nodded, but when we crossed near the main entrance, Aunt Avril's shrill voice stopped me short. "Rosalie! Sweetheart, come here."

My jaw was on edge as I turned to face her, dropping Bastien's hand to remind myself that I was engaged to someone else. "Aunt Avril. I can't imagine why you would want to talk to me after what you did."

Her eyes that had been welcoming now turned into

slits, dropping the veil of friendliness I'd fallen for all too easily. Her voice was quiet to keep any passing guards from overhearing us. "I took back what was rightfully mine."

"And you took three jewels that weren't yours. Roland tried to pin that theft on me, you know. Not that you care."

Avril touched her brow. "Sweetheart, I didn't mean to pin anything on you. I didn't accuse you of stealing the gem. I left with the extra ones because it seemed unwise to leave them so unprotected. I mean, if I could steal them, what's to stop anyone else?"

"Oh, and you were on your way to deliver them to Province 9, right? Is that where Roland found you?"

She stiffened. "My nephew misunderstood my intentions. But yes, I would have given them to Elaine and Roland. I am not Morgan; I wouldn't steal from my sister."

"You stole from your niece," I countered. It was her that had put it all into motion. Because Roland thought I'd stolen the gem, Bastien had made me strip down to be sure I wasn't a dirty thief. Yes, Bastien had to answer for his mistrust that I hadn't deserved, but it was her catalyst that tore Bastien and me apart, and I wasn't about to brush it all under the rug.

Avril's gaze drifted to my hand to stare at my ring finger. "Master Kerdik certainly let you make a spectacle of yourself today."

"Take it up with him, then. Kerdik's my friend, and he lets me be myself."

"Yes, well." She sniffed, as if I wasn't up to snuff with

what the world expected of me. I didn't argue. "Once word gets around that he's the one who gave you your ring, my sister will see to it that it's torn from your finger. You should keep it far away from Morgan."

I made a fist to keep my ring in place, but Bastien answered for me. "I'll make sure Morgan leaves Rosie alone. I'll be here to keep her safe."

"No, you won't," I said, though maybe I should've saved that conversation for another time.

Her amused gaze flickered between us. "A fiancé and a *Guardien* to warm your bed? My, my. Like mother, like daughter."

"Shut up, Avril," Bastien said with a glower.

Rage steamed in the balls of my feet. "Get out. This is my house, and you can't talk to me like I'm some stupid kid in here."

She tsked me, as if I'd spoken out of turn. "I saw the way your *soumettre* gazed at you during your coronation. Demi can sure make a girl feel special." She rolled her shoulders back. "I've been away for far too long. Demi was my *soumettre* for a time, you know. He kept me quite satisfied, though I'm sure you know how adept he is at that."

My blood ran cold. "Demi belongs with me now, and you'll keep your claws off him."

She tweaked my nose, and it was all I could do not to punch her. "It seems you have that ring and two other men to keep you company. Plus, you now have an entire crown from Master Kerdik himself. Demi will come to my castle until he looks at me with the same affection he doles out on you."

"What?" I was horrified, and grabbed onto the front of Avril's dress, jerking her forward so I could sneer in her face. "I don't think you want to threaten me, Auntie." My nose was an inch from hers, and I could tell by her wide eyes that she hadn't counted on me getting physical. "Demi is my boyfriend, and I don't appreciate him being threatened."

"Unhand me and fight like a queen," she snarled.

Bastien moved to separate us, but before he could, my fist lost its temper and whacked her twice in the temple, dropping her to her knees. "Didn't anyone tell you? I'm not a queen."

Bastien smacked his forehead, as if *I* was being the problem. "Was that necessary? All the royals do is idle threats and chess moves. She's not going to take Demi. She can't without your permission or Morgan's."

Avril blinked her world into view, glowering up at me with tears in her eyes. "That was a deadly move, Rosalie."

Instead of responding with a stupid threat, I leaned down and punched her in the same spot again, drawing blood when my ring sliced her skin. "Threaten me or Demi again, Avril! I friggin' dare you!"

Bastien sighed at my temper that wasn't all that far off from his. "Picking a fight with Master Kerdik's favorite person in Avalon? I didn't bring you back from the Forgotten Forest so you'd be this stupid. You can see yourself out," he cast over his shoulder at her as he spun me toward the stone steps that led to my room. "Upstairs, you." He sniggered as he followed after me up the steps. "That was awesome. I know I can get away with punching a royal because I'm Untouchable, but I've never been much for slugging women. To watch you in action? You're mine, Rosie. We're the exact same wild animal." A lazy grin spread over his features when we reached my hallway, making him more handsome than his usual scruffy perfection.

"Stop looking at me like that. What happened up there with the kissing and all of that? It was an accident. I'm still pissed at you, and I don't trust you like I'd need to if we wanted to start something up. Plus, I just started something up with Demi, and I'm not giving that up just because you turned your head my way. Deal with it."

I don't know why a small smile played on Bastien's lips, but it teased me all the same. "I know all of that, but I'm also not going away. Deal with it."

I pressed my hand to my chest and muttered Kerdik's name three times, summoning him the way he'd instructed me. Though I knew he'd come, for some reason I wasn't expecting him to already have appeared when I pushed my bedroom door open. "Hey, Kerdik. Morgan just woke up, so if we want to go visit my dad, maybe it should be now. Otherwise she might get suspicious if she finds out you were visiting him."

Kerdik ran to me, his hands ghosting over my front in

fear. "What happened to you?" His nostrils flared when he directed a silent accusation at Bastien.

"Oh, just scratched myself with your jewels. A girl's best hiding spot. I'm fine. We should get going."

"Very well. I'm not happy about this, though." He narrowed his almond-shaped eyes at Bastien. "I give her to you perfect, and you bring her back damaged."

I harrumphed, tugging on the sleeve of Kerdik's white dress shirt. "He wasn't even there when it happened. And I thought you said you weren't going to get involved with the jewels anymore. This falls under that category. Bastien's not my *Guardien*, so he's not responsible every time I break a nail."

Kerdik was still miffed at Bastien, but the two of them shut up about it as we ran through the castle to my father's room. When he spotted the two guards posted, he waved his hand, and they fell limp to the floor. "Just unconscious, so we could have some privacy," he assured me when my mouth fell open in horror.

Kerdik held my hand like a gentleman to help me over the slumped bodies. I felt like a mixture between a princess and a ruffian. It was hard to keep track of when I was supposed to be a proper lady, and when I was allowed to let loose and punch my aunt. When Kerdik was gentle with me, as if I was breakable, it really threw me. "Now remember, King Urien doesn't know who I really am. I'm Britney Spears to him, and that's how it's going to be."

Kerdik charged inside with me, locking Bastien out

and instructing him to keep watch, like a dog. It was a testament to Bastien's self-control that he did not argue, but folded his hands behind his back and puffed out his chest like the soldier he'd been trained to be.

I yawned, covering my mouth before I greeted my dad. "Hey, King Urien. I don't have much time, but I brought a friend who might be able to help you wake up."

"Britney? Miss Spears? Every time you leave, I convince myself you were a hallucination. But you came back."

I scooped up his hand. "Of course I came back. I won't leave you here to rot."

"Who is this friend?"

"Kerdik came to see you. He'd like to talk to you."

Kerdik cleared his throat. "Urien, can you hear me?"

Urien's voice was disapproving. *"Tell him that I can hear him, and that it's been at least twenty years since he last visited his dear old friend. In my book, that makes him no friend at all."*

"Oh, jeez. This is going to suck." I relayed the message exactly as it was given to me. I kept one of my dad's hands in mine, and reached out to squeeze Kerdik's fingers to calm him down, in case he had an Anger Management flare-up.

"I didn't know you were still in there. I was assured by the best healers that your mind was gone from you."

"Well, clearly that's not the case. Please tell me you got rid of that peasant's hat."

I loved that my dad wasn't afraid of Kerdik. Something in my chest swelled at the lion-like attitude I'd always hoped my own personal Superman would possess. "He's hoping you got rid of your hat."

Kerdik smirked at me, squeezing my fingers. "I only just recently found someone who would appreciate its beauty, though I can't say the hat's out of your life for good."

"Huh. You found someone you trust other than me and Lugh? My, how times have changed."

"He's shocked you found someone that you trust after all this time."

Kerdik drew closer, his arm wrapping around my shoulders to hold me, while his other palm rested atop the hand I'd clasped to my dad's. "I didn't come here to talk about trust, but to see what I could do to get you out of this bed. I daresay you've been lazy long enough."

My dad and I scoffed in unison, which made me chuckle. *"Yes, I've been having myself a good rest for the last twenty-one years."*

"Ro—Britney said Morgan poisoned you with Hemlock. Are you certain?"

"I'm certain it was her, and I'm certain it was Hemlock. I saved a piece I suspected from my salad one evening, and had it sent out for inspection after I'd begun to grow weak. I started to get stronger after that, but she found a way to poison me with it still. It has a sweet smell when it's burned, but by the time I realized what fragrance my room was being filled with, it was too late." He sighed, resigned. *"In all fairness, you did warn me Morgan would be the death of me."*

I relayed the message, feeling a little like a telephone operator from the early nineteenth century. "I warned her that if you ever did die, our truce would be off. No doubt that's why she's kept you on the brink all these years."

"What truce?" I asked, butting in.

Kerdik rubbed my back. "I promised I wouldn't take the vitality magic away from the Jewels of Good Fortune."

"Can you really do that?"

"Of course. It's me who put the blessing there in the first place."

"Kill Morgan, old friend. Avenge me."

I reluctantly relayed that charming message, and Kerdik snorted. "I promised you that I wouldn't harm any of the Daughters of Avalon." He tightened his arm around my shoulder affectionately. "They vex me on occasion, and my temper isn't always controlled."

My dad scoffed at the understatement. *"That promise was for your own good, and the good of Avalon. Your temper has no control, old friend."*

Kerdik sounded frustrated with himself when he continued. "I placed a blessing on them, making it so that the only killer that the Daughters of Avalon would face would be time, an occurrence of nature, or a death at their own hands. Not even I could kill Morgan, though I've wanted to many times. It was my way of sealing Avalon from the brunt of my anger after the way they fought over my gifts. Then I turned my back so I didn't have to watch while they slaughtered each other."

"Who's dead of the Daughters?"

I asked for my dad, and Kerdik replied with six names of my aunts whom I'd never met. "I told you they were no good, Urien. At least Elaine proved her worth. Your daughter's safe for now."

My dad's voice came back frantic. *"You know where she is? You've seen my daughter? Is she well? Does she know of me? Does she know that she was loved dearly?"*

I patted my dad's hand. "She knows." Something precious started growing inside my chest, begging me to believe that Superman was real, and that my father was a good man.

I really wanted to believe in Superman.

Kerdik seemed satisfied. "Now that I know it's Hemlock, I at least have a jumping off point. I was wary to try anything medicinal, not knowing if you were still in your body, or if you'd passed on into the mist. I searched that whole first year for a cure. I left Avalon soon after that, and haven't been back since."

"You can't abandon your creation just because I'm not awake enough to enjoy it with you."

When I relayed the message, Kerdik gave a contrite nod. I wondered if anyone else got to see him like this. "I'm sorry, old friend."

"You're the old one," my dad jabbed. When I told Kerdik what he'd said, Kerdik's arm dropped lower to squeeze my waist, as if the joke had been from me.

"Then I think it's time I put my considerable knowledge to good use. I have a date with a beautiful woman first, and then I'll be off to see what I can find that might work as a cure."

My dad made a few disparaging remarks about Kerdik fancying anyone, and the disaster that would lead to. I didn't translate those, since I knew Kerdik had been joking. "I'll be back tomorrow, King Urien," I said, squeezing my dad's lifeless fingers.

"I'm afraid it'll be longer for me, friend," Kerdik admitted.

"I impatiently await the moment you both return to me, and the moment I can return to you."

27

THE BEST BATH OF MY LIFE

I took Kerdik back to my room, and Bastien excused himself to go check on Mad, Link and Rousseau. He wanted to make sure the jewels had seen their way safely into Lane's hands. I caught his arm on the way out, cringing at the electricity that was still there, despite my best efforts to put him out of my mind. "Make sure Lane gets out of here now," I told him. "Before Morgan gets back on her feet, if you can."

"Of course, Daisy." He leaned down to kiss me good-bye, as if that was a thing we did all the time.

I jerked away, my cheeks flushing. "No, Bastien." There were a million reasons why he couldn't kiss me goodbye, and none of them needed restating. He knew them all, and still he gambled on me.

Bastien's caramel eyes hardened. "Lock the door while I'm gone, and don't open it for anybody."

I nodded and shut him out, latching the lock so he'd feel better, now that I'd listened to him on at least one point. I pressed my forehead to the door and exhaled, my lashes sweeping shut as I tried to collect myself. When my eyes opened again, I tried to act as if the whole implosion didn't matter one bit.

I turned to Kerdik with my best "I'm totally normal" smile in place, fake though we both knew it was. He motioned for me to come to him, understanding enough to know that I needed a hug to wash the day off me. I crumpled into his arms, seeking warmth and comfort against his hard chest. Kerdik radiated kindness and sweet affection, offering himself up to be the soothing balm I needed. My heart was dangerously close to freezing over, so I clung to the solace he gave me without hesitation. "Thank you," I whispered, hoping I didn't burst into tears, or do something totally embarrassing.

"My *Fleur,*" he scolded me, "how did it all get so broken?"

I didn't want to admit that I'd taken my clothes off in front of Bastien for such a horrible reason, so I chickened out with, "Wasn't it always?"

"You got engaged today, and got yourself a brand new crown. Yet here you are, breaking in my arms."

I gripped his bicep too hard out of desperation. "Don't let me break," I begged.

He tucked a stray curl that had fallen loose from my braid wreath behind my ear and kissed the top of my head.

"You are your father's daughter, darling. Too stubborn to break, but you still feel it all. It's hard to look away."

"I don't want to feel it all. I wish I felt nothing."

"Ah, but then you'd be your mother's daughter, and what a tragedy that would be."

I leaned back and shimmied the piece of parchment that had the portrait sketched on it out of my bloody bosom, earning a frown from Kerdik.

"Where is your *soumettre*? He's to tend to things like this."

I shrugged. "He's probably hiding from you. I didn't want him involved in the jewel business, so I sent him away for a little bit. I don't want Morgan going after him. I like Demi." I glanced down, unperturbed. "It's just a cut. I've had worse." I opened the paper and showed it to him. "Is this me?"

Kerdik's almond eyes softened, a small smile playing on his lips. "Indeed. Where did you find this? I gave it to your father so many years ago."

My mouth fell open. "You drew this?"

"Of course I did. Do you expect a mere mortal to have gotten the details so perfect?"

I sniggered at his cocky swagger. "I've never seen myself as a baby before. My best friend, Judah, has a million pictures of him as a baby, but mine started when I was two, and Lane finally got a camera."

He glanced down at me, his eyes sharpening. "Take this dress off. I'll see to having your healer sent up to look at you. I've seen a great number of graphic cruelties in my many years, but I admit, a small cut on you does me in. I would heal you myself, but I'd have to touch the wound." He glanced down at my breasts appraisingly. "I'm guessing we're not at the point in our friendship where I could get away with massaging your breasts?"

I shot him my best withering stare and placed the portrait on the table. "You guessed right, pal."

Kerdik smiled, and cupped my chin in one of his hands, angling my face up so he could examine each crevice. "I don't understand this hold you have on me."

I grinned up wryly. "It's called being a friend. I'm afraid there's no cure for growing a heart, K. Best get used to it. I feel the same way. I don't like when people shy away from you, like you're scary or something."

I don't know what was so funny about this, but Kerdik tilted his head back and let out a light laugh. "I prefer the fear, darling. I prefer the terror. It keeps people in their place. Now take off this dress and get cleaned up. I'm afraid I can't stomach the sight of blood staining your skin any longer."

"You're such a puppy. I'm alright." I leaned up on my toes and pecked his cheek, drawing out a coy smile from him that was absolutely precious. I went behind the partition and yanked off my dress, the hand-scrawled cursive note fluttering to the floor. I gulped, wishing I could understand what it said without letting Kerdik know I was a dummy who couldn't read. "I found a letter that Morgan wrote. It was stuffed in with one of the stolen jewels. Haven't had time to read it yet."

"Must be important to be hidden with the jewel."

I set the letter atop my ruined dress, and glanced around, realizing with chagrin that Demi always filled the tub for me, and that I had no idea where to get fresh water. "Uh, Kerdik? Can you call one of the people who work here? I don't know where to get water to fill the tub up."

"Silly girl. I'm all the water you need. I can help with that." He waited until I had a towel wrapped around me, and then came behind the partition with a mischievous gleam in his eyes. "I must say, that towel is far better than your bloody dress. It'll be the height of fashion if anyone sees you like this. Stunning."

My cheeks turned pink. "Oh, shush." The blood was half-dried but still sticky between my breasts, making me super uncomfortable. I shifted the towel around me and watched Kerdik kneel next to the tub, jumping in surprise when fresh water poured out of his palms. "Whoa, that's way cool, K."

"That's me. 'Way cool.'" He grinned as petals and whole flowers of all colors and varieties sprouted out of his wrists, severing themselves at the base so they could topple gracefully into the tub.

My hand went to my heart, moved at the beautiful above and beyond kindness. "You didn't have to do that." A yawn caught me out of nowhere.

"You're tired."

"Yeah. Used a lot of magic today. I'm alright." He extended his hand to me, as if he wanted to guide me into the tub. "Oh, you don't have to do that. I'm not a real princess."

"You're *their* princess, but you're *my* queen. I'll help you."

I shot him a miniature eye-roll. "I've been bathing myself since I was a kid."

"You're sending me away?" His face hardened, his mood swinging like a pendulum.

I shrugged, unsure what the rules were. "I guess you can stay, but you have to turn around. We are not naked friends, dude. And I can wash myself."

"Very well." He made a show of turning around and crossing his arms over his chest while I slipped into the tub. The water was the perfect warmth, and the petals lapped at my skin to soothe the suckiness of my day. He handed me the soap and sat on the floor next to the tub, letting the sounds of the water stroking my body fill the silence. I made good use of the hard gold-flecked rose soap, sighing at the luxury of being able to get good and clean. Kerdik smirked at my modest shifts under the surface of the water, and when our eyes met, I could tell he was experiencing the same kind of I-guess-this-is-something-we-do-now revelation. "Your *soumettre* is no doubt the envy of all the men in the castle."

"Ha, ha. Demi doesn't bathe me."

"A fact I'm sure he isn't pleased with."

"You're one smooth talker. You bathe any helpless young lovelies lately?" I tilted my head to the side to study him. "I never even thought to ask if you were seeing anyone."

"No. Intimacy is sort of difficult for me." He stood and folded the partition that separated me from the room, exposing the tub to the window's light. "There, that's better."

I waited a few beats for him to explain his intimacy comment, but he didn't, so I let that one go. "I heard it mentioned around the watercooler that you've been gone for a couple decades. Did you do anything cool while you were away?"

He shrugged, his forearms propped across his bent knees. "There are obscure parts of this world I escape to every now and again when life grows tiresome. The Daughters of Avalon were quite irritating after a while. When your father fell ill, there was nothing to stick around for." His eyes lost their focus, the corners of his mouth tugging down into a frown. "I can't believe he's been alive all this time. I thought his brain was asleep. I never would've... I tried everything. I never even thought of Hemlock. Urien's one of my few friends. He must think I abandoned him to Morgan. I guess maybe I did."

I reached my hand out of the tub and leaned over to clutch his fingers. "Hey, you didn't know. And now that you do, you're doing all you can to help him, right?"

"Of course. This afternoon I started cultivating a plant

that's been extinct for years. If harvested properly, it could be used as an antidote for the Hemlock."

"I didn't realize you cultivated things. I thought it was more like you rubbed your temples, thought of a flower, and blammo, it appeared."

Kerdik scooted closer to the tub with a small smile. "Sort of like this?" With his free hand, he made a fist. Two seconds later, a bouquet of yellow roses with short six-inch, thornless stems sprouted from his fist.

I dropped the soap in the tub when he handed the flowers to me, blinking at him with a surprised bashfulness. "For me?"

"Of course."

I gaped at the beauties, examining them from all angles. "No man's ever brought me flowers before. You seriously just did that?"

Kerdik chuckled at my astonishment. "You fall to pieces over the simplest things."

I inhaled the luscious fragrance, pressing the delicate softness to my nose so I could indulge in the full sensation of the gift. The petals were silky, caressing my cheeks with their loveliness. "Thank you, Kerdik. They're amazing." I tugged him closer, making sure my body stayed concealed in the tub when I reached out to peck his cheek. "You make beautiful things," I said quietly. My lips heated his skin by the smallest degree, drawing out a coy dimple from him that was positively adorable.

"Only for you," he admitted. "Anyone else would ruin them by searching for imperfections, or asking for more."

I settled back into the water, admiring my new treasure. "Well, I was going to ask you for a giraffe, but I guess that's shot now."

"What's a giraffe?"

I tried to explain the proper proportions of the animal everyone in my world knew like the back of their hand, but I think I only confused him more when I described a detailed vision of the long neck.

"You're making that up," he scoffed, turning his head when the first sounds of a storm reached us through the window. The smell of fresh rain wafted in, making us inhale in unison. "There's no such things as giraffes; I'm certain of it."

I guffawed at his blatant disbelief as the raindrops picked up, coming down faster than a drizzle. "That settles it. When you come to Common with me, we're going bowling first thing, then we're going to the zoo. Oh, and we're going to Doc Harvey's Ice Cream and Soda Shoppe." I frowned. "Wait, do you even eat? I don't want to wave the best butterscotch malts in the universe in front of your face if immortals can't eat or something."

Kerdik chortled through his nose. "I *can* eat, but I don't need to. Take me anywhere and everywhere, darling. Where else will we go?"

"Oh, there's this great park near campus. You'd love it. Not as pretty as Avalon, but it's got a running track and a whole series of quirky, handmade bird houses. Super awesome. Lane will tell you the one that looks like the post office is the coolest, but she's wrong. It's the cottage birdhouse that's the cutest. It's a birdhouse that's got a fake birdhouse in the design. That's like, way existential. Blows my mind every time."

Kerdik sniggered at my enthusiasm. "I can't imagine anything better," he allowed, pacifying me with his allegiance.

I loved our back-and-forth. When I was so turned around by everyone having hidden agendas, it was nice to have a real friend to share the afternoon with.

THE WORST BATH OF MY LIFE

I'm sure I was boring Kerdik with my mundane plans for what we would do if we could hang together in my world, but to me, simple fun was the one thing missing from my life.

"I'm afraid I don't understand. You're strapped to a machine that launches you into the air and whips you around, turns you in circles – and this is supposed to be fun?"

I grinned at him, not holding back on my explanation of the most harrowing roller coasters that Lane, Judah and I had ever ridden on. "If you come to Common someday, you can't be using your gifts to shazam yourself out of the harness. You have to go for the ride."

"It sounds frightening."

"The best things in life often are."

Kerdik's gaze turned soft and affectionate as he studied

my face. "You really spend time planning days for us to enjoy together in your world?"

I shrugged, wondering if that was weird. "Of course I do. Avalon is too harrowing. Simplicity. That's what you need." I fished around for the soap and ran the slippery bar over my toes, making sure my flowers didn't drop into the water. Thunder crashed in the distance, making me smile at the cozy feeling storms gave me (when they weren't accompanied by mind-warping leeches and what-not). "I didn't realize Lane's life used to be like this."

"You wouldn't have had much of a childhood if you'd stayed here, I imagine."

"Did you know your parents?" I wanted to know if he understood the loneliness that comes with being an orphan. If we were the same. We got along so easily; I wondered if that commonality was the reason. "Hold up, how does immortality here work? Like, were you ever even a child?" I asked, unsure if this was a thing everyone knew. "Were you born, or created as an adult?"

Kerdik's expression twisted, his tone turning sharp on a dime. "Why do you want to talk about that? I can't imagine how it's important."

I swallowed, my eyes on the soap. "You can't be short with me, especially when I'm vulnerable and naked like this. I was only curious to know more about you. That's normal, K. We're friends. It's good that I want to know more about you."

"You're prying."

My shoulders slumped, unsure how our easy back and forth got derailed so quickly. Apparently I had a bad habit of sticking my foot in my mouth when it came to all things Avalon. At this rate, I doubted I'd ever find a place to truly fit in.

I handed the bouquet back to him with a stalwart expression that told him he was being a jag for no reason. "Okay, *now* I'm sending you away. I was being nice, and you're treating me like I'm going to sell details of your childhood for a pack of cigarettes."

"You know," he accused me. The second crash of thunder made me jump. My birds flew in through the open window, screeching that a storm was here, and they wanted to hide out inside with me. Kerdik's temper swung with the hard rain that fell outside. "You know the answer. Why did you ask? Did Urien tell you?"

His accusation stung me. "Look, I don't know any of it, and I definitely didn't know it was a sore subject. I've only ever been nice to you. Go away. You're being a butthole."

The flowers I handed him crumbled to ash in his rage-filled grip, utterly destroying my beautiful gift. "You're only being nice to get information out of me! I see what you're doing. Taking your clothes off for me, too? Morgan's daughter, indeed."

I flinched at the verbal slap. I turned inward, going back to my introverted tendencies that had never deserted me when I needed them. I scooped water between my breasts, hissing at the sting from the gemstone as I rubbed the hard soap over the swells. I ignored his tantrum completely, and addressed the birds instead. "You can stay, guys. Tell the other birds out there to come on in, if they like. As many as you can fit in here is fine. Just leave my bed free so I can take a nap." I yawned again, a new layer of fatigue pushing my shoulders down into the water. The crows were talking over each other to tell me about the new nests they were building, the fun things they'd been up to, and where they were pretty sure a good stash of worms would come up in the wake of the storm.

"You can't talk to them this much, or you'll drain your magic," Kerdik scolded me with a scowl. His usual indulgent expression was gone, making it look like it had never even been there to begin with.

"Don't boss me. You can't be nice, then be a jackwagon, and then pretend to care about me in the same hour. I can figure it all out myself. I know talking to animals and using my Compass drains me, but I don't care. It's worth it to have friends who I know like me. No bird has ever snapped at me the way you're doing."

The birds kept cheeping, and then started singing to me a song about the rebirth the rain gave the earth. I loved their sweetness. I don't remember ever singing about rain with such passion as they did.

The water started to cool more rapidly than I anticipated. "What the..." My eyes widened when a slight fog started to rise from the surface, and the water turned painfully freezing in a heartbeat. "Kerdik, what's happening?" I tried to jump out of the tub, but I was stuck there. The water turned to a solid block of ice, ensnaring me in the tub. I screamed, afraid and in pain. "Help me!"

"You know about my beginnings!" he raged, and I realized with thunderous shock that it was his magic that did this to me. "You know I was the one who... You know! Why are you making me talk about it?"

"You're hurting me! Let me out!" I chattered, struggling to free myself from the ice that had me trapped. I was scared and pissed, and tried wriggling myself free from the block of ice with all the gusto I had in me. The edges of the ice sliced at my skin, scraping at my arms, back and breasts as I thrashed, still in prison, and mired in growing agony. The pointy edges ripped at my flesh in long cuts, warning me to be still, but I was too terrified to listen.

I heard a fist banging on the door. "Help!" I screamed. "Somebody help me!"

"I trusted you, but all you want is to find out my secrets so you can use them against me. The Daughters of Avalon are all the same. I can't believe you fooled me this long."

My teeth chattered so hard, I worried my words couldn't be understood. "I asked you b-because I d-d-didn't know, and thought it would be c-c-cool to learn more ab... ab...about you." I tried to squirm sideways, but nothing gave me more than half an inch of space. My ribs were barely contracting; the ice was more unforgiving than the corset. "I c-c-can't feel my toes!"

My birds were furious. They attacked Kerdik, pelting

him with their beaks and flapping their wings in his face to get him to stop. "Be gone!" he roared, and with a flip of his chartreuse hand, the entire flock fell to their deaths, thudding on my wood floor.

Stunned tears rolled out of me as I thrashed to get away, to go to them to see if there was anything I could do. "No! No! It's okay, b-b-babies! I'll fix it! I'll f-fix it!" Only there was no fixing it. They were motionless and splayed in unnatural positions. Who was I kidding? I couldn't save myself, much less them.

Blood started pooling onto the surface of the ice block, and for some reason this snapped Kerdik out of his blind fury. "Rosie, stop moving!" His hands came near my head, and I shrieked anew. He melted the ice back into water, but it was still too cold for me to feel it. My body convulsed recklessly, twitching as it went into some kind of shock.

The door burst open, and I heard Bastien calling for me. I didn't care about our fight; I cared that he was there. "Help!" I howled out my agony and fear as I lost control of my body and ended up completely submerged in the blood-streaked water.

Kerdik's hands jerked me up. His eyes were wild, his white dress shirt and pressed vest sopping as he held my seizing body in place so I didn't drown. He was scared, angry and too many other things for my brain to catalog. "Why did you ask me that?"

"Because I d-didn't know if you were s-s-sad, like me!" A spasm rocked through my body, renewing my shriek with each movement that jarred me. "You hurt me! Let go! Let go!" I thrashed against him, wanting to punch my way free, but unable to get my limbs to move from my body.

Bastien beelined for me, letting out a bleat of fear when he saw that the water had turned red with my blood. "What did you do to her?" he accused Kerdik, who was completely thrown into speechlessness by my honest answer.

Kerdik dropped me as if only just realizing what his hands were doing. He gaped at my body in horror, like he had no idea how we'd gotten to the place where I had ribbons of crimson streaking down my frozen skin. Kerdik glanced up at Bastien like a kid who'd gotten caught with his hands in the cookie jar. "I didn't mean to! She... I... She said..."

"*You* did this?" Bastien forgot his place in the pecking order and crossed over to Kerdik, socking him hard across the face. Kerdik didn't bleed, and he didn't retaliate. I heard Link swear, and then turned my head to see him backing away in fear.

"I want to go home!" I howled, unable to hide my pain any longer.

"Darling, I wasn't thinking. I..." Kerdik tried to cup the side of my face, but I screamed at him to go away. He looked down, his eyes shut to fend off the pain of my rejection. "I'll leave you, then. Please believe that I didn't..." Without another word, Kerdik vanished into thin air.

THE WORST TIME TO BE NAKED

"Mad! Link! Help me with Rosie." Bastien grabbed my towel and threw it at Madigan, who opened it without understanding everything that was going on. He trusted Bastien, and obeyed without question, turning his head to the side so he didn't see my body when Link and Bastien hoisted my frozen, seizing, naked and bleeding form out of the water. The worst time to be naked is in front of your guy's buddies, but we managed the four-tiered grimace with a firm code of "be cool."

The towel went around me, and Link tore the comforter from my bed to add another layer to fend off the cold and my nudity. Mad didn't need instructions, but ran out down the hallway, and came back a minute later with another blanket.

Bastien carried my crumpled body past the flock of

lifeless birds to the bed, laying us both down so Mad could cover us with the feather comforter he'd stolen from who knows where.

Link gaped at the floor in horror. "They're all dead, Bastien! What madness happened in here? Ye were only gone a wee bit."

I tried to reach for a bird, but my arms were frozen like a tyrannosaurus rex. "Bird!" I begged.

Mad lifted a dead crow with the edge of a hand towel and displayed it to me. "They're all dead, Rosie."

"I n-n-need it," I worked out through clenched teeth. "Give it h-h-here."

Bastien's body tried to warm mine, but it was useless. I'd gone past being able to feel the cold, and only felt numbness everywhere. "Easy, honey. I've got you. He's gone now, and you don't have to be afraid. I'm here."

I couldn't calm my body down, much less my terror.

Mad brought the bird closer, but I wasn't satisfied until the lifeless feathers brushed against my cheek. He rested it on the pillow so my tears could fall freely over its dead body. "I'm sorry! I'm so sorry!" I wept over the bird, feeling the weight of the death of the whole flock. They wouldn't have been there if I hadn't told them to come in out of the rain. They would be at their nests, and now their babies would have no parents. I'd orphaned an entire flock, and now the children would all live with that same sadness I'd carried – if they lived at all. I'd offered the birds a shelter, what they'd thought would be a safe harbor from the storm. I didn't realize the worst of nature was inside, and that I was no longer a safe place for innocent things.

A horrible cry broke from my lips, but Bastien didn't pull away. He took off his shirt and opened my blankets and towel so he could press his skin against me to warm my body. He nodded to Mad, who did the same. Though Madigan didn't give two rips about me, he would do whatever Bastien needed. In this case, it was get half-naked with a completely naked woman in bed with him. "Ah! She's an icicle, Bastien. Link, go fetch some hot water bottles. Broth, too."

I sobbed uncontrollably between them as sensation slowly started to come back to my outermost extremities. The numbness had been a kindness, and now it was deserting me. My arms and legs seized as if they were being stabbed repeatedly.

Mad rolled me onto my side so I could only see Bastien. He flinched at my cold when he pressed his bare chest firmly to my back to warm me. "Bastien, this is bad."

Bastien's expression was hard, his gaze drilling into mine mere inches from my face. "What did Kerdik do to you?" He undid his pants and slipped them off, so he was only in his underwear under the covers. This incited a fresh worry in me, but he kept his eyes locked in on mine. "Easy, honey. I'm just trying to get you warm. Here, wrap your legs around me. Skin to skin as much as you can."

"I'm w-w-with Demi," I protested, uncertain what the rules were in cases of hypothermia.

Bastien swallowed down the bitter pill with a nod. "I know. But I think Demi would like it if I returned you to him with all your fingers and toes intact."

I was too turned around to object further. My damp towel twisted away when I wrapped my arms and legs around him, locking into position with my rigid limbs. I sobbed, my breasts moving with shame as they pressed against his chest. "I don't like this!"

Bastien kissed my forehead and molded his arms around me, pulling Mad in so my bare back and butt were warmed by his BFF. I hated how naked I was, but knew this was standard procedure for frostbite. "My b-b-bird!" I wailed, calming to mere weeping when Madigan rested the dead bird on my shoulder without a word.

I snatched at the creature, my limbs as stiff as his, and tucked him under my chin. "Keep him warm," I begged, thinking that if maybe I could save the one crow, all wouldn't be lost. I nuzzled him between my chest and Bastien's.

Bastien was kind, and didn't call me out on my crazy. He took turns stroking the crow's feathers, and then running his knuckles over my cheekbone to soothe me. "What's his name?" he asked quietly.

My eyes swept shut as a new pain hit me. "I didn't even know it! They tried to attack Kerdik when he turned on me, and he waved his hand like it was nothing and killed them all! I'm so sorry!" I sobbed, ashamed that I hadn't been able to save them – that they'd given their lives up for me. "Go ahead. Say 'I told you so.' You warned me Kerdik was dangerous," I sniffled. It wasn't the assault that stung, it was the betrayal. I had so few friends here, and I'd counted on Kerdik being one of the good ones.

Bastien shushed me, touching his forehead to mine so he could look at the bird I was clutching like it was my lifeline. "I think we should name him. A good bird who defends my lady deserves to be buried with honor."

"Ah, jays," Madigan grumbled, his patience only going so far.

My lower lip quivered at the sweetness Bastien doled out like it was nothing. "Adam?" I said like it was a question.

Bastien nodded, moving my head with his through the prolonged marriage of our foreheads. "Adam is a good name."

I closed my eyes and willed all the magic in my Fae bones to finally do something. I didn't know how to cast charms or perform healings, but there was no time like the present to learn. "How do I heal him? Like, with my magic."

Bastien's eyebrows pushed together, reminding me just how much I loved his scarred brow. "You can't, honey. He's already dead."

Tears cascaded over my face and buried themselves in my pillow, no doubt to taint whatever dreams would haunt me tonight. "No! It can't go down like this. I'm not a useless princess. I can wake him up! If I'm really Fae, then I have magic inside of me. I can heal him!"

Link rubbed his jaw, taking it upon himself to select the short straw and clue me in on the harder truths. "It takes years of schooling to be able to heal even the smallest cut. Even if wee Adam were only mildly hurt, ye wouldn't be able to bring him back."

"I'm not stupid!" I shouted, more at all the kids who'd ever taunted me than at Link. "I can do this." I squinched my eyes shut and willed with everything in me for Adam to move on his own. I summoned up every hopeful thought and spread it over his stiff body like lotion meant for only the best kind of recovery. I even checked in with my gut, asking my Compass to show me the way to heal Adam, who had only ever been good to me. I held my breath, but when that didn't work, I tried deep yoga breathing.

I'm not sure how long it was before I finally conceded the fight to the Grim Reaper. I utterly wept in Bastien's arms, confronted with every single shortcoming that had led me to this moment. I was the gullible girl who played with monsters, and were shocked when they bit me. I was Remedial Rosie, powerless to save one small bird whose worst crime had been trusting me.

Bastien kissed my forehead and ran his hand lightly over my bird. "Rest in peace, Adam. Thank you for everything. Thank you for trying to save my girl."

I don't know how long Link had been watching us, but

his wary voice broke our hushed moment. "So someone snatched Bastien's brains out of his head and replaced them with roses and sweets, aye? Is tha the size of it?"

"Aye," Madigan replied. "Let me introduce ye to Bastien in love. Ye have to see it to believe it."

"A servant will be up soon with hot water bottles and broth," Link assured me. "It might do well not to be cozying up to a dead bird. Far be it from me to state the obvious."

Bastien didn't turn his head from me as he spoke to the guys. "Can you take all the birds out while I warm Rosie up? And give this one a burial, Link. His name is Adam."

My heart swelled for Bastien, tears of gratitude welling to replace the tears of pain and fear I'd been crying. "Thank you, Bastien. You get it. You get how sad this is."

Bastien closed his eyes at the sound of his name on my lips. "I do. We'll take care of it. I've got you, Daisy."

"Ye are serious? For a bird?" The way Link said "bird" almost sounded like "bard", which was exactly what Adam had been, singing to me just minutes before he died. Somehow Link's accent made the whole thing sadder. Now the world would be short one bard, which we needed now more than ever.

"It's for my girl. Give her whatever she wants."

I expected Link to argue, but he responded with a resigned, "Aye. At least your wee Rose is better than Nicholai's lady." Then for my benefit, he explained, "Katya only wants the finest clothes, and she don't care who

Nicholai takes them from. I guess a bird funeral is better than tha."

Madigan slipped out from the bed and tugged his shirt back on. He grabbed a basket from the corner and shunted the birds inside, his long fingers gathering two and three up at a time. "Just rest, Rosie. We'll see to taking ye out of here the second we have the jewels back where they need to be, and make arrangements for waking your Da."

It was a promise I put too much hope in. "Thanks, Mad. I'm sorry I'm naked." Tears rolled down my cheeks. "I know this is awful!"

Mad leaned over the bed and cupped my shoulder. "Don't think on it another second. If ye put it out of your mind, I promise I'll do the same."

I gulped down my hiccupped tears, and then nodded, grateful to Mad for so many things.

COLD GIRL, WARM BED, HOT GUY

Bastien waited until the guys had collected all the birds, including Adam, and vacated the room to bury their little bodies. My limbs were more pliable now, but they weren't ready to leave Bastien for a moment longer than it took for him to slide his flannel over my arms and button me up. The single layer of clothing gave me the freedom to wrap my body around his without shame. His hand had stayed as honest as possible, but found it couldn't resist the curve of my hips. His fingers traced from the outside of my thigh up my hip, dipping at my waist, and climbed up my ribs, guiltily thumbing the plump outer edge of my breast just to make us both shiver.

My body shuddered against his under the covers. I didn't even have the decency to be ashamed and pull away when a servant from the kitchen came in and tucked several hot water bottles under the many blankets. The bowl of broth was set on the nightstand, along with a jar of salve from Remy for my cuts. Then the man left without a word. I wondered where Demi was, though maybe it was best he didn't see me like this.

Bastien's lips found mine with a lazy allure as soon as the door shut. I didn't think it through, but surrendered, kissing the man I didn't want to want, and couldn't afford to need.

But I did need him. My body and heart wouldn't deny me the man who would come for me time and time again.

He kept the kisses light and languid, tasting and sucking at his leisure, as if we had all day and night to indulge in each other. The rain still poured outside, adding to the heat that thawed the ice between us. He rolled on top of me, rocking his body against mine and holding my arms above my head. There was no denying the need we had for each other. The kiss stayed measured and held back from the edge of wild passion. He knew I was fragile, and he didn't push me too far.

"I love you, Rosie," he sighed between kisses, his hips pressed to mine. My knees parted, and soon he was rocking against me in waves of seduction I wanted to drown in.

"Don't love me," I warned through a guttural groan. My toes curled as my body did what it wanted.

"Don't tell me what to do." His lips were soft and insisted that what we had could survive the careless things we'd done with the gift we'd found in each other. He carefully rolled us so I was on top, my arms and legs caging him in. He put me in the position of total control, so whatever happened next would be my own doing. He submitted to my whims, his hands on either side of his head in complete surrender. "Stop kissing me if you don't want me."

My lips betrayed me, seeking out his against my better judgment. "Shut up."

Bastien's hand moved under the covers to deliver a light slap to my left butt cheek. I yelped and jumped, pulling my head back to scowl at him. "Tell me the truth, Daisy. Tell me that you love me."

When I hesitated, he gave my butt another slap, the sting reminding me that I was keeping him waiting, and Bastien didn't do patience. The rain pounded the earth just outside my window, and try as I might, I couldn't tear myself from Bastien's warmth. I sucked on his lower lip before whispering a guilty, "You know I love you, even when you don't deserve it."

"See? Was that really so hard?" He leaned his chin up and kissed me, long and deep, making me swoon until my weary limbs decided they couldn't support me any longer. I collapsed atop him, too shaky to enjoy any more sexy moments. I knew I'd exhausted myself from the long day, the drama, the constant shivering, and the overuse of magic. Bastien kissed my cheeks lightly, and then rolled me off of him so I was laying on the mattress, my chin to the ceiling. He got out and pressed the small jar of salve into my palm. "Please tell me you need my help rubbing this into your cuts."

I managed a wan smile. "Maybe the ones on my back, if you don't mind." Under the covers, I rubbed the salve into my cleavage and around my chest and torso, finding more cuts than could be healthy.

Bastien waited until I turned myself over and slid the borrowed flannel off my shoulders, the dim light from the setting sun struggling to shine in through the rain to high-light the small slices peppering my back. Bastien straddled my butt and rubbed the oily cream into my skin, his calloused fingers letting me know just how capable he could be with a naked woman. Then he got up and rummaged through my drawers, coming back to slide a nightgown over my head, and underwear up my limp legs so he could have his shirt back. It seemed we'd come full circle from him ordering me to remove my clothes, to now him dressing me when I needed someone to be gentle, and take care of my body when I was too exhausted for the task.

He was careful with my fragile state, and didn't leave me while I slept. He kept his warm body pressed to mine, making sure his hands stayed honest while I dreamt.

The hard knock on the door came in the middle of the night, the rain still falling outside. I roused with a drowsy jolt, unhappy that I was being woken only a couple hours into my sleep cycle. When he made to get up, I gripped his shoulder, grateful he allowed my clumsy hands to pull him back down next to me. "Don't leave," I whispered, groggy and uncertain of everything I wished I had an answer for.

"Never," he promised me. I could tell in his voice that he was moved by my plea. "I'm just going to answer the door. I won't step a toe outside this room unless you're with me." He kissed my swollen lips, slid on his pants and shirt, and then kissed me again, as if he needed a hit of the oxygen I was to him every few seconds so he could breathe. He opened the door with a tightness to his shoulders. "The princess is unavailable."

"Her majesty most high demands the princess come to her chambers."

"Her majesty most high can bite me. I'm Rosie's *Guardien*, and I say she's sleeping."

I recognized Rigby's voice, humble but authoritative. "If you do not bring down the princess, her majesty most high will come up here in a most unfortunate disposition. Either way, there is no time for sleep right now."

Bastien swore and shut the door in Rigby's face. He came back to the bed and sat on the side, leaning down for another hit from my confused and guilty lips. "I think we should go down there and get this over with. The guys are in the parlor, catching up and making a mess of your mom's house."

I sat up against the headboard, pulling the covers up over the strappy nightgown. "Bastien, I don't know what got into me last night. I shouldn't have... I'm with Demi, if he'll still have me."

Bastien's face hardened, but to his credit, he didn't turn cold on me. "Demi's job is to make you happy. You don't owe him some kind of loyalty. It wasn't a real relationship."

My mouth drew in a tight line. "I'm sure there won't be any relationship at all after I tell him everything we've done. If you could give me a minute, I need to get dressed."

I expected Bastien to stomp out and slam the door with his signature temper, but instead he leaned in and traced my cheekbone with the pad of his thumb. "Take all the time you need, Daisy."

31

KERDIK'S PROTECTION

Morgan was awake, and pissed as a pit bull who couldn't reach her bone. I could hear her yelling all the way down the hall before I even reached her room. It had taken me a hot minute to make myself presentable for her, finding a dress that didn't rub too hard on my broken skin. Demi hadn't come back to my room. I'd hoped to find him on my way, but no such luck.

Bastien walked me to my mom's bedroom, and though she'd just been laid out for hours, she was dressed in a fresh ballgown, her hair redone, and nothing but vinegar in her soul. She didn't even bother disguising the vinegar as roses anymore, which was just as well. No one bought the ruse anyway.

"Rosalie, get in here and explain yourself!"

I took a deep breath to answer, but Bastien moved in

front of me. "Hey, Mom," I greeted her, as if nothing was wrong at all.

"'Hey, Mom?' That's all you have to say to me?"

"How are you feeling?"

"I'm feeling like I want to tear your head off! Since when do you know Master Kerdik? Since when did you become close with him, enough that he'd show up at random to your coronation? I've been trying to reach him for decades, and he's been at your beck and call this entire time?"

I scoffed at how little she understood the enigma that was Kerdik. "The fact that you think he's at anyone's beck and call shows how little you know him. So I had a friend you didn't know about. Newsflash, you know shockingly little about me. As soon as you found out my Compass abilities were gone, you shoved me away and haven't cared to engage in a single conversation with me that wasn't about your agenda. We've never even had a meal together."

"Like you need another meal." She gave a pointed look at my waist, which I gotta tell you, was spot on average for my size and age.

I was too tired to deal with her crap. "I was sleeping when you demanded I get out of bed and come down here. I know sleep isn't all that common here, but it's a nonnegotiable for me. When you wake me in the middle of the night, you're stuck with looking at your fat daughter in whatever state I show up. Deal with it."

Bastien hissed his disapproval. "Did you have anything

important to say to her? Just more posturing and throwing your power around? No one here's impressed."

Morgan fumed at Bastien, and though I knew she couldn't touch him, I didn't want him caught in her crosshairs. My voice softened to steer the meeting in a better direction. "You scared me, fainting like that. What happened? Some people are saying that you poisoned the crown you were supposed to give to me. Is that true?"

"Of course it's not true. I'm your mother. It was poisoned, though not by me." She stood from her bed, her face still pale, but no less threatening. "Your corset is to be worn every time you step outside your room. It's to retrain your figure, which is in serious need of help."

I sighed. "Fine. I'll have Demi put it back on when I go upstairs. You're the one who pulled me out of bed. Sheesh."

She picked up a rag that had been used to cool her forehead and whipped it at Rigby, who flinched at her temper, but said nothing. "Demi's gone. I'll send up another *soumettre* for you."

"What do you mean, gone? Like, out on an errand or something?"

"No, I mean your Aunt Avril required his services, so I sent him with her."

A fresh batch of ice ran through my veins. "What? Are you serious?"

"Of course I am. She required him, so I sent him on his way. After how things were between us when I saw her last,

I figured she needed a little appeasing. Demi is good for that sort of thing. You're to be married soon to that disrespectful Untouchable. What need have you for a specific *soumettre*? They're all the same, Rosalie."

My voice was shriller than hers had been. "I'm leaving to go to Province 8. I'll be back with Demi in a few days."

"He'll be sent back when Avril tires of him." An evil smile played on her painted lips. "Do you actually have an attachment to Demi? Do you think you have some claim on him?"

"Of course I do. He's my boyfriend!"

Morgan tilted her head back and let out a throaty laugh. "Oh, my! How glad I am to have heard you say such foolishness in person. Demi serves you faithfully until he's sent to placate whomever I deem needs pleasing. His allegiance is wherever I send it."

Bastien snarled at Morgan. "Are we done here?"

"By all means, let the girl go find her long lost love. Bastien the Bold, you may accompany her to my sister's mansion and see for yourselves how devoted Demi is to Avril at my command." She clicked her finger at Bastien. "Go ready two horses. I need a few words with my daughter before she rides off in search of true love." She said the whole thing like it was a joke – like *I* was a joke.

Bastien cleared the distance between himself and Morgan in two long steps, shoving her to the wall to knock the laughter off her lips. "You'll speak to Rosie with respect, Morgan. She belongs to the Brotherhood now."

My mother flinched at the use of her first name more than the assault. Rigby was at a loss, calling guards in, who were ready to attack, but lowered their weapons uncertainly when they saw it was an Untouchable who threatened their queen. They couldn't lay a finger on him, and everyone knew it.

Morgan fumed at Bastien, her nostrils flaring. "Rosalie belongs to me until she's been marked. I see no ink on her neck. I'll speak to my daughter as I see fit."

"It's only a matter of time until she's inked. Don't make me send Madigan the Formidable in here. He doesn't take kindly to his fiancée being pushed around."

"Get him off me!" Morgan screeched, but higher than the queen's command was the unshakeable code the soldiers lived by – if you were lucky enough to get out, you were free to live as you wished.

"I could gut you right now," Bastien seethed in her face. "But I won't do that in front of your daughter. I'll take her to Avril's mansion, and you'll have a fresh attitude when I come back. Otherwise I'll see to making you Madigan's little toy, like you've done with Demi. All the rumors about his ruthlessness? They're innocent compared with the truth. See how you like saying 'Yes, Master Madigan.'"

Morgan's face was red with rage, and she spat in his face in lieu of a threat.

When he turned back to me, he gave me a nod of solidarity. "I'll get the horses ready and meet you in the stables. We'll get Demi back for you, if that's what you want."

I couldn't believe he would go with me to retrieve the man I wouldn't cast aside for him. I was stunned at the selflessness I hadn't thought him capable of feeling. "Thank you."

He shoved the soldiers out and shut me in the room with Rigby and Morgan. Morgan straightened her dress and her hair, pushing Rigby out of the way when he tried to help her. "Avril said that your pal Master Kerdik gave you this ring," she said, cutting to the chase as she pointed to my finger in accusation. "Let me see it."

Wordlessly, I held up my hand so she could see my square-shaped aquamarine gemstone, accompanied by the three sparkling diamonds on either side of the white gold vine-like setting. I didn't correct her that Kerdik wasn't my pal anymore, and that he'd lost his temper and attacked me just a few hours ago. I hadn't even gotten to go bowling with him.

"Hand it here." She held out her palm expectantly. "Now, Rosalie. You wouldn't know the first thing to do with a gem from Master Kerdik."

Though I no longer felt the affinity for Kerdik I used to, my fist closed around the ring. "He told me not to take it off."

She snapped her fingers to Rigby, who summoned in four guards from the hallway. "Fetch me the ring from my daughter's finger. She's being particularly stubborn today, and doesn't deserve trinkets for her bad behavior."

Before I could protest, the soldiers closed in on me. I got in a few good punches, but it was four on one. Two held me still even after I'd punched out the third dude, who was asking for it. The two wrestled me to the rug and pinned my thrashing and terrified body. I screamed for Bastien, but he didn't hear me. I shrieked my terror at the implications of being helplessly pinned down by grown men who didn't even flinch at what they were doing. I normally like to think I can hold my own in a fight, but this was four full-grown military men on one tired me. The million-pound goon kneeled on my throat to stop my screaming and hold me more firmly in place. My hand was jerked over my head and pinned to the wooden floor, my fingers pried open.

Suddenly, there was a tingling in my hand that started in from my fourth finger. Something happened when the gold slid up my knuckle, sending a shiver through me and a flash of blinding light through the room. The soldier kneeling on my throat released me from the stranglehold, toppling sideways and falling off of me.

I coughed when I pulled in a full breath. The oxygen filled me with rage, expanding my ribcage with more fury than I could brush aside. I went spastic, knocking the other dudes off me in a battle of wild limbs before I realized the heavy goon with fat knees wasn't moving.

Morgan's voice was scared as she ordered them to fall

back. "What magic did he put in there?" Then the fear turned to zealous greed as she lunged for me. "Give me the ring!"

My heart splintered when I punched my mother across the face with my ringed fist, unsure what other course of action I should've taken. She stumbled off me, clutching her bleeding face with venom in her soul. She didn't look at Rigby as she spoke to him, her cheeks vibrating with rage. "Take her to the compound and give the soldiers a free pass to do as they wish with her. Tell them to make her wish she was never born. See if she won't part with the ring then."

Terror lit me like fire from the inside, but I held my ground, seething and readying for another fight.

Rigby was distraught, but stayed by Morgan's side. "Your majesty, they won't defile your daughter now that they've seen Master Kerdik's affections for her. No one would dare touch the princess and risk his wrath. That's not counting risking Madigan the Formidable's displeasure, which I know the men will not tempt."

Little did they know that Kerdik didn't give two rips about me anymore.

Rigby leaned down and felt the jugular of the soldier who'd tried to take the ring off my finger. "He's dead, your majesty. Kerdik's put a protection around her, and we'd all do well to respect it, rather than push its limits."

I gasped, horrified that I'd participated in someone's death who I didn't even know.

Morgan's nostrils flared as she held her stinging cheek-bone. I'd clocked her good, though I felt no triumph in it, only shame at raising my hand to the woman who'd given birth to me. "Very well. If I can't take the ring, I'll punish you until you give it over to me of your own free will." She snapped her fingers at Rigby and the three remaining guards. "Relieve her of her clothes and lower her down into the dried well on the back of the southern edge of the property."

Rigby swallowed hard, clearly not liking this order. "Your majesty, it's been raining. The well will not be dry. Surely Master Kerdik will retaliate if the princess drowns under your care."

Morgan hauled off and slapped Rigby across his face, stinging his heart more than his cheek. "Do as I say! Do you think I'm less than Master Kerdik? That *I* should cower? I cower to no one!" Her voice boomed throughout the room like the spoiled princess she was. "I am the Queen of Avalon! There is no one higher than me! Master Kerdik has magic? Well, so do I. Let him come for me. Let him see the country that he abandoned to ruin, and that I saved."

Rigby bowed his head, his voice stony and his soul running on empty. "Take the princess and do as the queen commands." Rigby broke what was left of my heart when he motioned for the soldiers to gag me, throw me into this giant black bag, and then drag my kicking and fighting body out of the castle.

32

GOODBYE, RIGBY

I had many acerbic things to spew at Rigby along the way, but none of them were heard behind the gag. The rain soaked through the sturdy black bag, and I was bumped and bruised as I was dragged for too long. I was stunned and furious, and couldn't believe Rigs would betray me like this. When the soldiers fished me out of the bag and stood me, bound and seething before him, Rigs removed my gag and cut my bonds. "Take your dress off, your majesty."

I spat in his face, though the rain dripping down his nose softened that assault slightly. "Friggin' make me! You want my dress, you're going to have to wrestle it off me, Rigs."

The use of the nickname I used for him cut deep, making him flinch at the sound. "Don't make this difficult, sweet girl. If you'd simply hand over the ring, this would all be a short, unpleasant memory." He brushed a stray curl from my sweaty face, his sad eyes locking in on mine. "I find it's easier to give her majesty most high what she wants. No one who opposes her lives to stand in her way for long. I would not see you cut down."

I didn't have the same sentimental attachment to the ring I used to, but if this was how it was all going to go down, Morgan could try prying it off my cold, dead finger. "And yet, here we are. Do it, Rigs. Strip me down. Hold me while I cry one day, and then make me stand in front of you in the outdoors stark raving naked the next."

Rigby lowered his chin and shook his head sadly, the slow motion distracting me while he raised his hand to the soldiers. "Get on with it, but see you don't hurt her."

"Why?" I challenged, furious and wanting to drive my point home. "Why can't they hurt me? Is there something wrong with hurting a young woman? Do you find it disgusting what you're asking them to do? But your precious queen commanded it, so how can it be wrong?"

Rigby nearly broke at my words. "What would you have me do, Rosie? Would you see my head severed from my neck? It would only mean someone who does not care for you ordering your clothes be taken, and they would not stop at that."

My fists clenched at my sides. "Oh, so I should thank you?"

"No matter what you think, you cannot possibly hate me more than I despise myself right now." Then my only friend left in the castle turned around so he didn't have to see the fight that was me trying desperately to keep the dress I hated, and three older, grown men tearing it piece by piece from my body. I'd managed to break two noses, got in a nut shot, three kidney jabs and knocked one of them clean out, but still they won.

I sported a fat lip, a sore knee, and zero pride to go with my naked skin. At least they left me my underwear and Madigan's ring that I wore on a gold chain around my neck. I sobbed into my hand, clutching my knees to my chest on the wet grass. The rain poured down on my bare shoulders, soaking me and making the grim evening seem that much more hopeless.

"I told you not to hurt her!" Rigby thundered, motioning to my scrapes that were mostly from Kerdik's icy temper. On instinct, he removed his red jacket and draped it around my shoulders, holding me to his chest while I wept. "Please, my sweet. Please just give us the ring. I cannot bear this!"

I felt lost and very, very afraid. I prayed for Bastien to come and find me, to have heard my cries when they were nearer the castle. I was so far away now, the castle small from this distance. I knew he couldn't hear me even if I howled. "Don't do this," I whispered, holding tight to Rigby's shirt.

Rigby let out a tortured howl before he took his coat

back and stepped away, leaving me to my fate. The soldiers wrestled me up and hoisted me into a bucket so wide that I could sit in it while it swung over the well. Rigby molded my fingers to the rope as they quickly lowered me down. I screamed and shook, my cries echoing off the stone, informing me that I had a long ways to go still. No one would find me in here, and this would be how I would die.

When I finally reached the bottom, the bucket landed with a splash, giving me something to hold onto when they cut the rope and sent the heavy cord crashing down on my head. The lower quarter of the bucket was submerged in rainwater, and I was too scared to test if I could reach the bottom of the abyss. I shook with icy fear, wondering how long I could hold onto the edges of the bucket and trust it to keep me afloat.

I was desperate, which is the only way I rationalized my actions when I pressed my ring to my heart and whispered, "Kerdik, Kerdik, Kerdik," as he'd instructed me to do when I wanted to reach him. Rigby rolled something over the well to seal me in the dark, alone with only my terror and the creeping desperation.

The world grew deafeningly silent, trapping me in the well with my rampant fear that I would die without Lane. She would scour both worlds looking for me, but my bones would rot in the bottom of this stinking well. I could smell mildew and something that could only be described as earth gone rancid. I heard nothing, save my own blubbering.

I bobbed, sobbing as I waited for anyone to come find me. I waited...

And waited.

Feeling just as wrecked as Rosie right now? Leave a review, which super way helps people find the books you love.

33

STUPID GIRL

Enjoy a free preview of *"Stupid Girl"*
Book four in the Faîte Falling series.

When the lid overhead opened up however many hours or days later, I couldn't open my eyes – the light was so painful. My blood boiled when I heard Morgan shouting down to me, her voice echoing off the walls and creating a confusing dissonance. "Are you ready to give me the ring?"

More rain entered the well, frustrating me that I'd have to keep waiting longer now for the walls to dry. They'd almost been sturdy enough for me to make an attempt, but not quite. "I can't get it off!" I shouted, trying my hand at lying to see if it would work.

"Then I guess you should make yourself at home down there," she spat back. "Enjoy your meal for the day."

I squeaked when something came flying down at me, hurling at a speed I couldn't counter, banging off walls and landing with a bloody splat in my lap. I shrieked at the dead quail that had been skinned for me, and still had lines of blood sliding down over its body. I was horrified at the lifeless creature in my arms, and unsure what to do with it. Without thinking, I tossed it over the edge of the bucket, letting it splash in the water as the well closed overhead. Then I panicked, guessing that an animal carcass would pollute the only water supply I had. Quickly, I tipped the lip of the tub I was hugging my knees in, filling it with rainwater to the point where it was almost non-buoyant. Though I could go without food for a while, I knew depriving myself of drinkable water would ensure I died quicker.

I had to stay alive. I had a new brother I was only just starting to get to know. Draper had recently been adopted by Lane, and the two of us had hit it off right from the start. Draper was desperate for family, and I didn't want him to finally get a sister who would fight for him, only to lose her so soon.

Lane and I were best friends. As much as I would never survive without her, I knew that same desperation existed on her end, too. She would find me.

I heard Morgan's cruel laughter above the relentless

rain. Then I was sealed in the darkness, unsure if I would ever feel the grass beneath my toes again.

Continue the Faîte Falling series
with *"Stupid Girl"* today!

ABOUT THE AUTHOR

USA Today bestselling author Mary E. Twomey lives in Michigan with her three adorable children. She enjoys reading, writing, vegetarian cooking, and telling her children fantastic stories about wombats.

While she loves writing fantasy, dystopian, and paranormal tales for her readers, Mary also writes romance under the name Tuesday Embers, and cozy mysteries under the name Molly Maple.

Visit her online at www.maryetwomey.com, and sign up for her newsletter, so you never miss a new release.

www.ingramcontent.com/pod-product-compliance
Lightning Source LLC
Chambersburg PA
CBHW010317100726
47906CB00006B/1024